SECRETS AT SUTHERLAND HALL

PIPPA DARLING MYSTERIES
BOOK 1

JENNA BENNETT

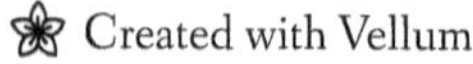 Created with Vellum

England, late April 1926

When Henry Astley, Duke of Sutherland, turns up dead in bed at the end of an afternoon spent calling his family on the carpet, everyone assumes that the excitement finished the old boy off. He was quite old and also quite vociferous in his opinions, so it isn't an unreasonable assumption.

It isn't until the next morning, when the duke's valet and confidant is found shot to death in the hedge maze, that the whole thing takes on a more sinister cast.

Bright Young Thing Philippa Darling, her best friend Christopher and his brother Francis, as well as their parents, Lord and Lady Herbert, have all been summoned to Sutherland Hall for a dressing down. So has cousin Crispin, the future duke, along with his parents, the Viscount and Viscountess St George. Everyone has a string of small peccadillos they're trying to hide, along with a few guilty secrets they don't want anyone to know about. The only question is, which secret was worth killing for?

Pippa isn't worried on her own behalf. She had no reason to want the duke dead. But when it looks like suspicion might fall on Christopher, she has no choice but to step up. She'll sacrifice Francis if she has to, and would throw Crispin to the wolves without a second thought, but Scotland Yard will arrest Christopher over her dead body.

And it might just come to that.

"Three may keep a secret if two of them are dead."

BENJAMIN FRANKLIN

ONE

"Christopher!"

I let the door slam behind me as I headed across the parquet floor of the foyer and deeper into the flat. "Kit! Are you home?"

"In here, darling."

The voice came from the first bedroom to the left—or more specifically, my bedroom. I veered in that direction and found my flat-mate and cousin seated at my dressing table, using my brush and rice powder to set his makeup. A pair of sky-blue eyes, perfectly outlined in kohl, met mine in the mirror for a moment before he spun the chair around to face me. "What's the matter? Didn't the interview go well?"

I shook my head, as I plumped my posterior down on the edge of the bed and crossed my ankles. "Mr. Bancroft said he'd consider my application for the position if I showed him my qualifications on the divan in his office. I told him no and walked out."

"And who could blame you?" Christopher said, and swung

back to the mirror. "You don't have to work, Pippa. I have enough money to keep us both."

"I know you do." And what's more, he was happy to spend it. But— "I don't want to be a burden."

He shook his head. "It's not a burden. You know as well as I do that you're the closest thing I have to a sister. You're my best friend. I don't want you to lower yourself to the divan in Mr. Bancroft's office when I have more than enough to take care of us both."

"I have no intention of lowering myself to the divan in anyone's office," I informed him. "Certainly not for a job. Even though I would adore working for The Bodley Head. They published *The Mysterious Affair at Styles*, you know."

"I know," Christopher said, eyes on the mirror as he painted his lips scarlet. "You told me, and told me, and told me."

He flicked his gaze up to meet mine again. "You know, you should just write a book of your own, Pippa. Your English is just fine now, and you're always going on about that Christie woman. And now there's the Sayers woman, too."

That was true. I had been reading Agatha Christie's mysteries since the first was released in early 1921 by The Bodley Head Press. Three or four or maybe five books to date. And now there was Dorothy Leigh Sayers and *Whose Body?*, which had been released in 1923, not by The Bodley Head. And—

"There's a new Sayers being released in a couple of months, did you know? Maybe I ought to apply for a job at T. Fisher Unwin instead. Maybe they'd let me have it early..."

I trailed off, as my mind delighted in the possibilities.

"Or you could just write your own," Christopher reiterated. "If they can do it, you can do it."

I squinted at him. "Oh, I don't think so, do you? I've never even seen a dead body."

"We'll find you one, if you'd like," Christopher said, with the air of someone happy to go to great lengths to please. "Although I'm not sure personal knowledge of dead bodies is necessary to write successful detective fiction. It's less about the body and more about the puzzle, isn't it?"

I supposed it was, really. "I could write about us. Two cousins who live in London and solve mysteries together. We could be like Tommy and Tuppence."

"But without the romance," Christopher said, since he'd also read *The Secret Adversary*, "naturally?"

I nodded. "Naturally. No one who knows us could possibly think we're anything but platonic."

Christopher looked relieved. I watched as he lifted a black, bobbed wig off the stand on the edge of the dressing table and lowered it, carefully, over his own slicked-back hair.

"Where are you off to?" As if I couldn't guess.

"Drag Ball at Lady Austin's." Christopher's eyes were on the mirror as he minutely adjusted the wig. He's a natural blond, but with his lashes and brows darkened, the black wig was ridiculously becoming, and made him look like someone completely different.

And I don't mean the obvious. Clearly, the makeup and wig and the evening gown I knew were waiting turned my cousin from a young gentleman into a young lady. But he also didn't look like Christopher Astley, second-youngest grandson of the Duke of Sutherland, in drag. Instead, when he walked out the door tonight, he'd be Kitty Dupree, belle of the ball, and I'd defy even those who knew him well to recognize Christopher under the wig and makeup.

I wasn't certain I would recognize him myself, had I not watched the transformation.

But nonetheless—

"Are you certain it's safe?"

Lady Austin, for the uninitiated, was not a lady, nor was her name Austin. Truth be told, I wasn't even sure she was a woman. I'd never met her, and I wasn't sure Christopher had. The lady—or gentleman—was elusive.

And for good reason. While Christopher's lifestyle had become more acceptable to the Bright Young Set in the second decade of the twentieth century, the London constabulary was not so sanguine. Raids were common, and the buggery laws were still in effect, and being in violation could lead to anything from fines to hard labor. Lady Austin—whoever he or she might be—was taking a big chance by hosting the balls, and so was Christopher and the others who attended them.

"It's been safe so far," Christopher said, his lips glistening red as he adjusted the sparkling headband over the short, black wig.

"I suppose that's true." We'd been in London for more than two months, and Christopher had attended several of the balls with no problems. "But surely the more often you tempt fate..."

"Don't worry so, Pippa." His eyes met mine in the mirror. "I promise to be careful."

"See that you are," I told him. "I don't want anything to happen to you."

"I don't want anything to happen to me, either. I'll be here by tomorrow morning, as always."

Before I could say anything else, he jumped up. "Did I show you my new dress? It's divine, darling. Absolutely divine."

He hustled across the room on men's size 42 patent leather pumps. Christopher has elegant feet, small for a man and with high arches.

I pivoted on the bed, so I could watch as he pulled open the doors to my wardrobe and reached in, turning with a pale blue confection of scalloped edge and beaded body clutched to his non-existent bosom. "Just look at this, Pippa! Isn't it the most stunning thing?"

It certainly was. "Lovely," I said, with the barest hint of envy that I hoped Christopher didn't notice. "You'll be the best dressed wo..." *Oopsie.* "—man there."

"That's the idea." He tossed the hanger on the bed before he pulled the dress over his head. "Give me a hand, darling?" his disembodied voice requested from inside the beaded creation.

"Of course." I went over and helped him smooth the dress into place before stepping back. "Oh, that's gorgeous. It does a beautiful job of bringing out your eyes."

Christopher is just about average height for a man, so he makes for a tall, but not outsized, woman. And he's slender, with that figure we're all longing for these days: totally flat fore and aft, leaving the nice, drop-waist gown to fall becomingly from the shoulders to the hem without getting caught up on anything unfashionable like breasts or bum.

"Thank you, darling." He turned this way and that in front of the full length mirror.

I bit my lip. "I don't suppose you'd let me come with you, would you?"

I was curious about the ball, I admit it. (I'm curious about most things.) But I was also a little worried, and I'll admit that, too. Something was scratching at the back of my neck in an unpleasant manner, and it wasn't the label in my blouse.

Christopher turned from the mirror to give me a look. "What's wrong, Pippa?"

"I don't know," I said honestly. "I have a bad feeling. Something feels like it's about to happen. Something... not good."

"You mean something bad?"

"I don't know what I mean. I'm just... uneasy. I'd feel better if I were going with you."

Christopher is the closest thing I have to a brother, slightly younger by a few months, and the idea of sending him alone into something I had reservations about, concerned me.

Christopher nodded, but said, "Well, you can't. Not only is it not a place for a well-bred young lady, but what if you're right and something happens, and I need you to come and get me from jail? If you're in there with me, I'll have to call Father to stand our bail, and that would definitely be not-good."

Definitely. For one thing, Uncle Herbert would yank Christopher back to Wiltshire so fast my hair would flutter in the breeze, and for another, he'd probably disinherit him. He might even lock him up in a sanitarium or asylum or monastery or something, and that would be the end of life as we knew it for both of us.

"I'll be prepared," I said. "Although it would be ever so much better if you could refrain from getting arrested in the first place. Are you sure I can't convince you to stay home tonight?"

He shook his head. "I can't, Pippa. Although I'll be as careful as I know how to be, I promise. I'll be observant, and I won't take any mad chances. And now I guess I'd better—"

He stopped at the sound of a knock on the hall door, and glanced at me. "Are you expecting someone?"

"Not me. Shouldn't Evans ring up before he admits anyone?"

Evans was the doorman in the mansion block in which Christopher and I shared a flat, and part of his job was to announce visitors before sending them upstairs, in the event the tenants should wish to be not-in to visitors.

Not-in as opposed to actually out, you understand. In the same way that not-good doesn't necessarily equate to wholly bad.

"He should," Christopher agreed. "Perhaps it's that young

woman from down the hall. The American one with all the teeth."

Perhaps it was. Or if not her, someone else who was already inside the building and wouldn't need to be announced. Perhaps it was Evans himself with a package. But just in case—

"You'd better hide. I'll go get rid of her."

"Bless you, my child," Christopher said. "I don't mind admitting she gives me the pip."

She didn't give me the pip, but then I wasn't the eligible grandson of a duke, and one who had no desire to marry.

"Just stay here and don't come out, no matter what you hear. I'll protect you."

I pulled the bedroom door shut behind me, and marched across the foyer to the front door. Which I yanked open without even peering out, so sure was I that on the other side would be the American manhunter with the teeth, heiress to a dime-store dynasty somewhere she called Toledo.

As a result, when I found myself face to face with an elegant young gentleman in evening kit, I fell back a step.

"Oh!" Good Lord. "How did *you* get up here?"

The young man took my involuntary recoil as an invitation to cross the threshold. Not my intention at all, I assure you. And I'm sure he knew that, but he didn't let it stop him. Instead, he glanced around the foyer with guarded interest (and a bit of a condescending sneer) before he answered my question. "Lift, of course. You didn't think I would climb the stairs, did you?"

Of course not. "You know that wasn't what I meant. Why didn't Evans ring up to announce you?"

Not that I needed to ask, really. While I had never had a problem telling Christopher and his cousin Crispin apart, the truth was that to a lot of people they looked the same, at least as long as they didn't stand next to each other. Evans, who to my knowledge had never encountered Crispin before, would have seen him come through the front door in his tailcoat and top hat, would have assumed he was Christopher, and would have waved him through. Politely.

Crispin's next words confirmed it. "He said, 'Good evening, Mr. Astley,' and went back to his newspaper. I decided not to quibble." He smirked.

"Of course you didn't." I folded my arms across my chest. "What do you want, St George?"

It wasn't technically his title yet, and wouldn't be until his grandfather, the Duke of Sutherland, breathed his last and Crispin's father, the current Viscount St George, moved into the duke's shoes, but it differentiated Crispin from Christopher (and his brother Francis) when they were all Mr. Astley, so I used it. It was better than curling my tongue around the syllables of his first name. Too familiar by half, especially when he didn't use mine.

The smirk spread. "Can't I come to visit my favorite cousin without incurring your suspicions, Darling?"

"You absolutely cannot. And why do you insist on addressing me like I'm your mother's lady's maid?"

He chuckled. "Because it's your name, Darling. Isn't it?"

It was, in a sense. Or at least it was a close approximation of it.

It's a long story, which goes back to the turn of the century and my late mother. She had been the younger sister of Christopher's mother, and while Aunt Roslyn had done the expected thing and married Uncle Herbert and proceeded to give birth to Cousin Francis, Cousin Robert, and, eventually, Cousin Christopher, my mother had run off to Germany and married a commoner. My parents had been very much in love, thank you, and my childhood had been as idyllic as anyone could ask for, but of course when I was eleven, The Great War started. Life on the Continent was no longer pleasant, nor was it safe, and I had been packed off to my aunt and uncle in England for my safety. Mother refused to leave Father, who had been drafted for the war effort, so it was just me. And since German sympathies, not unexpectedly, were at an all-time low in England, Uncle Herbert and Aunt Roz determined that it would be better to turn my last name of Schatz into English. It's German for treasure, something valuable or cherished or both, and it is also used informally as the equivalent of beloved or darling. Thus I was known as Philippa Darling from the moment I arrived on English soil.

If I had realized that I would one day have the Honorable Crispin Astley, future Viscount St George, standing in my foyer, smirking at me, calling me Darling in a way that set my teeth on edge, I would have put my foot down back then.

But there was absolutely nothing I could do about it now, so I rolled my eyes and asked him again, "What do you want, St George?"

And miracle of miracles, he stopped trying to antagonize me and came to the point. "Message from Grandfather. Kit is expected at Sutherland Hall tomorrow afternoon for tea and conversation."

"Just Christopher? Not me?" warred with a suspicious, "Why?" in my head. I settled for the latter.

Crispin raised an elegant shoulder. "Mine is not to reason why. I was coming up to Town anyway. Grandfather said to let Kit know he has an audience with His Grace."

"A little more notice might have been nice." Since Christopher was on his way out and it was likely to be a late night. Lady Austin's soirees always were.

"You're lucky I decided to indulge the old man in the first place," Crispin said callously. "But if you don't like it, you could always choose not to show up and see what happens."

Oh, yes. Brilliant idea.

"I'm sure you'd like that." One of the main aspects of his and Christopher's relationship has always been one of one-upmanship, the need for one of them to outdo the other. Or at least it has always seemed to be one of Crispin's main desires to outdo Christopher. Christopher is a bit more *laissez faire*, I suppose, live and let live. He's more concerned with his own life than Crispin's. But for Christopher not to answer his grand-father's summons would give Crispin the upper hand, a position he dearly loves.

He smirked, but didn't rise to the bait. "I have the H6, if you need help getting there."

As if I would voluntarily exile myself to several hours in a closed automobile with Crispin St George. Even if the Hispano-Suiza would likely get us there in half the time it would take to travel by train, I'd take the longer trip over sharing space with Crispin. "We'll manage on our own, thank you."

"Don't mention it," Crispin said, and glanced over my shoulder into the rest of the flat with a bright, expectant smile.

I winced, but gave in to the inevitable. To not offer would be rude, and I would surely hear about it tomorrow if I didn't. My standing with the duke, and with Crispin's parents, was already low enough. "May I offer you a cup of tea or something stronger?"

I was sure he'd jump on the opportunity to sit down and kick his feet up and drink Christopher's liquor and keep on annoying me for as long as I allowed it. I was rather surprised when he said, "I'm afraid I'm in a bit of a hurry. Although a quick look around can't hurt. You know Mother and Grandfather will ask me whether you and Kit are sharing."

Of all the cheek! But of course, if I refused to show him around, then he'd go home and tell them that, and then they'd think there had to be a reason why I was being secretive... and so I really was better served by letting him look, no matter how little I wanted to.

"Through there is the sitting room. Feel free to step through."

He did, and I followed, gesturing to the openings on both sides. "Kitchen and dining room to the right. Hall with two bedrooms and bath to the left."

"Cozy," Crispin commented. His face was impassive, and as such it was difficult to determine whether it was simply a comment on the size of the place—the whole flat could have fit into half a wing of Sutherland Hall, where Crispin still lived with his mother, father, and grandfather—or whether it was an observation on how closely Christopher and I shared space.

As a result, I wasn't sure whether to take offense or not. It's usually safe to do so when dealing with Crispin, but then there are those times when I jump to the wrong conclusion and he gets to smirk about it.

So I sniffed, but forbore to respond. "Mine is the closed door. Christopher's bedroom is at the end of the hall, with the bath between."

Crispin nodded, ambling down the hall to stick his head into Christopher's room. "Kit isn't home?"

I knew that Crispin could tell that someone lived in Christopher's room. All of Christopher's male paraphernalia was there: his clothes, his shoes, his shaving kit, and his suspenders. Anything Kitty used had always been kept in my room. Christopher had insisted. Now I was rather pleased by his foresight.

"He went out for the evening," I said.

Christopher had been as quiet as a mouse the whole time I'd been talking to Crispin. He no doubt knew his cousin was here, and figured that if anyone was liable to see through his makeup and wig, it was a boy who had known him since he was in nappies.

The latter eyed my closed door in silence for a moment before he arched a brow. "Not going to invite me to see your bedroom, Darling?"

"Absolutely not. Have you lost your mind?"

"Clearly," Crispin said dryly, and turned back towards the foyer and front door. "I'll be at Sutherland House until tomorrow morning if you change your mind about the motorcar. Rogers will pass on a message."

I thought about telling him we wouldn't change our minds, that there was no way I would willingly volunteer for several hours in a motorcar with him when I didn't have to, but in the end, I bit my tongue on the impulse and informed him, placidly, that I'd consult Christopher before we made a decision and then let him know if his services were required.

Then I followed Crispin across the foyer. "I'll see you down." And have a chat with Evans about the difference between Crispin and Christopher, and not to let the wrong Mr. Astley back upstairs without notice again.

Crispin smirked, like he knew exactly what I was thinking, but all he said was, "Delighted."

And then he proceeded to hold the door for me so I could pass in front of him, and to close it gently behind me once I was through and into the hallway.

TWO

I THOUGHT we would make it down to the first floor unmolested. We were at the lift doors and the lift was coming. Neither of us had spoken a word since we'd left the flat, so it wasn't like we were making any noise to attract attention. But nonetheless, just as the lift arrived on our floor with a cheerful *ding*, the door to a flat down the hall opened, and a strident voice called out, "Hold the elevator!"

Crispin stopped in the middle of pulling back the grille to watch as a vision in pink came storming down the hall towards us, scarves and chiffon panels fluttering and brown curls bouncing, teeth on full display. "Hullo, Pippa."

I cleared my throat. "Florence."

"Oh, don't stand on ceremony, sweetie! You know I've told you a thousand times to call me Flossie."

She turned to Crispin and stuck out a hand, all her perfect teeth on shining display. "There you are, Mr. Astley. I had started to worry you were avoiding me."

Crispin blinked, and I could see the thoughts following one another rapidly through his head. Of course he wasn't Christopher, so he had no idea who he was talking to—the American dime-store heiress from Toledo, in case you wondered—and so he had no way of addressing her by her last name. Since he couldn't in propriety use her given name when she hadn't used his, he was at a loss. I thought about what I might do to help, and then decided to let him sink or swim on his own. I didn't owe Crispin anything.

In any case, he ended up circumventing the issue rather expertly, by taking the hand she extended and—instead of shaking it—lifting it to his lips. When they brushed across her knuckles, Florence blushed a deep pink and tittered.

I rolled my eyes, even as I reflected that Christopher would most likely end up paying for that. "We were just on our way down to the lobby, Florence. Cris... Mr. Astley was just leaving, and I have to speak to Evans about something."

Crispin smirked, since he knew exactly what I wanted to speak to Evans about. Instead of saying anything about it, however, he handed Florence expertly into the lift and offered me his hand next. "Darling."

"I can manage," I told him coldly, and stepped into the box on my own. Crispin busied himself with pulling the grille across the opening, but not without a distinctly amused look on his face. Florence looked from one to the other of us with confusion. It was clear that she didn't understand why Christopher and I were acting so out of character towards one another, when we normally got on famously.

Nor is Christopher in the habit of calling me Darling, of course. Especially not in that smug, condescending tone.

"I know it's none of my business," she began, "but is everything okay?"

I managed a tight smile. "Everything's fine, Florence. Where are you off to this evening? That's a lovely dress you have on."

"Oh." She giggled. "This old thing?"

I refrained from rolling my eyes, since the dress was this year's fashion, and clearly worth every one of the not insignificant pounds she'd spent on it. "Are you going to a party?"

No one had invited me or Christopher to anything, or maybe Christopher just hadn't bothered to mention it, since he'd had other plans.

"Soiree at Lady Montfort's," Florence said, with a hopeful look in Crispin's direction. "Any chance that's where you're headed, too, Mr. Astley?"

But Crispin shook his head. "The Jungman sisters are having a Black and White party tonight. But if you'll allow me, I'd be pleased to drop you off on the way, Miss... um...Florence."

Florence grinned. Whether it was in response to the offer of a lift or the use of her first name was uncertain, but either way, she was clearly and obviously delighted.

"Behave yourself," I hissed to Crispin as we landed in the lobby with the usual accompanying noises I hoped would cover my words.

I wouldn't have bothered to admonish Christopher, who wasn't interested in Florence or her fortune, or for that matter in women in general, but Crispin had a reputation for much faster living. The Jungman sisters, Zita and Teresa, were firmly entrenched among the Bright Young Set, and besides, Florence believed he was Christopher. The last thing we needed was for Crispin to take advantage of the girl, and for it to blow back on Christopher when she ended up in the family way.

"Don't do anything Christopher wouldn't do," I told him, "or I will personally ensure that it's the last heir you sire!"

I expected a sneer. What I got was a broad grin. "Why, Darling, I didn't know you cared!"

He reached past me to pull back the grille as the lift door to the lobby opened.

"I don't," I said, stepping back out of the way so he could bow Florence out. Once she was safely in the lobby, hopefully out of range of hearing, I continued. "I mean it, St George. If you do anything to hurt Christopher, I will make you regret it. Don't think I won't."

He looked at me for a second with cool, gray eyes—so different from Christopher's warm blue ones—before he said, "I wouldn't doubt it, Darling. Now, if you'd be so kind?"

He nodded to the open door. "Places to go, people to see, you know."

I gave him one final threatening look before I stepped past the grille and into the lobby. Florence latched onto Crispin's arm the second he exited the lift, and swept him towards the front door with a jaunty wave over her shoulder. "See you around, Pippa! Come on, Mr. Astley!"

The bright blue panels of the Hispano-Suiza were clearly visible through the glass.

I waved back, a lot less enthusiastically, and bided my time while Evans held the door for them. And then, when he came back inside, while Crispin was occupied with getting Flossie and her chiffon panels settled in the passenger seat of his beloved H6, I approached Evans to explain, in painstaking detail, why he should never admit the Honorable Crispin Astley upstairs without first warning me, ever again.

WHEN I GOT BACK UP to the flat, Christopher—or more accurately, Kitty Dupree—was waiting for me in the foyer. The gorgeous dress was topped with a fur-trimmed evening cloak, and the rhinestones of the headband sparkled under the ceiling light. Christopher's eyes were worried. "What's going on?"

I closed the door behind me. "How much did you hear?"

"Crispin showed up and told you Grandfather wants to see me tomorrow."

I nodded. "Evans thought he was you, obviously, and let him up. I went back downstairs with him so I could make sure it won't happen again. Evans knows Crispin exists now, and if he sees the Hispano-Suiza pull up, he won't make the same mistake again."

"Unless Crispin parks somewhere else and walks in," Christopher muttered.

"Do you really think he'd bother? That seems like a lot of effort for not a lot of gain."

Christopher didn't look reassured, and I added, "I'm sure this was just an opportunity that presented itself, that he thought he'd take advantage of. He never misses a chance to irritate either one of us. But I doubt he'd be curious enough to make any extra effort to come back. Why would he?"

"Spying for Grandfather?" Christopher suggested.

That wasn't a bad suggestion, actually, and one I hadn't thought of. The Duke of Sutherland ruled the family with an iron fist, despite his advanced age and the fact that he spent most of his time in bed. Just look at the way he had summoned Christopher to his bedside and dispatched Crispin to tell him so, and they had both jumped to accommodate him.

But he wasn't able to get around to gather his own intelligence anymore. And Crispin had always bent over backwards to stay on good terms with his grandfather. With all that money, not to mention the title, at stake, it was hard to blame him, honestly.

"Crispin didn't see you while he was in the flat," I reminded Christopher. "He has no reason to know you're doing..." I gestured up and down over his figure, "—this. And he should be gone by the time you get downstairs. Florence

Schlomsky caught him going down and finagled a lift to Lady Montfort's soiree."

Christopher's eyes widened. "Crispin is going to Lady Montfort's?"

Considering that the aged Lady Montfort and her staid parties weren't likely to appeal to Crispin and his set, this seemed like a fair first question. But then before I could respond, Christopher shook his head. "Never mind that. The dime-store heiress caught him? Does she know he's him and not me?"

"I think she thought he was you," I said apologetically, and Christopher's eyes widened further. "But don't worry. I threatened to hurt him if he did anything to put you in a bind. I got the impression he believed me."

"I'm sure he did," Christopher agreed, "at least if he remembers the time you convinced him he'd get rounded up for the war effort and sent to France if he went into the village, and he didn't leave the grounds of the Hall for weeks."

We shared a moment of amusement before Christopher added, "So was it Crispin who set off your sense of something not-good happening tonight? Has it happened now, so I can safely go to Lady Austin's?"

I had no idea, and told him so. "I'm not a fortune teller, Christopher. I just had a bad feeling. Although I'll admit that St George showing up unexpectedly certainly qualifies as bad."

"He's a bit of a prat," Christopher agreed indulgently. "Although he's mostly harmless, you know. Just irritating. I'll head out, then?"

"I suppose so. He should certainly be gone by now. And Florence, too." The Hispano-Suiza was a race car, and while he couldn't properly race in London, I was sure Crispin wouldn't miss the opportunity to take off in a burst of speed and make Florence squeal and clutch at him.

"Then I'll see you in the morning, Pippa." Christopher brushed past me and out the door to the hallway. "Toodle-oo, darling."

"Toodle-oo," I told him, and watched as he swept into the lift and pulled the grille shut behind him.

THE FLAT WAS quiet after he left. I prepared myself a quick supper of cucumber sandwiches and tea, and ate while I leafed through a magazine I had picked up earlier in the day. I was tidying up after the meal when there was a buzz from downstairs. Evans had clearly taken my admonition about unannounced visitors to heart.

"Gentleman to see Mr. Astley, Miss Darling," he informed me. "Says his name is Grimsby."

The only Grimsby I could think of was Christopher's grandfather's valet, who certainly wasn't a gentleman in the usual sense of the word. But since he was the only one by that name I knew, I figured it had to be him. And while I wasn't Mr. Astley, and while Christopher wasn't here, maybe Grimsby had a message from the Duke. Maybe tomorrow's excursion had been canceled and we wouldn't have to make our way to Sutherland Hall after all.

"That's fine, Evans. Send him up."

"Right away, Miss Darling."

Evans disconnected and I headed to the front door and opened it so I would be ready for Grimsby when he arrived.

The lift clanged and whirred for a minute, and then the door opened and the grille was pushed back. Grimsby stepped out, tall and severe in a dark suit. "Miss Darling."

His eyes flickered over me and the hallway and the obvious lack of Christopher.

"Grimsby," I said. "Fancy seeing you here. Would you like to come inside?"

Grimsby indicated that he would, and I stepped back and gestured him into the foyer. "What can I do for you? Is everything all right at the Hall?"

He didn't answer, just looked around the foyer with hooded eyes. "I was hoping to talk to Mr. Astley."

"Christopher isn't here," I said. "Does this have something to do with tomorrow?"

He didn't answer, but he did turn to look at me. When nothing passed his lips, I added, "Crispin stopped by earlier to say that Christopher has been summoned to Sutherland Hall tomorrow for afternoon tea. His grandfather wants to see him?"

"His Grace has something on his mind," Grimsby intoned.

Clearly. "Would you happen to know what it is? Everything's all right, isn't it?"

Grimsby didn't answer. "When do you expect young Mr. Astley back?"

I pursed my lips. The way he refused to answer my questions was irritating, but I wasn't a Sutherland and so had no sway whatsoever with Grimsby. If he didn't want to tell me anything, there was nothing I could do about it. "Not until late, I'm afraid. He's out for the evening. But I'd be happy to take a message."

Grimsby looked at me. There was something slightly reptilian in the well-trained, black flatness of his eyes. "That won't be necessary," he said eventually. "I'll speak to him myself tomorrow, at Sutherland Hall. You *are* planning to make the trip?"

"Crispin didn't sound like it was optional."

Grimsby's lips twitched in something that might have become a smile, or perhaps a smirk or sneer, had it been given the opportunity to grow up. It wasn't. Grimsby is much too dignified for inappropriate displays of humor. "Thank you for your time, Miss Darling."

He dipped his head, a very modified sort of bow, and turned to the door.

"Don't mention it," I said, as he crossed over the threshold and into the hallway. "Safe home, Grimsby."

This time it was a curt—but not too curt—nod, and Grimsby was off. Once he was inside the lift and on his way down, I closed and locked the flat door again and went back to the kitchen.

THE FINAL INTERRUPTION came late in the night, after I had gone to bed. Nobody called from downstairs, and nobody knocked on the door this time. Instead, I was woken by the sound of the key in the lock—Christopher was home—and then by the sound of a quarrel in the foyer.

"—believe you'd be so careless!" a voice I didn't recognize snarled.

"—need your help!" Christopher hissed back.

"You certainly did tonight, you daft—"

"—not your problem!"

"I made it my problem! And you were lucky I was there at all. The only reason—"

"—don't care!" Christopher retorted. When I eased my bedroom door open a few more inches so I could creep into the hallway, I saw he was standing in the middle of the foyer, hands on his hips, still in the evening gown and T-strap shoes from earlier, but with the wig and sparkling headband hanging from one hand. His own hair was still slicked back, gleaming like wet wheat in the light from the small lamp I'd left burning on the sideboard, and the bright red lipstick had been partly gnawed off, either by Christopher himself or someone else. He seemed to have left the evening wrap behind, because it was nowhere to be seen. I surmised he'd been removed from the premises too quickly to have had the opportunity to collect it. His color was high, flags of heat riding on both his cheekbones, and his eyes were flashing with temper.

I crept forward another few inches and tilted my head to look at his companion.

Tall, dark, and handsome qualified, I decided. An inch or two taller than Christopher, although the heels on the strap shoes mostly made up for it, and a few years older, as well. He had brown hair, a sort of nutty color, with what I thought was a slight wave. I couldn't see much of it, since he was wearing a hat. Not the shiny evening topper Crispin had sported, but a more down-to-earth Homburg. He wore it with a brown tweed suit, which his shoulders filled out very nicely. Where Christopher—and for that matter Crispin—are slightly built and slender, still boyish at barely twenty-three (or still twenty-two, in Crispin's case), this man was broader, more muscular. I could only see him in profile, but he had a straight nose, high cheekbones—also flushed with color—and a square jaw that looked like he might be clenching his teeth. Both men were clearly irate, leaning towards one another, and whisper-yelling so as not to wake me. I don't think either of them had noticed my door opening or me slipping out.

"—acting like a gormless—" the man in brown said.

"I know what I'm doing!" Christopher snarled in response.

His opponent snorted. "Oh, clearly. You're lucky you're not languishing in a cell in the Old Bailey waiting for your father to get there to take you home. How could you be so bloody stupid?!"

It was the kind of question there's no real answer to, not unless you want to dig yourself deeper into the hole you're already standing in, and Christopher must have recognized it, because all he did was pout. After a few moments' silence, he managed a mutter of, "Thank you for making sure that didn't happen."

His... friend?... took a slow breath, too, and let it out. "You're welcome. In return, maybe you'd try to make sure it won't happen again?"

Christopher didn't say anything, but I recognized the mulish stubbornness of his expression, and so, clearly, did his companion, whose voice turned serious. "Listen to me, Kit. Next time, I'm not likely to be there. I was only there tonight because I heard about the raid beforehand. It's not my job to haul your arse out of the fire, and if I'm caught doing it, my actual job is on the line. You owe it to me to ensure that I won't have to do this again!"

Christopher muttered something.

"What was that?"

"I said I'll try."

There was a moment's pause, and then the man in the tweed suit said, "If that's the best you can do, then I suppose I'll have to be satisfied with it."

He turned on his heel and headed for the door. I waited to see whether Christopher would do anything to stop him, but he didn't. I could see his hands bunch into fists, but he didn't say a word, and didn't even watch, just kept his eyes on the floor, as his friend yanked the front door open and stepped through. "Good night, Kit. Lock this behind me."

He let the door go, and it dropped into the frame with a dull thud that I hoped hadn't woken any of the other inhabitants on our floor. A few seconds later I heard the grille get drawn across the opening to the lift, and then the sound of the box heading down. Christopher still hadn't made a move towards the door to lock it, so I abandoned my lurking in the hallway and brushed past him to do it myself.

"Who was that?"

He didn't answer, and when I'd turned the key and made sure the door was secure, I turned back to him and tried again. "Who's your friend?"

"Chap I used to know at Eton," Christopher muttered.

I parked my hands on my hips. "Did I hear him right? Something happened and you might have ended up in the Old Bailey? Was there a raid on the ball?"

Christopher shook himself and seemed to wake up. "I guess so. That's what he said. I was already out of there by then." He met my eyes for a moment, his own distant, as if he were thinking about something else, before he managed a slight smile. "Go back to bed, Pippa. It's late. We can talk about it tomorrow."

I contemplated him for a second before I nodded. "Of course. We'll have to be on the 10:35 train to make it to Sutherland Hall before two. Is that going to be a problem?"

Christopher shook his head. "Did you pack?"

"For both of us. I know what you'll need for a few days away."

"Thank you, darling." He bent and dropped a kiss on my cheek before he brushed past me down the hall towards his own bedroom.

"Sleep well, Pippa," he tossed over his shoulder. "See you in the morning."

"See you then." I watched him walk into the washroom and close the door behind him before I made my way back to my own bedroom and my own bed. I was still awake when I heard the toilet flush and Christopher turn out the light and head into his own room to go to sleep.

THREE

"Christopher, sweet!"

Charlotte, Viscountess St George, swooped in and pecked Christopher on the cheek as soon as we landed in the foyer at Sutherland Hall on Saturday afternoon.

She has always been a smidgeon too affectionate with the male side of the family, if you ask me. Not just Christopher, but his father as well. And of course she dotes on Crispin. Practically suffocates him with affection.

Me, on the other hand, she can take or leave, and I'm fairly certain her preference would be if I had decided to do the latter.

"And Miss Darling." She dropped her hands from Christopher's shoulders with a final graze over his upper arms, and turned to give me a polite smile. Her voice had cooled down several degrees by the time she got to my name.

"Lady Charlotte." I modified a curtsey into a quick dip in the knees while I wondered what I had done to upset her.

We've never been close. I was attached to the family on Christopher's mother's side, of course, and we weren't quite as prominent in society as the Sutherlands. Charlotte, as the daughter-in-law of a duke, might feel that my mother's antecedents as the daughter—and a younger daughter, at that—of a younger son were too plebeian to bother with. And then, of course, there was my father.

But she should have had plenty of time to come to terms with me by now. I had lived with the Astleys for more than a dozen years. Robert's death was almost a decade in the past. And while the happenings on the Continent had been terrible for everyone, Aunt Charlotte and Uncle Harold hadn't lost anyone in the conflict. Crispin was their only child, and he had been too young to serve. It was Uncle Herbert and Aunt Roz who had lost Robert, and if they could love me and care for me in spite of my father's nationality, I saw no reason why Lady Charlotte should have a poor attitude.

She looked at me as if I were something that had made it into the house on the bottom of her shoe, however. I glanced at Christopher to see if he had any idea what was going on, but he looked as perplexed as I was.

"Something wrong, Aunt Charlotte?"

Her expression cleared. "Of course not, darling boy." The endearment was accompanied by a pat of his cheek, before she tucked her hand through his elbow. "Come along. Let's go into the parlor while we wait for your grandfather to finish speaking to Francis."

She click-clacked her way across the marble of the foyer, tugging him along beside her. I hadn't been invited to accompany them, so maybe she had expected me to take myself upstairs with the bags, but Christopher called out to me. "Come along, Pippa. And don't dawdle. Don't you want to see Mother and Father?"

Of course I did. I also had a shameful desire to put Aunt Charlotte's nose out of joint. Both of those desires were warring inside me as I crossed the foyer and stepped across the threshold into the parlor behind Christopher and Lady Charlotte.

FRANCIS NEVER CAME BACK—NOT into the parlor—and Crispin wasn't there to begin with, but after ten minutes or so, Grimsby appeared in the doorway and spirited Aunt Roz upstairs. She didn't come back, either. I wondered if she might have gone to talk to Francis, if the audience with the duke had upset him enough that he wanted his mother. He doesn't handle conflict terribly well, not after spending several years shooting at others and being shot at in return, and if the Duke of Sutherland is a master at anything, it's conflict.

At any rate, Grimsby came back at that point and told Christopher that it was his turn to see his grandfather.

It isn't usually the valet's job to summon guests for the master of the house, so I think we had both been a bit surprised to see Grimsby come and go as the duke's emissary. But Aunt Charlotte didn't bat an eye, just waved her hand regally. "Go on, Christopher, darling. Don't keep your grandfather waiting."

Christopher arched his brows, but stood and buttoned his jacket. I shot to my feet, as well. "I'll go with you."

Grimsby turned to me, and so did everyone else. Before anyone could say anything, I added, "I'll wait outside the Duke's Chamber. But I'll accompany you upstairs."

I didn't want to be left in the parlor with only Aunt Charlotte and the two uncles for company, after all. I knew that Christopher would likely appreciate the moral support on the way up, and besides, I had a cunning plan.

Christopher nodded, of course, and crooked his elbow at me. I slipped my hand through and let him escort me out.

Grimsby closed the door gently behind us before anyone in the parlor could articulate what they were thinking. "This way, if you would, Mr. Astley, Miss Darling."

He led the way to the central staircase.

About halfway up, Christopher found his voice. "Miss Darling told me you stopped by the flat last night, Grimsby."

Grimsby didn't even bat an eye. "Yes, Mr. Astley. I wanted a word."

Christopher waited, but when Grimsby didn't take the opportunity to explain what that word might be, he said, "I suppose now is not a good time?"

"I'm afraid not, Mr. Astley." Grimsby's voice was perfectly polite and unassuming. "His Grace is waiting. And it's something that would be better discussed in private."

Christopher opened his mouth, seemed unable to come up with anything to say—although I could see his complexion turn pale—and closed it again.

"I'll come to your room, if I may," Grimsby said blandly, "after your talk with His Grace, and we'll have our own chat."

Christopher blinked. I did the same. It was, at the same time, so very polite and so egregiously brazen that it was hard to find words.

By now we had reached the top of the stairs, and the upper corridor in the main wing of the house. I glanced at the door to the Duchess's Chamber, unused since Christopher's grandmother died some ten years before, and stopped. "I'll meet you in your room after your visit with your grandfather, then, Christopher?"

Christopher nodded. "Yes, Pippa. Please." He hesitated. "That is... if Grimsby doesn't...?"

Clearly he wasn't used to worrying about whether the valet would object to me being in his room or not. Nor was I, if it came to that.

Grimsby looked bland. "It is entirely up to you, Mr. Astley, if you want an audience for our discussion."

He continued on towards the Duke's Chamber while Christopher and I exchanged a look behind his back. It had sounded quite ominous. Then I squeezed Christopher's arm in support before I dropped my hand and headed in the other direction, towards the door to the Duchess's Chamber. Christopher went to meet Grimsby, who was lingering in front of the duke's bedroom door.

I heard a brisk knock and then Grimsby's voice, "Your Grace? Mr. Christopher Astley to see you," before I was too far into the Duchess's Chamber to hear the response. A moment later, Grimsby's steps came back down the hallway towards me. For a moment, I was concerned that he would open the door and order me out, but then the steps continued down the staircase, and I started to breathe again.

And just to have it said: I know I'm not a child anymore, and it wasn't Grimsby's job to order me about. But with the high-handed way he was behaving, it was difficult to guess exactly what he might do, and I felt off-balance.

Although he was gone now, and I could yet again concentrate on the task at hand.

I couldn't hear anything that was going on inside the duke's bedchamber. There were two dressing rooms between me and where Christopher was standing right now, in front of his grandfather's bed. But there was a way for me to get closer.

Or rather, there were two. Now that Grimsby had descended to the ground floor, I could go back out into the hallway, sneak down to the duke's door, and press my ear to it. But if I got caught, by Grimsby or by someone else, I would look very silly trying to eavesdrop in plain view in the main corridor of the house, and it would also be uncouth in the extreme for me to do so.

That was why I had ducked into the Duchess's Chamber in the first place. Because I knew, from childhood memories of playing in Sutherland Hall, that there was a not-so-secret passage running between the Duke's and Duchess's Chambers, along the exterior wall of the manor behind the two dressing rooms. The original duke, who had been responsible for building the hall back in the mists of time, must have wanted a way to visit his wife for congress without traversing the main hallway with his candle at night. Every time we had played hide-and-seek as children, we could usually find someone—most often Crispin, who knew the Hall best—hidden in the passage between the Duke's and Duchess's Chambers, or in one of the other out-of-the-way passages or stairwells tucked away against the outer walls of the manor.

In this case, I made my way past the obvious door into the duchess's (now empty) dressing room and over to the paneling in the corner of the room, where the semi-secret entrance to the passage lay. Slipping my fingers into the small crevice that hid the latch was a matter of a second's work, and then part of the paneling swung out and exposed the narrow stone passage. I probably shouldn't have been surprised to see Crispin at the end of it, ear close to the wall of his grandfather's bedroom.

He looked up when the door opened, either because the paneling had made a sound swinging into the room or because the light from outside suddenly flooded the usually gloomy narrowness of the passage.

For a second we stared at one another. I'm not sure whether it took that long for him to recognize me, or whether he was just surprised that I'd disturbed his eavesdropping. Either way, it gave me that moment or two to calculate the situation and my choices.

From where I was standing, I figured I had two. I could join Crispin at the other end of the passage, and listen to what the duke had to say to Christopher along with him. I wanted to know what that was, of course, otherwise I wouldn't be here.

On the other hand, it would put me in close proximity to Crispin, where I didn't want to be.

And also, it would give him the opportunity to continue to eavesdrop on what the duke had to say to Christopher, and I'm sure neither of us—Christopher or I—wanted that to happen. We didn't know the exact reason why Christopher had been called here—we had discussed it on the train down—but we were both certain it couldn't be for anything good. The duke might have found out about Christopher's proclivities for dresses, makeup, and drag balls, which would be disastrous, or he might simply object to Christopher's choice to live with me in our own service flat in London, and not at Sutherland House, the duke's Town residence. If he insisted that we move into the ancestral town house, most of Christopher's freedom and all of his choices would be gone, and so would most of mine.

In the end, it only took that one second to make the decision. The choice was obvious once I thought about it. Christopher would certainly tell me what the conversation had been about if I wasn't in a position to hear it myself. Crispin, on the other hand, had his entire life ahead of him to cause trouble. Long after the duke was dead and buried, Crispin could continue to be a thorn in both our sides if he learned any of Christopher's secrets now.

And so I scrambled down the uneven stone floor of the passage, wrapped my fingers around his wrist, and tugged.

"You horrible sneak! Get out of here!"

Crispin sniggered, but didn't budge. "Quiet, Darling. They'll hear you."

"I don't care if they hear me," I hissed, yanking on his arm. "At least that way they'll know you're in here, eavesdropping. Come out immediately, or I'll cause a scene and make sure your grandfather knows what you're doing!"

Crispin smirked. "Maybe he knows already. Maybe he put me here so I would overhear."

I faltered for a second. Was that a possibility?

It might be, actually. Although if the duke had wanted Crispin to hear his conversations with the other family members, surely he would have kept him in the bedroom instead of having him hide in the secret passage? No reason not to keep that out in the open, was there? Not if you were the head of the family and could do whatever you wanted?

And anyway, Uncle Harold was downstairs in the parlor. If the duke had wanted someone else to hear, surely it would have been his son, his successor, and not his grandson? Surely Crispin had enough misdemeanors and peccadillos to deserve his own talking to?

"I don't believe you," I said, although it might not have been quite as staunch as I would have liked it to be.

"Believe what you want, Darling." He twitched his wrist out of my grip. "Run along now, so I can hear what's going on."

"I'll scream," I told him, snatching for his arm again. "Your grandfather can't do anything to me. I'm not his grandchild. He has no control over me. If he kicks me out, I'll go back to London and be just fine. But if he finds out that *you've* been eavesdropping..."

"He'll laugh," Crispin said.

"Are you sure about that? What exactly did you and Flossie Schlomsky do, when you left last night? Where did you take her, and what happened?"

"Nothing," Crispin said, but he grimaced. "Fine. Let go of me. I'll come out."

I dropped his arm and headed down the passage towards the Duchess's Chamber. Half a second later, Crispin followed. He made sure the secret door had melted back into the paneling before he turned to me. "You're a horrible cow, Darling. How dare you threaten me?"

"How dare you eavesdrop on your family?" I shot back, sticking both hands on my hips to glare at him. "How terribly ill-bred of you, St George!"

He smirked. "Are you telling me you weren't planning to do exactly the same, Darling?"

Of course I'd been planning to do the same. But I wasn't about to admit that to him. So instead I said, poisonously, "I knew you'd be in there, you know. You aren't subtle at all. When you weren't downstairs in the parlor, I knew you'd be up here, creeping along in the wainscoting like a cockroach!"

The humor dropped from his face and he flushed, flags of hot pink on both his cheekbones. "You're awful, Darling. Truly. I can't imagine what Kit sees in you."

He saw his best friend, obviously. His pseudo-sister. To suggest anything else was ridiculous.

"And I can't imagine what your various women see in you," I fired back, since rumor had it that he had had plenty of them, difficult as that was to believe.

And then I smirked, just as evilly as he'd done a minute ago, as I drove the metaphorical knife in. "Oh, wait. I forgot. It isn't you at all, is it? It's the money and the title. Without those, you wouldn't have a thing to interest a woman!"

He sneered. "Shows what you know, Darling."

I opened my mouth to retort, something clever and cutting, when I realized I had no stinging comeback. So I tossed my head instead. "You're deplorable, St George. Truly."

"Maybe so," Crispin agreed, a bit too readily. "Although I'll have you know I don't have to listen in to know what Kit's hiding. I was still there when he came outside yesterday evening, you know. And that American gold-digger you saddled me with was happy to tell me all about your 'friend' Kitty Dupree. *She* might be stupid enough not to realize that Kit is Kitty, but *I'm* not!"

"She's not a gold-digger," I said fairly, even as my stomach dropped. "Perhaps she didn't tell you, but she's a wealthy heiress. Her father is a businessman in Toledo."

"Where?"

"Somewhere in America. But that's not important. What matters is that she's one of those heiresses from across the pond who's looking to trade American dollars for a British title. You could do worse, St George. She obviously liked you."

"Nice try, Darling," Crispin said dryly, "but you're not going to make me forget what we were talking about. I've known Kit for twenty-three years. I recognize him, even when he's wearing a wig and a dress."

I grimaced. "I suppose we have you to thank for this, then?"

This being the conversation taking place in the other room, of course.

Crispin sniffed. "Don't be absurd, Darling. I told you yesterday that Kit was expected today. At that point I hadn't seen him yet."

"But I'm sure you immediately ran back here and told everyone in the household what you'd discovered, didn't you?"

He opened his mouth, probably to deny it, but I cut him off. "You're a sneak, St George. How completely in character for you to be up here, pressing your ear to the wall!"

"Just exactly what you'd be doing right now if I hadn't been here first," Crispin retorted.

"That's different! I'm concerned. You're just looking for something you can use to cause trouble."

Crispin's lips twitched into a smirk. "Oh, indeed. Would

you like to know what's going on with your Cousin Francis and your Aunt Roz?"

I sighed. Of course I wanted to know. But it was galling to have to ask Crispin for the information. "Is something bad going on?"

"You could say that," Crispin said, with what I can only describe as a snigger. "Cousin Francis has a drug habit. Aunt Roslyn has been selling gossip to the London tabloids to pay for it."

I scowled at him. "That's hardly a laughing matter."

"Of course it is," Crispin said. "Aunt Roslyn selling her friends' secrets for money? News about who's sleeping in separate rooms and whose piles are acting up? How can you say that isn't funny?"

Of course that part of it was funny. Or perhaps not so funny to the people with the piles who were dealing with the separate rooms. But that wasn't what I'd been referring to, and Crispin knew it.

He took in the look on my face, and added, "Oh, come off it, Darling. You're no more concerned about Francis than I am. Besides, it's not like it's news. Anyone who knows him, and knows anything about self-medication, can tell what he's been up to. It's been going on for years."

"Why didn't you tell someone?"

"It's none of my affair," Crispin said, "is it? If Cousin Francis needs something to help him cope with what happened in the war, who am I to get between him and his crutches?"

"But..."

"We all cope in our own ways, Darling. Francis is a grown man. If this is how he chooses to deal with his problems, it's his concern."

"But that's unkind! It's unhelpful!"

"He has the right to go to hell in his own way," Crispin said coolly. "And I have problems of my own."

I snorted. "Let me guess. A balance at Fortnum & Mason? Some girl you talked into thinking you care, who won't leave you alone now that you've gotten what you want from her?"

He leaned closer, teeth gritted. "Listen, Darling..."

But before he could continue, something behind my shoulder snared his attention, and he straightened, the sneer dropping off his face in favor of bland nothingness. "Kit."

"Crispin." Christopher glanced from me to him and back. "I heard you all the way down the hall."

Crispin took a step back and shot his cuffs. Christopher waited another moment to see if he was going to say anything else, and when he didn't, turned to me. "We have to go, Pippa. Meeting with Grimsby, remember."

I nodded. "Did everything go all right next door?"

He was a little pale, to be honest, as if the conversation had been more taxing than expected. Or perhaps it was just a reaction left over from the events of last evening. Late night, early morning, exciting escape from a raid in the company of someone tall, dark, and dangerous.

Or perhaps it was the prospect of talking to Grimsby, whose demeanor had certainly come across as ominous. I thought I saw a glint of interest in Crispin's beady eye, but it was easily extinguished when I glared at him. He arched a brow my way, but didn't say anything.

"Fine," Christopher said. "We'll see you later, Crispin."

He took my arm. Crispin murmured something polite and non-committal, and stayed behind in the Duchess's Chamber when Christopher towed me through the door and into the hallway.

"He's going to go back into the passage as soon as we're out of the way," I informed Christopher when I thought we had traveled far enough that Crispin wouldn't hear me. "That's what he was doing when I came in."

"Hard to blame him for that when you were planning to do the same thing, isn't it?"

He didn't look at me as he said it, just kept pulling me along towards the bedroom he usually stays in when we're visiting the hall.

"He must have been up there for a while," I said. "Long enough to hear about both Francis and Aunt Roz."

Christopher slanted me a look. "Something going on with my mother and brother?"

"Francis has a drug habit," I told him, "and apparently your mother is supporting it by unearthing secrets about the upper classes and selling them to some tabloid in London. I'm not sure exactly how it works, but that's what Crispin said was going on."

"My mother is keeping my brother in illicit drugs by exchanging gossip for money?"

Christopher turned the corner into the east wing of Sutherland Hall, tugging me along.

"That sounds rather unlikely, Pippa, if you'll forgive me for saying so. Are you sure Crispin wasn't just pulling your leg?"

"He didn't sound as if he was." Although anything was possible. Crispin did have an annoying habit of saying things just for the attention they would get him. "Your grandfather didn't bring it up?"

Christopher shook his head.

"What did he want to talk about? Anything I should know?"

"He thinks it's time I get off my duff and propose."

He pushed open the door to his bedroom and pulled me inside. The weekender bag I had packed yesterday evening was sitting in the middle of the bed, unopened. Perhaps Grimsby hadn't gotten around to emptying it. Or perhaps that was to be his excuse for the time he planned to spend here in Christopher's room shortly.

"Pardon me?" I said.

"He thinks," Christopher enunciated, as if the problem had been that I hadn't heard him the first time, "that it's time I propose."

I blinked. "To who?" Or whom?

"To you," Christopher said.

FOUR

I'll ADMIT that for the first moment or two I wasn't sure whether to laugh or cry. Part of my mind insisted that it had to be a joke, that the duke couldn't possibly be serious, and so laughter was in order. The other part knew perfectly well that the Duke of Sutherland had no sense of humor whatsoever, and that Christopher wouldn't choose to jest about this.

As a result, the laughter got stuck in my throat, and I needed Christopher to pound on my back so I would stop coughing. Once I could breathe again, I asked, "I'm sorry, but what did you say?"

"I have ruined you," Christopher pronounced. "We've been living together without benefit of clergy, or for that matter without a chaperone, for several months. No one else will want you now. And while your heritage is clearly subpar for the grandson of the Duke of Sutherland—German, and a commoner to boot..."

"You keep quiet about my heritage!" I said, insulted.

Christopher arched his brows. Crispin can do one; Christopher has to do both. "You know I don't care about your heritage,

Pippa. Nor does it matter, you know. I have no plans to marry you."

Of course. "I'm sorry. You took me by surprise."

"*He* took *me* by surprise," Christopher said, and then stopped when we heard the sound of footsteps in the hall outside.

We exchanged a look, and Christopher put a finger to his lips before dragging me over to the edge of the bed, where he pushed me down and sat next to me. He transferred his grip from my elbow to my hand, which he folded between both of his. "Just in case he's planning to report back to Grandfather after this."

The footsteps stopped just outside the door, and Christopher called out, "Come in," before Grimsby could knock.

The door opened and the valet stood on the threshold. Those reptilian eyes flickered between Christopher's face and mine, and then down to our intertwined hands for a moment, before he glanced at Christopher, politely inquiring.

"Pippa stays," Christopher said, with a touch of belligerence, as if Grimsby had questioned it. "You can say whatever you need to say in front of her. We have no secrets from one another."

That wasn't true at all, actually. Whatever Christopher gets up to during those drag balls he attends, is something he never talks about. He hadn't been particularly forthcoming about the chap he knew from Eton, either, even though I had raised the subject again on the train this morning. And I did occasionally encounter something that I didn't see it necessary to share with him, either, if it came to that.

I'm not sure I'd call those things secrets, though. At least in my case, they weren't things I particularly wanted to keep from him, just things he probably didn't need to know. And just because I hadn't shared them yet, didn't mean I wouldn't share them at some point if the situation seemed right.

At the moment it didn't matter, anyway. I certainly didn't want to leave the room before Grimsby had had his say, so I was willing to play my part in this farce we were putting on.

Grimsby's face retained its façade of bland nothingness. "As you wish."

He closed the door behind him. The quiet click of the latch was loud in the silence. "Would you like for me to unpack for you, Mr. Astley?"

His glance flickered to the bag on the bed behind us.

"I'll do it," Christopher said, and I got the impression that he didn't want Grimsby's hands on any of his belongings.

Not that there was anything untoward or compromising in the bag. I was the one who had packed it, so I knew exactly what was inside. But Grimsby's demeanor right now was such that it gave the impression that anything he touched would be just a bit tainted.

"I'll get to the point, then." Grimsby stood just inside the door to the room, hands behind his back and his face the proper bland expressionlessness of the well-trained servant. Only his eyes gave him away. The black was lit from within with what could only be malice. I recognized that expression, having seen it frequently in Crispin's eyes growing up. "His Grace the Duke has recently been looking for information about what his heirs have been up to while not under the roof of Sutherland Hall."

"As is his right," Christopher said evenly, whether he truly believed it or not. As far as I was aware, he didn't. We both agreed that the duke was a meddlesome, ill-spirited old man who didn't understand how things worked in the modern age, and who would be better off leaving his children and grandchildren to live their own lives as they pleased out from under the ducal thumb. But of course neither of us could admit that to Grimsby, who would be sure to pass the intelligence right back to His Grace.

Grimsby... well, he didn't exactly smirk. No servant in his right mind smirks, not if he wants to keep his job. But there was the distinct impression of a smirk somewhere on his countenance, even if it wasn't visible. "Of course, Mr. Astley. To proceed, I spent a couple of days in London last month, and I know what the two of you are up to."

Well, that was coming right out with it, wasn't it? Nothing subtle about that. Christopher and I exchanged a look before we both turned back to Grimsby.

"What exactly is it you think we've been up to?"

"Not this," Grimsby said, with a glance between us that took in, and dismissed, the way Christopher's hand was holding mine. "You—"

He looked at me, "—have been seeking employment with various publishers and publications. Looking for a job. Looking for independence."

He made it sound like a bad thing, when I'd rather thought I'd been doing something admirable. Looking for a way to support myself rather than live on the charity of Christopher's allowance and the handouts from Aunt Roz.

"I would have thought His Grace would rather I support myself than angle to marry his grandson," I said.

"If it were Master Crispin and the title," Grimsby answered with a grimace; I grimaced, too, at the idea of marrying Crispin, "then yes, His Grace would rather you support yourself than become involved with the family any further than you already are."

He'd rather I jumped off a bridge somewhere, too, clearly.

"But since it's Master Christopher, His Grace would rather the two of you do things the proper way."

"And marry?"

"That would be His Grace's preference," Grimsby said blandly. "However—"

He turned to Christopher, who went a shade paler, "—then there's you."

Christopher opened his mouth, probably to argue, and Grimsby shut him down promptly. "I have been employed in His Grace's household for many years. I have watched you grow up. Dressing yourself in your flat-mate's clothes and using your flat-mate's makeup isn't enough to disguise you from those who know you."

Clearly not, if Crispin had also recognized him. I realized, with a stab of guilt, that I hadn't even had a chance to tell Christopher that yet.

"Grandfather didn't say anything about it," Christopher said. There was a hint of defiance, or maybe a question, in his tone.

Grimsby's lips curved. It was so slight it was almost invisible, but it was there. Satisfaction. "I thought perhaps it was something you would prefer His Grace not learn about. Or for that matter Lord and Lady Herbert."

I honestly didn't think Lady Herbert—Aunt Roz—would care what Christopher did in his spare time. She'd worry about the dangers, of course. She'd worry about arrest and prison and hard labor, and ostracization and ridicule and whatever else might come along with Christopher's preferences. But I didn't think she'd truly *care*, not about anything but her youngest son's happiness. If dressing up in gowns and wearing lipstick made him happy, why would that matter to his loving mother?

Uncle Herbert, on the other hand, might care a bit more, especially about the ostracization and ridicule. And of course His Grace the Duke would be fit to be tied.

"I suppose you thought I might like to show you my appreciation in a monetary way?" Christopher asked dryly. His hand had tightened around mine to the point where it was almost painful. His voice shook slightly, but I wasn't certain whether it was from anger or fear, or perhaps a bit of both.

Grimsby inferred, as politely as you wish, that he had indeed thought such might be the case.

"How much?" Christopher asked. Again, I didn't know whether he was too angry or perhaps too worried to be more circumspect, or whether he had simply decided to be shockingly blunt.

Grimsby suggested that perhaps a thousand pounds might be a suitable amount, and I could hear Christopher's breath catch. Mine certainly did. A thousand pounds is a lot of money, especially when you have no income beyond the allowance you get from your doting father.

A father who might not continue to be doting, and so might not continue to be generous, if the cause for the blackmail is revealed.

"I'll need a little time," Christopher began, just as footsteps hurried past outside in the hallway. A moment later, a door slammed nearby, and we all jumped, even Grimsby.

A second later it happened again, and then there was the sound of muffled voices.

The valet had clearly been recalled to himself. "Perhaps we might discuss the matter in private at some later point," he said. "I should attend to His Grace."

"Outside the house," Christopher said. "There are too many people here."

Grimsby nodded politely. "As you wish, Mr. Astley. I shall make myself available in the formal garden at eleven tonight. Will that suit?"

Christopher allowed as how that would suit very well, and Grimsby gave him—gave us both—another of those modified bows that wasn't servile at all before he disappeared into the hallway with another discreet click of the lock. I turned to Christopher and opened my mouth, but he shook his head. "Let's have a stroll across the grounds. Work up an appetite before tea."

Outside the house, away from listening ears, was what he meant. Like he had asked Grimsby to do.

"Of course." I was still wearing my traveling costume from the train ride, so I was quite well dressed for a stroll across the grounds.

Christopher took a left out of the door, towards the end of the east wing instead of the central wing and main staircase. "We'll take the servants' stairs down. It'll be quicker."

I nodded.

In addition to the semi-secret passage between the Duke's and Duchess's Chambers, Sutherland Hall is practically honeycombed with other passages and stairwells. There are servants' stairs at the end of each wing, of course, along with servants' halls to and from the below-stairs, and one of those was what we were heading for. But there's also a narrow stairwell from the study downstairs to the linen closet in the corner of the central wing upstairs, for those times when someone had to get around quickly and quietly. And there's a priest's hole tucked behind the chimney in the library. It even has a spy-hole in the paneling, for when the occupant wanted to watch what was going on in the library itself. And at the top of the house, in the vast space of the attics, there's a built-in cabinet that opens into a rather spacious room where someone could conceivably spend a not-uncomfortable week or two, should it be necessary. There's even a damp and miserable little room below-stairs, that Crispin used to tell me was a dungeon where people had died and been turned to skeletons. Even this many years later, I had no desire to see that room again.

And speaking of Crispin...

"Your cousin still lives in the rooms across from you, doesn't he?"

Christopher nodded, "Is that him, yelling? Wait, no. It's Uncle Harold, isn't it?"

It was. The voice clearly belonged to the Viscount St George, Crispin's father, and he was just as clearly reading his son the riot act.

"—utterly ruined," he snarled. "Your grandfather won't hear of it, nor will I or your mother!"

Crispin's voice interjected something, but it was too low for me to make out. From the context, I could perhaps guess that he had informed his father he was of age, because Uncle Harold's voice came back, just as vicious as before. "If you want to be treated like a man, then you'd better step up and start showing some maturity and responsibility towards your family and heritage. The way you've been carrying on—"

Crispin said something else, and again I couldn't make it out. I glanced at Christopher, who met my eyes, but shook his head.

"Don't you sass me, boy!" There was a bang from inside, loud enough that both Christopher and I jumped. Crispin made a noise, almost as if his father had socked him in the stomach, although he couldn't have, because Crispin got his voice back too quickly for that.

"Father! Wait, you can't—"

"I can do what I want, and you'd better remember it!"

Uncle Harold's voice got louder and clearer as he approached the other side of the door. Christopher and I started to scurry away, but not before I'd caught another sentence or two. "I'm your grandfather's heir, the future duke, and I can absolutely approve or disapprove of who you want to marry. So if you want to keep the viscountcy and your place in the hereditary line, you'd better not even think of defying me."

There was a pause, in which I thought Crispin might have tried to say something, but got cut off, yet again, by his father. I had suspected before that their relationship wasn't all it ought to have been, but I had never realized it was this bad. It was almost enough to make me feel bad for Crispin.

However, Uncle Harold sounded a little calmer now, or at least he wasn't yelling anymore, although his words fell with at least as much vitriol. "You can't have her, and that's that. Find someone else to marry. Keep her as a mistress if she'll have you. But you will not destroy this family and your future by marrying some common chippy, and one who is a foreigner to boot!"

"Don't you—" Crispin's voice rose, and that was the last thing I heard before Christopher yanked open the door to the servants' staircase and pulled me through and into the dusky grimness of another stone passage.

We clattered down the steps in silence, or at least silence apart from the sound of our feet hitting stone. At the bottom, Christopher pushed open the door to the hallway, and then nudged me ahead of him into the conservatory, which happens to sit at that end of the house. Two minutes later, we were outside in the fresh air, strolling, rather quickly, along one of the graveled paths towards the front of the house.

It was Christopher who broke the silence. "Whew."

I nodded. "I had no idea he wanted to marry anyone. Did you?"

My impression of Crispin was of a social butterfly, or perhaps something more like a social mosquito. He flitted around, landed occasionally, and stuck his stinger in first this woman, then that one, but he never stayed long before he flew off again, looking for his next victim. Of anyone I knew, I would have guessed he'd be the very last to want to get married.

Well, the very last aside from Christopher.

Who shook his head in response to my question. "No. Although I must admit I'm more concerned about my own marriage than about Crispin's right now."

"That's right," I said. "Your grandfather wants you to propose to me."

"So it seems."

"Your grandfather thinks we're living in sin? You and me?"

Christopher nodded.

"That's mad. Surely Aunt Roz and Uncle Herbert know better?"

"Mum does," Christopher said. "She wouldn't have allowed it otherwise. You know she looks at you like a daughter. To her, I'm sure it's no different than if we'd really been brother and sister."

I nodded.

"I'm not sure about Father. But he certainly never said anything about it."

"Probably wouldn't dare," I said. "Your mother would have him for breakfast."

"No offense, Pippa," Christopher answered, "but at the moment I really have bigger concerns than whether or not my grandfather wants me to marry you."

Of course. "The blackmail."

He glanced at me. "That's what it was. Wasn't it? I thought so, but I wanted to be sure."

"It was absolutely blackmail. He knows about Lady Austin and the drag balls, and he wants you to pay him to keep quiet about it. A thousand pounds."

We took a few steps in silence, the quiet only broken by the crunch of our shoes on the gravel and the singing of birds in the copse of beech trees on our right.

"I don't have a thousand pounds," Christopher said.

I shook my head. "I don't, either."

There was another break, and another few steps.

"What are we going to do?"

My heart warmed. We were still a team, it seemed, even if Grimsby's extortion hadn't included me. I slanted a look at him. "Your mother is supporting Francis. Maybe she can sell a few more secrets and make enough for you, too?"

A thought struck me, and I added, "Maybe we can figure out who Crispin wants to marry. The news that the scion of the Sutherlands wants to marry a commoner, and a foreign one at that... that ought to be worth something to the tabloids, don't you think?"

Then another thought struck, and I derailed myself this time. "Wait. You don't think he meant Florence Schlomsky, do you?"

"The American heiress?" Christopher fought off a shudder while he thought about it. "Rather him than me. Although I suppose it isn't out of the question. She's about as common as muck, for all her money. And she's definitely foreign."

"But they just met yesterday. I introduced them."

Or not. Not only had I not introduced them, actually, but I truly had no idea whether they'd ever met before yesterday. Flossie clearly hadn't realized that Crispin wasn't Christopher, but he could have pretended to be Christopher last time, too. He could have been skulking around our building on multiple occasions, thanks to Evans not realizing who he was. He and Florence might have met before. And Crispin might have fallen for...

That's where the rub was, honestly.

"I can't imagine anyone wanting to marry Florence

Schlomsky," Christopher said, echoing my thoughts. "Least of all my cousin. She'd drive him mad within a fortnight, wouldn't she? And it's not like he needs her money."

"If he thinks he's about to be disinherited, he might."

Christopher looked at me. For a long moment, before he shook himself. "This is madness, Pippa. There is no way Crispin would consider marrying the American manhunter. He has his faults, but he has always, reliably, shown good taste."

"She isn't that bad," I tried, but then an image popped into my head, of Crispin waiting at the altar, in full morning dress, Christopher at his side, while Flossie swept down the aisle the way she'd swept up the hallway in London last night, only this time she was wearing white ruffles and orange-flowers and a full, flowing veil, and my brain shut down. "You're right. There's no way St George would be pining for Flossie Schlomsky. Someone else, then. And if we could find out who, I bet it would be worth..."

"No," Christopher said. "I'm not going to ferret out my cousin's innermost secrets so I can sell them to the highest bidder. I wouldn't want him to do that to me. I'll get the money some other way."

"We could get engaged," I suggested. "You and me. That might be worth a bit to the gossip columnists."

He looked at me, and I added, "Your grandfather might like it, too. There might be some money in it. A betrothal gift, or something like that. I'd break the engagement later, obviously. I don't want to marry you, either. But it might work for long enough to pay off Grimsby."

Christopher didn't speak. Too overcome with the idea, probably.

"Or we could ask Flossie," I added. "Maybe she'd lend it to us."

"We'd never be able to pay her back," Christopher

protested. "And then I'd probably end up having to marry her eventually anyway, because I'd have no other choice."

"So Aunt Roz?"

"It will probably have to be," Christopher said morosely. "Francis doesn't have any more money than I do. You don't, either. Nor does Crispin, for that matter, although he could probably raise some on his expectations. Grandfather isn't going to live forever. But he wouldn't do that for me. Why would he?"

No reason at all. "So Aunt Roz."

"Or your version of an engagement. It's worth thinking about."

"Then give it some thought," I told him. "If you decide to propose, let me know. Or not. It might be better if I look surprised."

Christopher said he'd keep that in mind, and we walked on in silence as he—presumably—gave it some thought. Or pondered how he might come up with a thousand pounds to pay off Grimsby. Which was the same thing, really.

We went back inside before tea and separated at the top of the stairs, for Christopher to go into the east wing and me to go into the west. For some reason, which was especially inexplicable now that we shared a flat in London, Aunt Charlotte had seen fit to put us on entirely opposite sides of the house. My room was as far into the west wing as Christopher's was into the east. It would be a ten minute walk to get from one to the other should we decide to visit one another, and it would have to be done along the main hallway, since there was no secret passage leading from the west wing to the east.

At any rate, I trudged along to my room, where I removed the skirt, blouse, jacket, and shoes I had traveled and walked in, and slipped into an afternoon dress I thought Lady Charlotte might not object to. It was a navy blue and white crepe de chine, with a floppy bow on one hip and a big, flouncy collar, and it reached below my knees, so wasn't too terribly daring. I paired it with pale gray stockings and blue strap shoes with gray trim, and since I wouldn't be wearing a hat inside the house, I tucked a jeweled bobby pin into my hair just above one ear, turned back and forth in front of the mirror, and called it good.

There didn't appear to be anyone else rooming near me, or at least I heard no voices as I walked the corridor towards the central branch of the house. Francis was next to Christopher in the east wing, I assumed, across the hall from Crispin's set of rooms, and I knew Uncle Harold and Aunt Charlotte had rooms over there, too. Uncle Herbert and Aunt Roz took the matching rooms on this side when they were visiting, and in the old days, when we'd all come to Sutherland Hall together, all three of the boys—Francis, Robert, and Christopher—had been in the rooms surrounding mine. Now I was the only one left. If I screamed in the night, no one would hear a thing.

Not that I was likely to scream in the night, I told myself. That kind of thing only happened in detective novels.

The main hallway was just as empty as the west wing had been, and I made my way to the top of the central staircase and started down. I could hear a murmur of voices from the salon, and the clinking of porcelain and, possibly, crystal. Whatever else had been going on today, everyone seemed to be getting along now.

My heels clacked across the marble floors, and then I appeared in the doorway, to see that there was a good reason for that. Uncle Harold was missing, and so was Aunt Charlotte. Francis was likewise gone. Christopher and Crispin were engaged in a low-voiced conversation on one side of the room, while Aunt Roz was manning the teapot. She glanced up when

I walked in, and gave me a smile. "That's a lovely dress, Pippa. Tea?"

"Yes, please." I looked around. "I expected there to be more people here."

Over by the fireplace, Christopher and Crispin both turned at the sound of my voice. The former gave me a sweet smile, and the latter a sneer. I rolled my eyes and turned away, but not before contemplating, again, how different two men can be when they look so much alike.

Christopher and Crispin were born within a couple of months of each other, and of course they share the same last name, even if Crispin adds an Honorable to the front of his. When they went to Eton as part of the same year, everyone thought they were siblings. And not just brothers, but twins. Perhaps even identical twins, who aren't truly identical if you look at them closely, but certainly fraternal twins.

They're the same height, and probably the same weight, too. Their features are almost identical, with the same heart-shaped face, slightly pointed chin, and wider cheekbones. Christopher's nose is perhaps just a shade longer, while Crispin has a scar above his left eyebrow where he ran into a tree at one point and cut his skin open. His hair is a shade lighter, more ashy than Christopher's, due to Aunt Charlotte being a silvery blonde, but that difference isn't terribly easy to spot when they both keep their hair slicked back. And of course his eyes are a cool gray, whereas Christopher's are a warm sky blue.

And that's really where the difference lies. Their features are mostly the same, but the expressions they put on them are vastly different. Christopher looks warm and friendly and approachable. Crispin, like his mother, looks like he's constantly enduring a bad smell. At the moment, he was eyeing me like something that had crawled out from under a flat rock.

"Honestly," I told him across the room, "if you're not careful, your face will stay that way, and then what will you do? You won't get a girl to like you if you look like you can't stand to be in the same room with her, you know."

Aunt Roz smirked, but kept her face averted from her son and nephew while she poured and doctored my tea. Milk and one sugar.

Crispin rolled his eyes. "I've gotten plenty of girls to like me, Darling. Which you know perfectly well, as you brought it up earlier. All on your own, too. Pretty much the only girl who doesn't like me, is you."

"Well, that's certainly true," I told him. "And small wonder, really. What's wrong with the way I look, exactly? Why are you looking at me like that?"

His face immediately turned bland. "Like what?"

"Like I smell and you don't like my new dress. Or my shoes or my ankles or my stockings or my calves."

I stuck out a foot and wiggled it. He flushed, which would have been endearing in anyone else, and was frankly laughable in someone with his reputation. But before I could tweak him about it, Aunt Roz handed me the cup and saucer. "Here you are, Pippa. Why don't you find yourself a seat? I'm sure the others will be along shortly."

It was an order more than a request. I was pushing Crispin, and she wanted me to stop.

When Aunt Roz asks something of me, I tend to do it, so I abandoned the quarrel and headed for one of the sofas, where I crossed one leg over the other and stirred my tea without making the spoon *clink* against the inside of the cup while I waited for something to happen.

When it did, it wasn't what I expected. After a few seconds, Christopher muttered something to Crispin—"Watch this," maybe—and came over to me. But instead of sitting down beside me so we could converse, he dropped to the floor in front of me instead. "Philippa Darling," he intoned, and from somewhere else in the room—Crispin, or more likely Aunt Roz—I heard what was surely a quickly indrawn breath.

But that was as far as any of us got, because now the proposal—if that was what it was going to be, and I assumed, from the fact that he was down on one knee in front of me, that it was—was interrupted by a lot of noise from outside the room.

It came from upstairs, and increased in volume as it came closer. With the shrillness of the delivery, it was difficult to make out the words, but eventually they isolated themselves into the same three syllables, over and over. "Dead! He's dead! Dead!"

FIVE

It was Aunt Charlotte who was screaming, and who subsequently rushed through the door. By that point, Christopher had given up on whatever it was he'd been doing, and I had put the tea and saucer on the table next to the sofa and gotten to my feet, too. So had Aunt Roz. But it was Crispin who was first across the floor, and who scooped up his mother before she could collapse into a heap on the Bokhara.

"Dead," she told him, as she clutched the lapels of his jacket, peering up into his face like the overwrought heroine in some desert drama. "Stone dead!"

And then her eyes rolled back in her head and she slumped. Crispin blinked, but held on. For a moment we all stood there gaping, then Aunt Roz pulled herself together.

"Here." She shooed her son and me away from the sofa. "Put her here, Crispin. Brandy, Christopher."

I stepped out of the way as Christopher hurried off to the bar cart and as Crispin hauled his mother over to the sofa and dropped her, none too gently, onto the sage green damask. She made an "Oof"-sound when her back hit the rather firm cushions, so perhaps she wasn't as overcome as it had seemed.

"Match," Aunt Roz snapped out, and Crispin obligingly lit one and blew it out, before handing it over so Aunt Roz could wave it under Aunt Charlotte's nose. Christopher, back with two fingers of brandy in a glass, hovered uncertainly on the other side of the sofa while Aunt Charlotte's eyelids fluttered.

"There, now," Aunt Roz said briskly—she has never been one to suffer fools gladly; probably the result of raising three boys and then an orphan girl. "You're all right, Charlotte. Have a sip of this—" She grabbed the glass Christopher held out, and raised it to Aunt Charlotte's lips, "and tell us what happened."

"Dead," Aunt Charlotte said. Another sip restored a bit of color to her cheeks, and seemed to have prodded her brain out of the track it had been in, into one with a few more words. "I brought the tea up, and found him."

"And he was dead," Aunt Roz clarified.

Aunt Charlotte nodded, clutching the glass.

"Henry?"

Another nod. Christopher drew in a sharp breath, and Crispin blanched. It's hard to tell, admittedly, because he's so pale to begin with—Aunt Charlotte is, too—but all the color vanished from his cheeks, leaving him like an alabaster statue, all white skin and colorless eyes.

"St George," I said, and it was hard to get the words out, both because my lips felt weirdly stiff and because it was now truly his title, used properly for the first time. "Perhaps you should go upstairs and look?"

He eyed me, and then Christopher, and then me again. And then, finally, Christopher. "You're older."

"Two and a half months," Christopher said. "You're the heir."

"You're just as much his grandson as I am."

"But this is your home, not mine."

"Go together," Aunt Roz said, "and stop behaving like children. I'll take care of Charlotte."

Christopher and Crispin glanced at one another again, and then moved as one towards the door. Since I hadn't been told to stay, and since I felt no compunction to take care of Crispin's mother, I only hesitated for a moment before I scurried after them. "I'll be back," I told Aunt Roz over my shoulder.

She waved me off. "I've got it under control. Go hold their hands. They're both clearly unequal to the task."

I wasn't sure I would say that, exactly. They were both moving steadily towards the staircase now, even if Crispin was still too pale and Christopher practically green. He looked like he was trying to keep himself from vomiting. When he heard my heels clacking on the floor behind him, he glanced over his shoulder. "Pippa?"

"I'm coming with you. Dead body, remember?"

The corner of his mouth twitched before he got it under control again. "You don't have to."

"I don't mind," I said, as they started up the stairs with me two steps below. "Unless you don't want me there. He wasn't my grandfather, after all."

And there had never been much love lost between us. Like Aunt Charlotte, and to a lesser degree Uncle Harold—and of course Crispin—the duke had never seemed to like me much. I probably didn't have the correct feelings about this situation. Mostly, I had been angry with him today, for telling Christopher he had to marry me when he didn't want to marry anyone. I certainly had no feelings of loss at the news of his death.

But he had been Christopher's grandfather, and Christopher was my best friend. He had been there for me when I got the letter saying that my mother had died, and I wanted to be here for him now. I even felt a tiny bit bad for Crispin, to be honest. Not that I planned to act on that in any way. I just knew how hard it is to lose family.

"Don't be silly, Pippa," Christopher said and reached a hand back for me. "Of course we want you." His fingers wrapped around mine. They were a bit cold, but steady. I curled mine back around his, for support.

He turned to Crispin. "I don't suppose there's any chance your mother is mistaken, is there?"

Crispin glanced over at him. "I don't imagine so. My mother can be overly dramatic, but she isn't stupid."

Christopher nodded. "We have to assume, then, that he's truly dead. What's next, do you suppose? Ringing the doctor?"

"The doctor won't be able to do anything if he's dead," I pointed out, and they both turned to look at me.

After a moment, Crispin said, "Aunt Roslyn will know what to do. She seems to be handling this better than either of us."

Probably because there was no love lost between Aunt Roz and her—presumably dead—father-in-law, either. It's easier to be pragmatic when your feelings aren't involved.

"Where's Uncle Harold?" Christopher wanted to know, and Crispin shrugged.

"I have no idea. Uncle Herbert?"

"No idea, either. Pippa and I spent the afternoon together, but we didn't see either of them."

"Perhaps they're together?" I suggested. "Perhaps they decided to have a walk down to the village pub after all the yelling this afternoon?"

There was a moment while we all contemplated the yelling. Crispin was undoubtedly thinking of the row Christopher and I had overheard between him and Uncle Harold in his rooms earlier, but of course he didn't know that we knew anything about that.

"I can't imagine Uncle Harold and my father lifting a pint together in the Fox and Hare," Christopher said, and Crispin shook his head.

"Father may have locked himself in his study. He does that sometimes, when something's on his mind. And I suppose Uncle Herbert might be in there with him. Although it's surprising that neither of them seemed to have heard my mother carrying on."

By now we had reached the open door to the Duke's Chambers, and all our feet checked for a moment as the conversation fizzled.

Christopher and Crispin exchanged a glance.

"You're older," Crispin said, and Christopher rolled his eyes.

"Are we doing this again?"

"I'll go first," I told them. "I'm older than both of you."

Which was true, even if it was only about four months in Christopher's case, and about six in Crispin's.

I dropped Christopher's hand and stepped across the threshold before either of them could stop me. I'm not sure they would have tried, although Christopher's hand twitched when I let it go, and Crispin's mouth opened for a second, then closed again.

This is probably where I admit that I had only been in the duke's bedchamber once or twice before. It had been off-limits during those long-ago games of hide-and-seek, and I had rarely been called on the carpet before him. Not earlier today, and only a very few times previously. Usually, it had been when one of us had accidentally managed to break some heirloom or other during play, and we were summoned as a group to make account.

The chamber looked the same as I remembered it. Old and stuffy, full of heavy, dark furniture that likely hadn't changed in the two hundred years since the Hall was built. The bed had velvet draperies that matched the dark blue and gold damask that covered the upper half of the walls, above where the wainscoting—the one that hid the secret door—ended. The bed itself was huge, mounded with pillows and blankets, and the bottom right corner also held a tray with a teapot and cup, cream and sugar, tongs, and plate of biscuits. Aunt Charlotte must have put it down somewhere semi-safe before succumbing to the vapors.

After taking in all that, I could no longer avoid looking at the occupant of the bed.

He was half sitting, half lying against the pillows, and from where we were standing, just inside the door, he didn't look particularly dead. More surprised at our entry. His jaw had relaxed, and it gave him a look of open-mouthed astonishment. It was only when one stepped closer, and realized that the cloudy blue eyes didn't follow our approach towards the bed, that the thought of death would have presented itself. And of course, once we got closer, it became more obvious, too. The skin was waxy and a bit yellow, the pupils dilated, and the eyes bloodshot and staring, while the narrow chest below the striped pyjamas didn't expand or sink with breath.

Crispin's hand shook when he reached out and put it against his grandfather's throat.

"Cool," he said after a moment, and his voice shook, too. We each took a step back, as if we had synchronized it. Crispin brushed his fingers against the outside of his trousers once and then again.

"I don't see anything to indicate foul play," I remarked, looking around. "No sign of a struggle, no odor of almonds."

Crispin's eyebrow inched up, and he looked at Christopher, who told him, "Detective fiction."

Crispin's lip twitched in a sneer. After a moment, Christopher added, "The excitement probably killed him. All that yelling and carrying on. Telling everyone what to do and how to do it. And then the disappointment when we didn't all immediately jump when he said to."

"He was quite an old man," I agreed. "He must have been close to ninety, surely?"

Christopher nodded. "Not surprising at all if his heart should give out at that age, after an afternoon of browbeating his descendants."

"His heart was weak to begin with," Crispin said. "He had the doctor in just a few weeks ago."

There was a moment of silence while we, all three, contemplated the old man in the bed.

"I'm sorry for your loss," I said, formally, to both of them. "If there's anything I can do…"

"We should close up the room," Christopher said, "and then we should go downstairs and tell Mum to call the doctor."

"Not the police?"

He glanced at me. "Let's start with the doctor. If he thinks there's a reason to call the local constabulary, then I imagine he will. But as far as I can tell, this was an old man with a bad heart who died from too much excitement."

He hesitated for a second before he added, "If Francis is around, perhaps he could have a look. He has more experience with dead bodies than the rest of us."

And more problems with them, too, judging from what Crispin had told me earlier.

"I should think that would be a good reason for him not to have to deal with this one," I said, "although I suppose it couldn't hurt to ask, if you can find him. Then again, I'm sure none of the bodies Francis came across in the war died in bed of natural causes."

Christopher shook his head. He grabbed my hand again,

and started to back away from the bed. I followed, and so did Crispin. It seemed impolite to turn our backs until we were halfway across the room, and once we had, we scurried for the door so quickly that there was a crush to get outside into the hallway. Crispin shut the door behind us, a little harder than was strictly necessary, and then we stood there looking at each other.

"I'll go speak to Mum," Christopher said after a moment.

I nodded. "I'll go with you."

"I'll be down in a minute," Crispin said, with a glance over his shoulder down the hall. "There's something I... um... something in my room. I'll knock on Francis's door on the way, and see if he's there. And my father's door, as well."

"We'll see you later, then," Christopher told him and turned towards the stairs. I gave Crispin a strained sort of smile, one that resulted in a twitch of his lip that wasn't quite a sneer, but wasn't quite anything else either, and then the two of us headed down while Crispin strode down the hallway towards his suite of rooms. He wasn't running, but his stride covered ground just as quickly. I wondered whether he was trying to get to a private place before he broke down in tears, or whether there was another reason he wanted privacy.

And then we were downstairs in the foyer, on our way back to the salon, and the thought flew out of my head at the murmur of voices from within.

Aunt Charlotte must have been feeling better, because Aunt Roz had her sitting up instead of reclining on the sofa. And she was sipping from a cup of tea instead of the glass of brandy from earlier. It had been discarded on the side table next to my now-cold cup of tea, although the glass itself was empty, so Aunt Charlotte must have fortified herself on the contents before switching to the genial beverage.

Or perhaps Aunt Roz had poured it into the two cups the

ladies were drinking from, and so they were being fortified by both tea and brandy at the same time.

When we walked in, they both looked up. After a moment, Aunt Roz's attention focused on her son. "Well?"

"He's definitely dead," Christopher confirmed. "Cool to the touch, no pulse."

Aunt Charlotte squeaked. This should not have come as news to her, so perhaps it was the somewhat callous phrasing she objected to. If Crispin was upset about his grandfather's demise, Christopher was quite clearly the opposite.

Unless Crispin hadn't been upset, either, and had simply wanted to get to a place with some privacy before his elation could give him away.

"We think it might have been a heart attack," I said, "perhaps brought on by all the haranguing he did earlier today."

Aunt Roz nodded and put her cup down. "I suppose one of us ought to ring up the doctor."

She glanced over at Aunt Charlotte. And really, as the lady of the house, it was properly Aunt Charlotte's duty. But she made no move to put down her own cup of tea, so it was Aunt Roz who got to her feet and headed into the hall to the telephone.

"Tea?" Christopher asked me. "If you'll give me your cup, I'll refresh it for you."

"Please." I took the cup from the side table, tossed the cold beverage into a convenient aspidistra, and handed the empty cup to Christopher, who proceeded to fill it. "Thank you."

"It's my pleasure." He smiled.

"You're such a lovely boy, Christopher," Aunt Charlotte said dreamily. The brandy had quite clearly done a number on her. "Tell me, darling, what was it that I interrupted when I came in earlier? It seemed like you were doing something of consequence?"

Christopher looked blank. So did I. Until it hit us both at the same time, and we turned to one another with identical expressions of horror.

"Oh, no," Christopher said, shaking his head determinedly. "That was nothing."

"Nothing at all," I agreed, since, with the duke dead, there was no need to carry on the charade. No one else was likely to pressure us to marry. Aunt Roz certainly had no interest in losing a daughter only to gain the same person back as a daughter-in-law, and I'm sure Uncle Herbert was hoping for far better for his youngest son.

Not that he would get it, of course. Not unless he forced the issue, at any rate. Which I sincerely hoped he wouldn't. There was no point. Francis would eventually marry and provide an heir for the secondary Sutherland line. And if he didn't...

Well, if he didn't, then we'd worry about that if we had to.

But for now, Christopher had no desire to marry me, or for that matter anyone else. Nor I him. So whatever Aunt Charlotte thought she had seen, it behooved us both to nip it in the bud as quickly as possible. The last thing we wanted was someone else thinking a union between the two of us would be desirable.

"Oh." Aunt Charlotte looked disappointed. "I'm sorry to hear that."

"We were just having some fun," Christopher said. "Weren't we, Pippa?"

I nodded. "Of course we were."

"Well." Aunt Charlotte looked desperately brave about it. "I'm sure your mother will be sad to hear that, Christopher."

Christopher and I exchanged a glance. "She'll live," Christopher said.

I nodded. And changed the subject. "Hopefully there

won't be any problem getting the doctor to come out. Or any problem with the death certificate."

Aunt Charlotte blinked. "Why would there be a problem with the death certificate, Miss Darling?"

"No reason," Christopher said firmly. "Pippa has read too many detective stories, that's all. He was an old man who spent the afternoon yelling at his family. Small wonder if his heart gave out."

Aunt Charlotte nodded, looking grateful. "Of course, Christopher. I'm sure that's exactly what happened. Nothing more and nothing less."

AND SO IT proved to be. We sat around the parlor sipping tea and making small talk—very small—while we waited for the doctor. Aunt Roz came back after a few minutes, with the information that Doctor Meadows from the village was on his way up to the Hall, and she started pouring out tea with a steady hand. A few minutes after that, Crispin came back downstairs, looking more composed than he had earlier. I didn't want to stare, but I did examine his face surreptitiously for long enough to determine that his eyes weren't red. Whatever he'd been doing upstairs, it didn't appear as if he'd been crying. He accepted a cup of tea from Aunt Roz and went to sit beside his mother, with the news that there had been no answer from either Francis or Uncle Harold when he'd knocked on their doors.

Slowly, the others started to trickle in, too. Francis was first, and a little unsteady on his feet as he came through the front door and into the foyer. We could hear the unevenness of his steps as he crossed the marble floor towards the door.

"Good gracious." He took us all in as we sat around the parlor balancing our cups. "What a collection of long faces."

"Come in, Francis," Aunt Roz said, in a voice that brooked no argument. "Have a seat. I'll pour you a cup of tea."

Francis opened his mouth—presumably to tell her that he wanted to go up to his room, or perhaps that he'd prefer something stronger than tea—but one look at her face and he must have thought better of it. "Yes, Mother."

He pushed off from the door jamb and made his way, with a bit of listing, towards one of the empty chairs, which he dropped into rather heavily. "What's happened?"

He looks like an older version of Christopher and Crispin, or perhaps more like a younger version of his father. Fair-haired and -complexioned, but a bit heavier in build than his younger brother. And now that I looked more closely at him, especially after a few months of not having seen him at all, I could clearly see the signs of dissipation. His skin wasn't just pale, it was pasty, with dark circles under bloodshot eyes, and deeper lines around his nose and mouth than I remembered having seen before.

Truthfully, he didn't look much better than the corpse upstairs, and that was saying something.

"Grandfather's dead," Christopher said, and it was only Aunt Roz's hand still holding onto the teacup that kept Francis from fumbling it. He murmured an apology to his mother and took the cup from her hand, carefully, only to put it down without taking a sip, onto the small table beside the chair.

"Dead? Grandfather?"

Christopher nodded. Francis looked at him for a moment, before his eyes traversed the rest of us. When they landed on Crispin, he said, "Congratulations, St George."

Crispin flushed, while Aunt Charlotte sucked in a breath.

"Francis!" Aunt Roz exclaimed.

"Well, it's a step up, isn't it?" He moved his attention back to Christopher. "You all right, little brother?"

"Fine," Christopher said. "He was an old man. I never thought he was going to live forever."

Francis nodded, and moved on. "Philippa."

"Francis," I said. "How have you been?"

He flapped a hand. I imagined it was intended as an insouciant gesture, but it came across more as if he couldn't control the movement the way he had planned to. "Oh, you know."

It was all he said, and I nodded. "It's good to see you. Even under the circumstances."

Francis grinned. "You too, Pipsqueak."

That horrid moniker has been my nickname since I showed up on Aunt Roz's and Uncle Herbert's doorstep, skinny and awkward at eleven years old, and between you and me, I wasn't sure whether I hated it more or less than Crispin's drawling use of my last name. "I wish you wouldn't call me that."

"I know," Francis said. "Why do you suppose I do it?"

This time the corner of Crispin's mouth quirked, and Christopher's eyes narrowed in amusement. I rolled my eyes at both of them.

"So what happened?" Francis wanted to know, but before any of us could enlighten him, there was the sound of more footsteps in the foyer. This time it was Uncle Harold who appeared in the doorway, tall and thin and flushed, presumably from a walk or perhaps a ride in the great outdoors.

Like Francis, he stopped in the doorway and took in the assembly. Unlike Francis, he didn't appear to have had anything to drink while he'd been out. His voice was firm and no-nonsense when he ignored the rest of us to address his wife. "Charlotte?"

Aunt Charlotte flushed. I have no idea why, because it wasn't like she was clutching a tumbler of brandy anymore. "Harold. I'm so sorry to have to tell you..."

She ran down without coming to the point, and Uncle

Harold shifted his attention from her to Aunt Roz, and then to his son.

"Grandfather's dead," Crispin said.

For a moment, Uncle Harold's jaw dropped, and he turned pale. Then Francis piped up with a, "Congratulations, Your Grace," and Uncle Harold's face flushed an alarming shade of puce.

SIX

THE DOCTOR ARRIVED at the same time as Uncle Herbert, and was conveyed upstairs by Aunt Roz, since Aunt Charlotte still didn't seem equal to the task. Uncle Herbert went with them, since he hadn't yet seen his father's corpse. Nor had Uncle Harold, but he was still processing what had happened, I guess, and perhaps also Francis's irreverent remark from earlier, because he didn't go upstairs. All the men had switched from tea to something stronger by now, and I was sipping from a glass of sherry, while Aunt Charlotte still nursed her cup of tea, with or without alcohol mixed in.

It didn't take the doctor long at all to come to a conclusion. "Heart failure," he announced when he was ushered into the salon by Aunt Roz just a few minutes after going upstairs in the first place. "I understand he's had an exciting afternoon?"

Someone snorted. I think it was Francis, although it could have been Crispin. They were over there on the same side of the room, and Francis frequently acts on instinct, while Crispin has no problem being deliberately rude.

"Quite," Aunt Roz said blandly. "A lot of exertion and high emotion."

"That's what did it, then. I told him last year, peace and quiet is the ticket." Doctor Meadows—a small man with a fringe of white hair—clutched his bag with both hands as his gaze roved over the assembly.

"Can I offer you some tea?" Aunt Roz asked, "or perhaps something stronger?"

"Very kind of you, Lady Herbert, but my wife will have supper on the table soon. I'll contact the mortuary and have a car out tomorrow, to transport the remains. You can coordinate the details with them."

He addressed us in turn, and in descending order of importance. "My condolences, Your Grace," Uncle Harold, "Your Grace," Aunt Charlotte, "Lord St George." Crispin.

He then moved his attention to the rest of the family. "Lord Herbert, Lady Herbert, Mr. Astley."

His eyes lingered on Francis for a moment, before moving on to Christopher, "Mr. Astley," and, finally, to me. "Miss...um..."

We had met before, but he clearly couldn't place me, or at least couldn't lay his mind on my name. I opened my mouth, but before I could get it out, someone got there first. "Darling," Crispin said with a smirk.

The doctor's eyes darted from him to me and back. "Are congratulations in order?"

"God, no," escaped my mouth, while Crispin said blandly, "Miss Darling is Christopher's intended."

I was hardly Christopher's intended, but it also wasn't something I wanted to deny in public, in front of everyone. So — "I'm Christopher's cousin," I said. "On his mother's side."

The doctor looked more confused than ever now, which I had to admit was fair. "I should perhaps warn you that while legal, consanguineous marriages can produce offspring that lacks some of the healthier—"

Crispin stifled a snigger, and both Aunt Roz and Aunt Charlotte sent him quelling glances.

"Thank you," I told the doctor, since I'm well aware that marriages between close relatives can be unfortunate for the health of the children. Just look at King Tut.

However, it wasn't something I wanted to discuss over tea in the salon, especially since there was very little chance that Christopher and I would ever produce offspring. I'd marry him if I had to. I'd bed him only at gunpoint, and I was certain he felt the same way.

The doctor took his leave, a little ruffled, and I turned to Crispin. "Really, St George? Your grandfather's lying dead upstairs, and this is how you get your jollies? By suggesting that Christopher and I are getting married?"

He arched that infernal brow. "Was that, or was it not, a proposal that was interrupted earlier?"

It had been, I guess. Or at least that had been my impression of it when it was going on.

However—

"Interrupted is the operative word here," I said, and glanced at Christopher.

He said, "Mind your own, Crispin," to his cousin.

"Of course." Crispin smirked. "Just let me know when the deed is done, and I'll package up a nice fish spade."

"Just what every married couple wants," I said, and pushed to my feet. "If you'll excuse me, I'm going to my room."

I'd had enough of the assembly for the time being—had specifically had enough of Crispin—and besides, I did feel a little out of place. I was the only person here who hadn't been related to the late duke, by blood or marriage, and although no one specifically let me feel that I was *de trop*, I felt like an intruder nonetheless.

"Supper at eight," Aunt Roz said. "I don't think we'll bother dressing tonight, given the circumstances. Have a nice rest, Pippa."

"Thank you." I escaped with as much of my dignity as I had left.

I HAD THOUGHT that Christopher might stop by during the time between tea and supper, but I didn't see him, so he must have found other things to do. For all I knew, the family had spent the entire time in the parlor, discussing what had happened and what would happen next. As a result, it wasn't until after the (quiet) meal was over, and after everyone had dispersed, that I was able to get Christopher alone to discuss this evening's events. Both the ones that had happened already, and the ones that were about to.

"I'm sorry about your grandfather," I said, tucking my hand through his arm as we promenaded back and forth on the terrasse after supper.

He glanced at me. "I'm not. I mean, of course it's sad that he's no longer with us. But he was a cantankerous old bully most of the time. And I can't believe he sent Grimsby to spy on me!"

Which was precisely the other thing I'd wanted to talk about. "Do you still want to meet him tonight? Now that your grandfather—his employer—is gone, do you think he might have given up the blackmail as a bad idea?"

"I imagine he'll want the money even more now," Christopher said. "He might lose his job, after all. Unless Uncle Harold or Crispin wants to take him on. But Uncle Harold already has a valet, and I doubt Crispin would want one. Especially Grimsby. He might be blackmailing Crispin, too."

"What has St George done to be blackmailed over?"

"Let me count the ways," Christopher said, and then shook his head. "Never mind. I have no idea what Crispin's been up to, other than what everyone knows. Dalliances, drinking, dope, debt..."

"All the usual vices, in other words."

He nodded. "And he hasn't made a secret of any of them, either. But I don't know if he's worthy of blackmail if it's all out there in the open, and if there is more, I don't know whether Grimsby has done anything about exploiting it. Blackmailing me is one thing. Blackmailing the future duke is quite another."

Yes, I could see that. "But you're still going to meet with him?"

"I don't see how I can avoid it," Christopher said. "If I don't show up, and he does, he'll think I've refused to pay, and then he'll start spreading my business to anyone who'll listen, and I'm sure there are plenty of people who would."

No doubt.

"I haven't had a chance to talk to Mum, though, and I'm not going to tonight. Not with everything else that's going on. So I'll just have to head him off until I can work out how to get the money."

"That's if he shows up at all."

He glanced at me. "Why wouldn't he?"

"I don't know. But this—what happened to your grandfather—has been a shock to the whole household. That might have been the worst roast duck I've ever eaten."

Christopher nodded. "I'll go to the meeting, but I think you're right. He might not show up. Although if he doesn't, I won't make the mistake of thinking I'm off the hook."

"Probably better if you don't," I agreed. "But at least it

would give you—give us—some breathing room, and time to figure out how to come up with a thousand pounds without falling short over the next few months. I can live on beans on toast for a while, if it would help."

"You're a corker, Pippa." He squeezed my hand, where it lay in the crook of his elbow. "The best friend any chap could ask for. But I don't want you to have to do that. We'll figure something out."

"We'll manage," I agreed. "We always do. But you know I would do it for you if I had to, Christopher. I'd do a lot more than that."

"I know. And on that note, it was lucky Aunt Charlotte found the body when she did. Otherwise we'd be engaged right now."

I shuddered. "Lucky, indeed. Just imagine having to pretend we're planning a wedding. Aunt Roz would be devastated when she found out the truth."

"Mum loves you," Christopher said.

"I'm well aware. But she doesn't want me to marry you. Or you me."

He shook his head. "I imagine my mother has a better idea of what's going on than most of our relatives."

Probably so. "Aunt Charlotte seemed more invested in the idea than I would have guessed. I got the distinct impression, when we arrived this afternoon, that she disliked me."

"Aunt Charlotte dislikes most women," Christopher said. "I think it comes from being so much younger than Uncle Harold, and blond. She always has to feel like she's the most attractive woman in the room."

"Well, she's certainly much prettier than I'll ever be." Blonder, too. "But I'm at least twenty years younger, and that has to be worth something."

"Indeed," Christopher sniggered, and sounded, for a

moment, unnervingly like his cousin. "Maybe she's afraid you're going to vamp Crispin."

I snorted, in a very unladylike manner. "No chance of that. St George's disdain for me is only outdone by mine for him. I'll marry Crispin St George when hell freezes over."

Christopher had nothing to say to that, and I added, "It sounds like he has someone else in mind, anyway. I wonder whether the late duke's demise might have helped with that."

"Or hurt it," Christopher said. "Uncle Harold might be more against it than Grandfather was. He sounded like he was frothing at the mouth during that conversation we overheard. For a moment, I was afraid he hit Crispin."

I nodded. "I thought the same thing. You don't think he did it, do you?"

"I'm sure he has at some point," Christopher said. "You have to admit, Crispin is eminently hittable."

Of course he was. But that didn't mean I wanted his father to abuse him.

Christopher must have been thinking the same thing, because he squeezed my hand. "It's nice to have parents who don't care who we marry, isn't it?"

They were his parents, not mine, but if he wanted to share them with me, that was very nice of him, so I squeezed his arm back and smiled. "It is."

Of course, the moment of amity dissolved into thin air when I informed him that I intended to go with him to his clandestine meeting with Grimsby.

"I don't think that's a good idea, Pippa."

"Why not? He knows I know. I was there when he extorted you."

"I'm aware," Christopher said. "However, I'd rather you stay inside the house. That way, if there's a problem with me getting back inside—if someone locks the door while I'm outside in the garden—you'll be able to let me back inside."

That made a certain amount of sense. However— "You could always bring a key, you know."

"I wasn't planning to leave through the front door," Christopher said. "Or for that matter the back door."

"What, then? One of the secret passages."

He nodded.

"They open from the outside, too, don't they?"

"Not the one in the study," Christopher said.

I squinted at him. "And does it have to be the one in the study?"

"It's nearest to my room."

"I actually think the door from the conservatory is closer to your room." And there were lots of places to hide in the conservatory. Among all those plants.

He thought about it. "If we make it the conservatory, will you stay inside?"

"Of course." It would be much easier for me to see what was happening through the panes of glass there. The passage from the study was stone, and ended in a heavy wooden door. I would have no opportunity to see anything whatsoever. So yes, I could agree to stay inside the conservatory while Christopher ventured outside.

"Knock on my door at quarter till eleven, then?"

I promised I would, and we went back inside for the game of whist that was shaping up in the billiard room after supper.

The house was silent and dark when I left my room just before ten forty-five that evening. Most of the inhabitants had gone to bed, it seemed, or if not that, at least they were in their rooms being quiet.

My wing was the most deserted, of course. I saw no sign of life as I pulled my door shut, wincing at the sound the latch made as it broke the depth of the silence, nor as I tiptoed down the carpet runner in my bare feet, shoes dangling from my hand.

There was a faint stripe of light where the west wing dead-ended into the central wing, in the spot where Aunt Roslyn's and Uncle Herbert's room was. From this, I deduced that they —or one of them, at least—was still awake. From the faintness of the light, I further considered that Aunt Roz might be reading in bed. Uncle Herbert is not a big reader, but she enjoys a good mystery.

I held my breath as I tiptoed past, careful not to disturb the air too much with my passage. Aunt Roz raised three boys, and as such, has a well-tuned ear for noises at night.

The main wing was faintly lit by the light from the foyer on the first floor, that shined up the main staircase and illuminated the area right in the middle of the hallway. The Duke's and Duchess's Chambers were, of course, dark and silent, and I'll admit to feeling the slightest frisson of discomfort as I passed the Duke's Chamber, at the memory of what—or who—lay beyond the closed door.

Then I was past the door, as well as out of the glow of the light, and on my way down the hall towards the other half of the manor.

Aunt Charlotte and Uncle Harold kept rooms in this corner of the hall, and unlike Aunt Roz and Uncle Herbert, they had separate sleeping chambers. It seems a very archaic way of doing things. Especially in our day and age, when people not only admit to having congress, but admit to liking it. They must have been together as man and wife as some point, after all, or Crispin wouldn't exist. But perhaps Uncle Harold snored and Aunt Charlotte had the sensitivities of the princess on the pea, and so separate arrangements worked better for them.

Now, I assumed, they would be moving into the Duke's and Duchess's Chambers, and wouldn't even have to share a wall.

There were no sounds coming from either chamber, nor was there any light peeping out around the jamb. If Uncle Harold snored, he hadn't yet gotten to that level of sleep, and Aunt Charlotte was not twisting and turning in her bed, at least not as far as I could make out.

Then I was past that corner, too, and on my way down the hallway towards Christopher's room.

Here, there were a few more signs of life. Light shone under the door of what had to be Francis's room, although when I stopped to listen, I heard no sounds from within. Not even the turning over of a page in a book or the scratching of a pen across paper. Christopher's light was out, of course, but on the other side of the hall, I could see the outline of the door to one of Crispin's rooms. He had a full suite, not that I had been in his rooms for probably close to a decade. But back in the days when we'd all been running around the Hall playing hide-and-seek, there had been a bedroom, a dressing room, and a sitting room for him to call his own. If I remembered correctly, the light was on in the sitting room, so perhaps he had just forgotten to turn it out when he went to bed.

Alternatively, he was sitting in there reading, or smoking, or contemplating the unfairness of his life, and that was certainly his right, as well, even if the unfairness of being Crispin St George couldn't compare to the unfairness of being almost anyone else.

I didn't go across the hall to check. Instead I stopped in front of Christopher's door and turned the knob carefully. It made the slightest squeaking noise as it turned, of metal against metal, but someone must have oiled it quite recently, because it was a very small sound. It nonetheless sounded much bigger in the silence of the sleeping house, and I froze for a moment before Christopher's voice hissed from inside. "Either get in or get out. The longer you stand there, the more likely someone will see you."

That was certainly true, so I pushed the door open enough to slip through, and shut it again behind me. "Ready?"

"Almost." Christopher was peering at himself in the mirror. "It feels a bit silly to put on a hat for a clandestine meeting in the garden just before midnight, but I glow like a beacon, don't I?"

He didn't. Not remotely. Although he would certainly show up a lot better than I would once the moon hit that head of fair hair.

My own bob is a sort of soft medium brown, and I hadn't bothered to tuck it under a hat, since I didn't think I'd be leaving the house.

"Put on a cap if you want to," I said. "But if someone sees you through the window, it's no big deal. You have every right to walk around the gardens at eleven-thirty if you choose to. You're an adult now, and your parents or aunt and uncle can't order you back to your room for being out too late. And it's been a strange day, after all. Perhaps you couldn't sleep and thought the fresh air would help."

He gave himself a dissatisfied look in the mirror. "I suppose so. Although I'd feel better if I wasn't so immediately visible from above."

"I don't think you have to worry about it," I told him. "The lights were out in Uncle Harold's and Aunt Charlotte's rooms, and I figure Francis has better things to do than sit at the window staring down into the garden. Your parents have rooms on the other side of the house, so they won't see you, and Crispin's windows look out at the front drive and the courtyard.

Nobody's likely to see you if you just stick to this side of the Hall."

"I suppose. Although if I had my wig..."

"If you had your wig and someone caught you wearing it, that wouldn't be a good thing at all."

"Perhaps not," Christopher admitted. "Although Grimsby knows anyway."

"Yes, but what if it wasn't Grimsby?"

The conversation reminded me that I still hadn't told him that Crispin had recognized him as Kitty last night, but when I glanced at the small ormolu clock ticking away on the mantel, I came to the conclusion that it had to wait, again. "We'd better hurry, or you're going to be late for the meeting."

Christopher took his eyes off his own reflection to check the time. "You're right. Ready?"

We opened the door again, carefully, and Christopher stuck his head around the frame and looked back and forth down the hall in both directions before he waved me out. "Go on. I'll be right behind you."

I scurried past him into the hallway. Behind me, Christopher shut his door and followed. We vanished behind the door into the servants' staircase, and I took the time to slip on my shoes before we headed down. Nobody was likely to hear our steps through the thick stone walls anyway, so I figured it was safe. I wasn't planning to go outside, of course, but the floor in the conservatory is tile, and cold, and sometimes wet from the plants, so I'd really rather have shoes on my feet than not.

Besides, just because you don't plan on doing something— like going outside—doesn't mean you won't find yourself out there after all. Might as well be prepared.

Christopher had brought a torch, which he used to light the way down the worn stairs, before clicking it off again as we reached the bottom floor. "We'd better make sure no one's walking around before we pop out."

He suited action to words, and then dragged me out of the staircase and through the door into the conservatory when he had determined that the coast was clear.

Here, we didn't need the torch. There was light coming through the glass panes above our heads, not only from the stars and moon, but from Francis's lighted window.

It wasn't enough light to see much, of course. The plants and flowers were black outlines along the windows, just a bit more solid than the darkness beyond, and they moved slightly in what I had to assume was some sort of breeze. There was a faint rustling as leaves and fronds brushed. It sent a shiver down my back. Perhaps we were the ones who had set them off with our passage, or perhaps there was a window open somewhere in the conservatory, which wasn't impossible. But whatever it was, it was eerie. Movement where there shouldn't be movement. When we stopped beside the door at the other end, the one leading out into the formal gardens, part of me wanted to beg Christopher not to leave me behind.

I didn't, of course. Christopher had to keep his appointment with Grimsby, and I couldn't go with him. And I didn't want him to feel bad about leaving me when I was scared, so I pushed the feelings of unease to the back of my mind and gave him a brave smile. "Go on. It's almost eleven. Don't keep him waiting."

Christopher nodded, and glanced around the dark conservatory. "Tuck yourself away among some of these bigger plants. If anyone comes through, you don't want to be standing here in full view."

No, I didn't. Because if that happened, then someone would surely ask what I was doing, and I would have to admit that I was waiting for Christopher, and then I'd be asked what Christopher was doing, and then I'd have to lie.

So yes, much better to avoid the entire scenario.

"I'll be back here," I said, taking a few steps away from the door, into the dark corner where I would be half hidden between an orange tree and what felt very much like some sort of prickly pear. A cactus of some sort, or perhaps something more like a yucca.

Christopher stared for a moment at the place where I'd disappeared, and then he nodded. "Don't follow me."

"I won't."

"I'll see you in a bit. Hopefully I can talk sense into him. Or at least convince him to keep his mouth shut until I can get my hands on a thousand pounds."

"We'll figure it out," I said, hidden among my fronds. "Just go get it over with, Christopher. It's late. I want to go to sleep."

He nodded, and turned towards the door. "Wish me luck."

"Good luck," I said. "I'll be here when you get back. Just be careful, Christopher. Don't say anything that'll make him want to spill the beans to anyone else. Even with your grandfather dead, this news probably wouldn't do you a lot of good with anyone else in the family, either."

Christopher nodded before ducking out the door and shutting it behind him. I melted into the corner behind the plants and tried to make myself as comfortable as possible while I waited for him to come back.

At first nothing at all happened. I stood there for what felt like an eternity, shifting from foot to foot, and then I checked my wristwatch, and saw that only a few minutes had passed. We were past the scheduled meeting time now, but there were no sounds from outside. However, the formal gardens took up enough room that if Grimsby was on the far end, I wouldn't necessarily be able to hear anything that happened anyway.

I shifted back and forth again. Outside the conservatory, the wind rustled through the trees. Inside the conservatory, the plants made the occasional sound, like a sigh or small *plop*, perhaps from a dry leaf hitting the floor.

Suddenly, from out of nowhere, I was plunged into darkness. It was so sudden and so shocking that I let out a gasp, loud in the silence. It took my eyes a few seconds to adjust—it was a cloudy night, and something was covering the moon, so it was even darker than it might have been otherwise—and then it took me a few more to realize that the reason for the sudden descent into darkness was bog simple: the light had gone out in Francis's room upstairs.

As my pupils dilated, I heard a sound outside. I spun towards the panes, so close that I could feel the tip of my nose brush against the cold glass, but there was nothing to see. It had sounded like the scuff of a foot on the gravel of one of the pathways, but I couldn't see anyone or anything.

I stood there for what felt like a long time, several minutes, just staring into the darkness. Trying to discern movement, or anything else that might help me figure out what might be happening outside.

And then there was another sound, louder, but from farther away: this one a sharp crack, like a gunshot.

I jumped and scanned the side of the house and what I could see of the gardens frantically.

The moon peeped out from behind cover, and illuminated the area of the lawn beside the house. There was no one there.

I closed my eyes again and forced myself to breathe slowly and regularly while I waited for my heart to settle back down. Standing here in the dark telling myself stories about gunshots wasn't helping my state of mind one bit. Besides, what was more likely, was that Christopher, or perhaps Grimsby, had trod on a dry branch, and it just sounded like a gunshot.

And even if it had been a bona fide gunshot, it was much more likely to be poachers than anyone trying to kill Christopher. I was being silly.

And then another sound caught my attention, one which sounded like it came from inside the house this time. Perhaps even the inside the conservatory. It appeared like a brush of fabric, a sleeve or hem, against the floor or wall or perhaps the furniture. A soft rustle. I froze and held my breath while I waited for it to come again.

When it didn't, I told myself I must have misheard, that it had just been the sound of one palm frond brushing against another in the breeze from whatever window was open. I'm not sure I convinced myself, but the sound didn't come again, and there was nothing whatsoever I could do about it. I couldn't leave my corner to go exploring—or rather, I could have, I suppose, but I had promised Christopher I wouldn't, so I didn't. I put my back to the windows once more, and kept my attention forward into the room, and my eyes peeled.

Minutes passed with no more sounds. My heart rate slowly settled down into the normal range again. I was honestly starting to get tired when something moved across my foot.

To this day, I can't tell you what it was. All I know is that I felt it, and then I jumped about a foot in the air with a shriek, and stumbled back, into the plants in the corner, until I knocked my elbow against the window with enough force to bring tears to my eyes.

And then the door to the hallway burst open, and I jumped again, although at least this time I had enough sense to know I had to be quiet, so I forced myself to stand still with my teeth clenched and tears running down my face, to keep in the whimpers of pain that were threatening to escape.

A figure filled the doorway, a black silhouette outlined by the light behind it.

"Who's there?" it asked, threateningly, and I was rattled enough by everything that had happened that I couldn't immediately place who the voice belonged to. It could have been Uncle Harold or Uncle Herbert, Francis, or one of the staff, like Tidwell the butler, or Grimsby himself.

Or perhaps not Grimsby, since he was supposed to be in the formal garden.

It wasn't Christopher, of that I was certain, and I felt fairly strongly that it wasn't Crispin, either. The outline didn't look like him. The man in the doorway both looked and sounded like someone older than twenty-two or -three.

When no one answered the query, the shadow vanished again, as abruptly as it had come, with a slam of the door, and I was once again alone in the conservatory.

By now I was feeling pretty rattled, even if some of what had happened had surely only taken place in my own mind. There was no one else in the conservatory with me, obviously. The rustling I'd heard, that I had taken for cloth, had been the animal that ran—or perhaps slithered—over my foot. It might have been a mouse, a lizard, or a snake, or something else I didn't want to think about, but that's all it had been. Some little pest that had stumbled inside, or one that made the conservatory its home.

The gunshot, if it had been a gunshot, had sounded like it came from too far away to be of any importance to us. Poachers in the wood behind the Hall, most likely. Certainly no one aiming at a son of the house standing in full view in the formal garden.

And then I stopped thinking about any of it at all, as the next second, the door from the conservatory to the outside opened and Christopher stepped through.

SEVEN

I removed myself from the corner and the yucca, and threw myself at him. "Thank God you're all right." I patted his arms and shoulders, searching for blood or anything else of concern. "You *are* all right, aren't you?"

"Of course I'm all right," Christopher said, grabbing me by the shoulders and holding me at arms' length, peering down at me. "Why wouldn't I be?"

After taking in my no doubt frazzled expression, his own changed, and he added, "What's wrong, Pippa?"

"Noises," I said. "Outside, inside... Something ran across my foot, and the door opened, and someone was there, but he didn't come inside." I glanced at the door. "I just hope he didn't lock it behind him when he left. And I thought I heard a gunshot..."

"You did," Christopher nodded. "It came nowhere near me, though. It was behind the Hall, probably well off the property. Poachers, most likely. I don't think you have to worry about anyone having been shot tonight."

"We're probably the only ones out here, anyway. And Grimsby, of course."

"Not Grimsby," Christopher said, as he turned me towards the door into the hall and gave me a shove.

"No?" I glanced at him over my shoulder as I made my way through the conservatory. "You didn't see him?"

"Not where I was waiting. I walked all over the formal garden, and stood by the fountain for rather a long time. I don't see how he could have missed me, or I him."

He shrugged. "Between you and me, Pippa, I'm just grateful I didn't have to deal with him again today. It gives us a little more time to try to figure out what to do about the money."

"We'll work on it tomorrow," I said, as we reached the door.

The knob turned under my hand, of course, but the door didn't open, and Christopher rolled his eyes. "That's just perfect, isn't it? " He applied his knuckles to it. "Tidwell! Where are you, Tidwell?"

In-between knocks and yells he glanced at me. "You couldn't have stopped him from locking us out? That was the entire reason you came along, wasn't it?"

It hadn't been the entire reason, not in my mind, but there was no point in saying so. "I didn't realize he'd be locking *this* door," I said instead. "I thought he'd lock the one from the conservatory to the outside, not the one from the conservatory in. If he had locked the exterior door, I would have been there to open it for you."

Since I had a point, Christopher didn't say any more about it, just renewed his assault upon the door. "Tidwell! Where are you? Tidwell!"

The key turned in the lock, and we stepped back. The door opened.

It was not Tidwell on the other side, however. Instead, it

was Crispin's eyebrow that crept up his forehead as he took in my no-doubt disheveled appearance—the orange tree and yucca had both had their fingers in my hair, and of course I hadn't bothered to refresh my lipstick before I left my room earlier—and Christopher's less than formal dress, with open collar and no hat or tie. "Midnight stroll?" he drawled.

"Sod off, St George." I pushed past him and into the house.

It was incredibly rude of me, of course. Aunt Charlotte would have been appalled. Aunt Roz might have been, too.

Crispin wasn't. He grinned, and it turned him from haughty young man to malicious little boy as he turned to watch me go. "The experience wasn't to your liking, I take it?"

"A snake slithered across my foot," I said stonily, and the grin widened.

"Was it the kind with two legs, Darling, or the kind with none?"

"None," I said. "Like you, St George. It slithered along the ground, and—"

At this point, Christopher nudged Crispin out of his way, none too gently. "Leave off teasing her, Crispin. Can't you tell she's about to blow?"

The corner of Crispin's mouth turned up. "Of course I can, old chap. That's why I'm doing it."

"Well, don't," Christopher said, as I pulled open the door to the servants' stairs. "What are you doing down here, anyway?"

"Waking the old man," Crispin said, "what else?"

"There's not enough liquor in your own room for that?"

Crispin shrugged, and I told them both, "It's late. I'm going to get some sleep. You two can do whatever you want. Stay down here and drink all night if you want to."

Crispin opened his mouth, but before he could say anything, Christopher shook his head. "I'll go up with you."

He entered the staircase behind me, and so, a bit to my surprise, did Crispin.

"Would you like me to walk you to your room, Darling?" he asked when we'd come out of the staircase into the upper hall and were standing between his and Christopher's doors. "Make sure the creepie-crawlies don't get you?"

"Don't be silly," I told him crushingly. "Nothing's going to happen to me between here and the west wing."

"Then I'll say good night." He stepped up to his own door with a nod for each of us. "Darling. Kit."

He ducked inside and we heard the key turn in the lock. If he stepped away from the door, I didn't hear his footsteps, however.

Of course, there could have been rugs. There probably were.

But just in case, when Christopher asked whether there was anything else we needed to talk about tonight, I told him no.

"Will you be down for breakfast?"

He said he'd be down bright and early, so we could plan our return to London in the afternoon, and then he ducked into his room and pulled the door shut behind him, too, while I slipped my shoes back off for the trip back to my own room.

I had changed out of my clothes into pyjamas, and had walked over to the window to pull the curtains closed against the moonlight and clouds scudding across the sky, when I caught a movement out of the corner of my eye, out there in the darkness beyond the house. I stopped, hands up and clutching the sides of the drapes, as I peered into the night.

At first I saw nothing. The moon was tucked behind a cloud, and the stars were not enough by themselves to illuminate the garden, and by now, Tidwell had turned out all the lights on the lower level, so the house was blanketed in darkness. But then the moon peeped out from behind the clouds, for just long enough to illuminate the apex of a fair head, gliding above the top of the hedge maze behind the Hall.

The next second it was gone again, so quickly I couldn't be certain I'd even seen it.

Except I was. Certain, that is. So certain that I dropped the curtains like they had burned me, and bounded across the room and out the door into the hallway, where I proceeded to pelt down the length of the west wing into the central hallway, and from there through the door into the Duchess's Chamber, and over to the window.

Or at least over to the bed, where I stubbed my foot on one of the ornately carved legs. I ended up hopping the rest of the way, biting back moans of pain, certain I had broken my little toe.

And it was all for naught. By the time I got to the window and could examine the view at my leisure, the moon had once again disappeared behind a cloud, and the garden maze lay quiet and mysterious under the changing sky. I gave it up as a bad job, and limped back to my own room and into bed without looking out the window again.

"Could it have been Grimsby?" Christopher wanted to know the next morning over breakfast.

I thought about it for a moment before I shook my head. "I don't think so, Christopher. Grimsby has dark hair. Almost black. This was someone fair-haired, as far as I could tell. You know, from the one-second glimpse I got."

"He uses quite a lot of brilliantine, though," Christopher pointed out, "so it's possible the moonlight on top of his head would make it reflect like that for a second."

Perhaps. "I don't know why you're so insistent on it being Grimsby. Why does it matter?"

"I just find it strange that he didn't show up last night," Christopher said, and took a bite of kipper. After masticating and swallowing, he added, "There's a thousand pounds riding on it. Why would he choose to give up all that money?"

His relief at having avoided the conversation with Grimsby last evening had clearly turned to questioning and dread overnight.

"I don't know that you can say he gave it up," I said fairly. "He'll probably make contact with you today, to start negotiating. The below-stairs might have been too discombobulated last night for him to get away. We don't know much about what goes on down there, but I imagine there must have been turmoil. So many of the servants had been with your grandfather for such a long time."

Including, of course, Grimsby, who might have been devastated by the loss of his employer. Not to mention his steady income.

Christopher didn't have an answer to that, so I continued. "Or, if it was Grimsby I saw—" which I wasn't convinced it had been, but there was no point in repeating it, "—maybe he was just running late. Perhaps you're not the only family member he has on his hook. Maybe he was meeting with someone else, too, before you, and the meeting went longer than expected, so he didn't make it to your part of the garden until after you'd left. He probably wouldn't have scheduled two meetings in the same part of the garden, for fear the two of you might see each other."

Christopher looked reluctantly assured as he chewed his fish. "Who do you suppose he might be blackmailing? Other than me?"

"I have no idea," I said. "St George heard about Francis's

drug use and your mother's sideline by listening in on the conversations in your grandfather's room. If the old boy knew about those things, Grimsby wouldn't have been in a position to blackmail either of them with those secrets. You can't blackmail someone with something someone else already knows."

Christopher nodded.

"He certainly wasn't blackmailing me. That leaves your cousin, your aunt and uncle, and your father."

"I can't imagine what Father might have to hide," Christopher said. "He never does anything except shoot partridges and visit his club. And surely Aunt Charlotte would know whatever Uncle Harold has been up to, and vice versa."

"I guess that depends on how close they are." And they weren't sharing a bedroom, so perhaps not as close as a married couple ought to be. "Although it's probably St George. He's getting up to all sorts of things in Town, if the rumors are true."

"You just don't like him," Christopher said, which was certainly fair. I didn't. "If there are rumors about what he's doing, his actions are hardly a secret, are they? And from that conversation we overheard, it sounds like Uncle Harold is well aware of what Crispin has been up to."

"Unless he's doing something else. Something his father doesn't know. Something nobody knows."

"Something Grimsby discovered? I suppose that's possible. If he was sneaking around after you and me, he was probably sneaking around after Crispin, as well."

"We can just ask Tidwell where Grimsby is," I said, "if you're ready to get it over with."

I looked around for any sign of the butler.

"No," Christopher said, which was just as well, since the breakfast room was empty except for the two of us. "I'll wait for Grimsby to contact me. I don't want to see him any sooner than I have to."

This was honestly contrary to my own habit of grabbing whatever problem I have by the ears and shaking it into submission, but if Christopher preferred to put off the inevitable until he could avoid it no more, who was I to stop him?

"That's fine by me. I'm sure he'll show up sooner rather than later, to be honest."

I took a bite of fried tomato and chewed it carefully before I added, "Although I really don't think it was him I saw last night. It was only a glimpse, but I really got the impression it was someone with fair hair. You, your brother, your cousin, your father..."

"It certainly wasn't me. You walked me to my door and saw me go in, Pippa. I doubt I would have had the time to run back downstairs, out through the conservatory, and all the way around to the hedge maze by the time you looked out your window."

Perhaps not. Then again, I had changed out of my clothes and into my pyjamas by the time I went to pull the curtains, so it was possible. It had been five minutes, at least, from the time we had parted ways outside Christopher's room. He would have had to hurry, certainly, but I thought he could probably have made it there.

And by that measure, so could Crispin. When he'd come upon us last night, perhaps that's where he'd been going. Out, to meet Grimsby. Maybe he hadn't been, as he put it, waking his grandfather at all. And when he ran into us, he had walked upstairs with us to make sure we were settled and weren't going to come after him before he went back downstairs and out.

He had even offered to walk me all the way to my door, hadn't he?

Although that wasn't the important thing right now.

"Of course I don't think it was you, Christopher. Don't be

silly. You had no reason to gallivant around the hedge maze close to midnight."

"I can't imagine that anyone else did, either," Christopher said. "Who would?"

It was the perfect opening to present the theory I had just worked out. But before I could get the first words out, someone else spoke first—and a good thing, too.

"Not me," Crispin said. "What are you suggesting, Darling? That I would rendezvous with the parlor maid in the garden maze with Grandfather lying dead upstairs?"

I sniffed. "Certainly not. I would hope you'd at least offer poor Sadie the dignity of a bed if you were going to descend to that level, instead of going about it like an animal on the grass in the maze."

The tops of Crispin's ears grew red. "You have a truly foul imagination, Darling, and a worse mouth."

I didn't answer beyond an offended—and offensive—sniff, and he added, "For your information, I'm not in the habit of seducing the staff, but if I were to 'descend to that level'—"

His tone made the quotation marks his fingers didn't make, "—and what a horrible expression for you to employ, Darling, since we're on the subject. Who are you, to suggest that Sadie is someone I would have to 'descend' to?"

I opened my mouth to snap at him that he'd clearly misunderstood what I'd been saying, because I didn't consider Sadie to be below him at all. In fact, I would consider very few people below Crispin St George, and that included every one of the parlor maids. But before I could get any of that out, he'd gone on.

"—but I'll have you know that when I do take the trouble to bed someone, I do it with all appropriate pomp and circumstance, which certainly includes a feather bed, and furthermore, I've not had any complaints about my technique, so you can just keep your vile mouth and horrid insinuations to yourself from now on!"

He walked out of the room while the air was still ringing with his final declaration. I opened my mouth and then closed it again, while his footsteps echoed across the floor of the foyer and then vanished with the punctuation of a slammed door.

"Ouch," Christopher murmured.

I turned to him, expecting amusement or commiseration or eye-rolling or *something*, but he wasn't even looking at me. So I opened my mouth again. "For goodness's sake, Christopher..."

"You know, Pippa—" He flashed me a rueful glimpse of blue, "I know you don't like Crispin, and I'll be the first to admit he can be trying, but he was right about one thing. You really do have a foul imagination when it comes to him and all his misdeeds. And you have no compunctions about verbalizing your thoughts, either."

I glared at him across the table. "Am I supposed to feel bad about that?"

"You're supposed to realize," Christopher said, "that in this case, at least, he was the one who brought up the parlor maid and the hedge maze, in the sense that he wouldn't shag her there—"

"Don't be vulgar, Christopher."

"—and there was no need for you to take offense at the way he treats his—hypothetical—conquests."

"I hardly think they're hypothetical," I said with a sniff. "We've both heard the rumors. And it's not like he's modest about it. 'I've had no complaints,' hah!"

"You know," Christopher said, tilting his head to contemplate me, "someone who didn't know your history with Crispin might listen to what you say and think there's a reason you're so angry about that."

I stared at him.

"You know, as in—"

"I get it, Christopher!"

My voice had gone shrill, and I took a breath and lowered it. "I get it. Someone might think I have tender feelings for Crispin—eurgh!—and that I'm saddened and—again, eurgh!—jealous that he's shagging his way around London—yes, I know, Christopher, I just told you not to be vulgar, and now I'm using the same word myself—but someone would be wrong then, wouldn't they?"

"I'm sure they would," Christopher said, his lips curved with amusement, "but you would have to excuse them for wondering, with the way you carry on."

He shook his head. "He didn't deserve the way you lit into him, Pippa. I know he can be annoying, but this morning he did nothing wrong. You need to go apologize to him, so the two of you can go back to your usual manner of semi-polite bickering. I can't handle this level of animosity. I have enough unpleasantness on my mind."

"Fine." I pushed my chair away from the table with an impolite shriek. (The chair legs on the floor, not me.) "But if I end up slapping him, I'm blaming you."

"Don't slap him," Christopher said. "Do you want me to come with you to make sure that doesn't happen?"

I shook my head. "You being there will only make things worse. If I have to humble myself in front of St George, I'd rather do it without an audience."

"Best of luck, then," Christopher said, and wiggled his fingers in the direction of the foyer and the front door. "Off you go."

I took two steps in that direction and turned around. "Any idea where I might find him? He went outside, not upstairs to his room."

"I'd try the hedge maze," Christopher said, "if only because we were just talking about it."

Right. "I'll see you back here after I've finished humiliating myself?"

"I imagine I'll be upstairs by then," Christopher said. "It might take a while. He'll want to luxuriate in it, no doubt."

No doubt at all.

"But don't worry," Christopher finished brightly, "my room doesn't overlook that part of the garden."

At least there was that one thing to be grateful for. I headed out, with the dragging feet—or at least the sinking feeling—of Marie Antoinette walking towards the guillotine.

THE FRONT DOOR, quite obviously, opens into the front of the Hall, and out to the courtyard. I opened it and peered out, but there was no sign of Crispin. No sign of anyone else, for that matter. The fountain in the middle of the courtyard burbled quietly in the morning sunshine, but that was the only sign of life.

I'll admit I had half expected to hear the roar of the Hispano-Suiza's engine, that Crispin's first instinct had been to jump into the motorcar and take out his aggression on driving too fast down the winding roads to the village, but other than the fountain and the birdsong, there was nothing to hear.

Nonetheless, I closed the door behind me and trudged across the courtyard and over to the carriage house. The Hispano-Suiza was still parked where it had been upon our arrival yesterday, between the duke's—the late duke's—more staid Crossley Touring Car and the Astleys' Bentley Tourer. Crispin was nowhere to be seen. I even called his name, and got no answer.

The hedge maze is located behind the house, so next I

turned my attention, and my feet, in that direction. He could be anywhere, of course, but we'd certainly used the word 'maze' enough that it might have made an impression, so it seemed a logical place to continue my search.

I wandered through the formal gardens, past the fountain where Christopher said he had waited for Grimsby last night, toward the back of the Hall.

The European hedge maze arrived on British soil during the reign of William III, perhaps better known as William of Orange, who was king for a couple of decades during the late sixteen-hundreds. By then, hedge mazes had already been popular on the Continent for a few hundred years, and hundreds of them were constructed all over England over the next two centuries. The Sutherland Hall maze was one of those.

It wasn't terribly large, and although I had gotten irrevocably lost the first few times I'd ventured into it (goaded by St George, of course) and had had to be rescued (by a gloating St George), the experience had mostly borne in upon me the necessity for figuring out the pattern of the maze so it wouldn't happen again. As I recall, I had been twelve when I traversed the maze with a notebook and pencil in hand, endeavoring to draw myself a map. That done, I went to my room and memorized the path. After that, I was never left to weep by myself, surrounded by green hedges, again. St George had been fit to be tied when he'd realized it, too.

But I wasn't supposed to be thinking about that. I was supposed to be planning my sincere apology, a concept which filled me with the most horrible sense of nausea.

I did not want to apologize to Crispin.

Not because he didn't deserve it, because in hindsight, I could see that I had perhaps jumped a little too briskly to berating him for something he absolutely had not suggested he would do. In fact, I had no reason whatsoever to think that Crispin would pick lovers from below-stairs at the Hall, or for that manner from the staff at Sutherland House.

Indeed, between his grandfather—until yesterday—and his father and mother, I would have guessed Crispin would have been made absolutely aware of what would happen should he do something so ill-advised.

Besides, whatever his other faults may be, and I knew without a doubt that they were plentiful, I didn't believe seducing the staff was something he'd stoop to. He'd think it was beneath him, and not in the way I had made it sound earlier. Not that Sadie the parlor maid—who, by the way, had to be at least ten years Crispin's senior, and who was as round as a dumpling—was beneath him, but that sexual relations with the servants was. For all his other faults, I couldn't see him exerting his dubious charms on anyone who wasn't both upper-class, stunning, and rich.

No, the reason I didn't want to apologize was because I knew I was wrong, and I knew he would rub it in if—when—I gave him the chance. Because he was Crispin St George, and he'd never let an opportunity go by to get beneath my skin. He was going to make me grovel, and I wasn't looking forward to it.

It had been a decade since we'd played in the garden maze, but the twists and turns came back to me as I entered the cool greenness of the paths and turned right.

The maze was created from common English yew trees, evergreens with red berries, none of which were in evidence at this time of year. Its shape is roughly square, and unlike some mazes, the paths are perpendicular, not serpentine, which made the map a lot easier to draw back in the day. Right, eight steps; left, seven steps; left, nine steps... And while I was now several inches taller than I had been at eleven, the hedges inside the maze still topped my head by a bit. Right at the front, where the entrance was, they were shorter—five feet instead of six or seven—but once I got into the maze, they got taller and the gloom got deeper. Because it was early and the sun was close to the horizon, the maze itself was shady and a bit cool. I wrapped my arms around myself as I trudged towards the middle of the labyrinth.

The center of the maze opens into a clearing with a couple of benches and a sundial. It's a nice place to sit and breathe after traversing the maze, and the sundial is a lovely piece of art, with a base carved from marble and a weathered copper face. It must have started out bright, but has since oxidized to a pale green, and it is inscribed around the edges with Roman numerals.

Normally, it's the first thing I look at when I reach the center of the maze. This time, my gaze was arrested by the two figures next to the sundial instead. A man, flat on his back on the dewy grass, the toes of his black shoes pointing straight up at the sky. And the other man, kneeling beside him, head bowed.

I MUST HAVE MADE A SOUND, because Crispin's head jerked up, and he spun around to face me, his eyes large and startled in his pale face. When he recognized me, he slumped. "Oh. It's you."

"Who did you think it was?" I looked past him without waiting for an answer, and added, "Is that Grimsby?"

Crispin nodded. "Don't look."

"Why wouldn't I look? What's—?"

And then I moved far enough to the side that I could see for myself what he didn't want me to look at. "Good Lord."

My head started swimming, and I took an involuntary step back.

All right, so perhaps I staggered. That's how Crispin described it to Christopher later, and I won't say he was wrong. Although I did object to his further statement that I would have fainted dead away had he not taken hold of me. I would not have fainted, thank you very much. I do not faint.

But he did at any rate grab me by the arm, and yanked me over to one of the two benches in the clearing. There, he pushed me down and put his hand on the back of my neck. "Head between your knees. Breathe."

There was absolutely nothing tender or concerned about any of it, by the way, although I will say for him that what he told me to do worked. I stared at the tweed fabric of my skirt, up close and quite personal, and breathed into it. After a couple of inhalations, I thought the desire to succumb to the vapors had passed, so I asked, "What happened?"

"Who knows?" Crispin said, with his hand still at the back of my head. His fingers had somehow wound their way into my hair. "I found him like that."

"Is he dead?"

He snorted. "Of course he's dead, Darling. Why else do you suppose he'd be lying there?"

I turned my head to the side, because talking to my knees was starting to feel ridiculous. This way, I could at least address my questions to Crispin's knees in baggy gray flannels. "I suppose I thought there was a possibility he was drunk."

"At nine in the morning? Not bloody likely, is it?"

Perhaps not. Not when he put it like that.

"You can let me up now," I said, and when he untwined his fingers and removed his hand and I had raised my head, I added, "I thought perhaps he had been drunk last night—his employer died, after all, so it didn't seem out of the realm of possibility that the servants would have decided to wake the old duke, too—and then he decided to sleep it off here."

"No," Crispin said. "He's quite dead, I assure you."

I risked another glance over at Grimsby, and contemplated the blood. There was rather a lot of it. Not so visible against the black fabric of his jacket, but the shirt underneath was red, almost all the way up to his collar, and there was also rather a lot of blood on the grass around the body.

My vision developed small bright spots around the edges, and I closed my eyes again. "Gah."

"I should go get help," Crispin said, rocking back and forth on his heels. "I was making sure there was nothing I could do for him, but he's been dead for hours. We have to call the constabulary."

He turned towards the path out of the maze, and I snatched at his sleeve before he could move away from me. "Don't you dare leave me here with... with him!"

He sniggered. He'd been pale when I'd first stumbled upon him, but the opportunity to annoy me seemed to have put him back in countenance, because his cheeks showed a hint of color again. "He's not going to rise up and attack you, Darling."

"I didn't think he would," I said, "but I still don't want to be left alone with him."

He raised a shoulder. "Fine by me. No one has to stay here and mind the body. He's been lying here all night, as far as I can tell. If someone was going to cart him off, they would have done it by now."

"Then let's go." I held out a hand. It might have been the first time I had willingly accepted Crispin's help with anything, let alone actively asked for it, and the arch of his eyebrow showed that he knew it. But he took my hand and hauled me to my feet. And then he kept a hand under my elbow while I found my footing and made sure I wasn't going to develop another bout of dizziness. I seemed to have gotten over the instability I had felt earlier, so I nodded to him. "Lead the way."

"You know the way out of the maze, Darling."

"Don't antagonize me," I told him. "I came out here to apologize, but if you upset me again, I might forget to do it."

Both his brows rose this time. "You? Came to apologize to me?"

I grimaced. "Christopher convinced me I had misjudged you."

He laughed. Not just sniggered, but actually laughed. Out loud. "That was kind of Kit, but I assure you, you haven't. I'm everything you think I am, and more."

I refrained from rolling my eyes, but just barely. "Whatever else you are, apparently you're not someone who would shag the parlor maid on the grass in the hedge maze."

"No," Crispin agreed, as we made our way along the shady paths between the yew hedges. "I suppose that's one thing I'm not."

"And as such, I shouldn't have suggested you were. I've heard stories about your escapades, so you'll forgive me for believing you capable of practically anything."

"Of course." His voice was perfectly bland and courteous, in spite of the rather hair-raising things I was saying. "Just out of curiosity..."

"No," I said. "I'm not repeating them. You have a reputation, as I'm sure you know."

"I'm aware." He smirked, even as he tugged me around a corner of the maze, just as comfortable with the right and left turns of it as I was. "I didn't realize *you* were."

"All of London is, I think."

We walked another few steps in silence before I added, "Christopher and I overheard some of the conversation you had with your father yesterday afternoon, for your information."

And yes, the biggest reason I brought it up was to wipe that annoyingly self-satisfied expression off his face.

I hadn't expected a stumble, nor did I get one, but his steps did check for a fraction of a second. Just long enough for me to notice the lack of smoothness. When he turned to look at me, he had lost a little color. "What did you say?"

"You and your father had a conversation yesterday afternoon, in your sitting room. After the incident with you and me and the secret passage in the Duchess's Chamber."

"Oh." On the face of it, it looked as if he might be relieved by that explanation, which was interesting. Perhaps there had been a different conversation—one that had included his grand-father? The conversation that had sent him hurtling down the corridor and into his room in the first place?—and that was what he'd been afraid we would have overheard?

"Christopher and I were passing by your room," I explained, "and we heard your voices."

"Without putting your ear to the door at all, I assume?"

"Totally without." I grinned at him. "Neither of you was precisely quiet, you might remember. So who have you lost your heart to, St George? Flossie Schlomsky and her dime-store empire? Or some unsuitable waif from darkest Calcutta with no money and fewer prospects?"

He gave me a look down his nose that could have wilted the yew hedges, just as we escaped from the entrance to the maze and started to make our way towards the Hall. "Neither. And I'll thank you to keep your impertinent questions to yourself, Darling. It's none of your business who I..."

He stopped, with a sound like he was gagging.

I giggled. "It's all right to admit you have feelings, St George. It's hard to believe, I agree, but—"

"For God's sake, Darling, have you no sense of decorum? You can't ask a man about his feelings the same way you ask if he'd like butter with his crumpets."

He yanked on one of the double doors to the drawing room and, when it opened, pushed me through. The room within was empty, and Crispin gave it a single comprehensive look before he raised his voice. "Tidwell! Where are you? Tidwell!"

A moment passed, and then there was the sound of running footsteps outside in the hall. When the door into the drawing room burst open from the other side, though, it wasn't Tidwell in the doorway, but Christopher. He stood framed in the opening for a second, eyes wild, before he took a couple of long steps into the room and yanked me away from Crispin. "Pippa! What happened?"

"Grimsby," I said into his shoulder. "Dead. In the maze."

It was Christopher's turn to stagger, and yes, it was absolutely a stagger. I grabbed for his arm, and so did Crispin, so for a second we were both keeping Christopher upright. Then he shook us both off. "How?"

"Shot," Crispin said, which was news to me. I honestly hadn't thought about it, or looked around for a weapon. Or noticed one. There had been no knife handle sticking out of Grimsby's chest—I would have noticed that much—so a bullet made sense.

I grabbed Christopher's arm again. "The shot. Last night, when you were—"

He snapped his eyes to me, and I stopped. For a second, no one said anything. Then...

"You heard a shot last night?" Crispin asked. His voice was pleasant, not demanding at all.

I nodded, and made a point not to look at Christopher as I did it. "Around eleven-fifteen or eleven-twenty, maybe. We thought it came from farther away. That it was poachers. But now..."

"Now it looks very much like we heard the shot that killed Grimsby," Christopher said grimly. "We'll have to... Oh, Tidwell. There you are."

"Mr. Astley." Tidwell gave him a look, before he glanced past me, "Miss Darling," and fixed his attention on Crispin. "My lord."

Crispin blinked. Perhaps it was the first time he'd been

addressed as such. "Tidwell. Grimsby has been shot. He's in the middle of the garden maze."

"Dead," I added, since I didn't feel that part had been clear from Crispin's explanation.

There followed a humming sort of moment, before Tidwell said, "Very good, my lord. I'll call the constabulary in Little Sutherland, shall I?"

"If you please, Tidwell. And let my father know?"

"Of course, my lord." Tidwell withdrew, as placid as if murders in the garden maze was a weekly occurrence.

We stood in silence for a moment, until— "I need a drink," Crispin said.

I glanced at the clock ticking away on the wall. "It's not even ten in the morning. On a Sunday."

He shot me a look. "Is it more acceptable to drink before ten on the other days of the week?"

"I'm with you," Christopher said. "And I didn't even see the body. A drink sounds like just the thing."

They headed for the door to the hallway. I trotted after. "Maybe just some whiskey in a cup of tea? It might make it look less like alcoholism and more medicinal?"

"If it'll make you feel better," Christopher said with a shrug. "I'll get the whiskey. You pour the tea?"

"Fine by me." I headed for the breakfast room, where the warming dishes were still ranged along the sideboard and the tea was still warm. After I had lined up three cups and as I started to pour tea into each of them, the clicking of heels outside the door warned me that company was coming, and most likely of the female variety. I turned my head, just in time to see Aunt Roz breeze through the doorway. She took in me and the three teacups in a single glance, and arched her brows. "Goodness. Having a party this morning?"

"Christopher, St George, and I are having whiskey," I said.

Aunt Roz blinked. "What is the occasion?"

"Grimsby's dead." I put the teapot down and plopped the cozy over top of it, so the contents would stay warm. "St George just found the body in the middle of the garden maze."

"Dear me," Aunt Roz said. "Has anyone called the police?"

"Tidwell went off to do it. Christopher and Crispin went to find the whiskey."

"Better pour me some, too," Aunt Roz said, and reached for a cup and saucer, which she put next to the other three.

I reached for the pot again, while Aunt Roz added, "Who would want to kill Grimsby?"

I imagine she meant it rhetorically, and it probably meant that Aunt Roz, at least, had not been one of Grimsby's victims.

"I can't imagine," I said, while I focused on keeping my hands steady. "Perhaps he killed himself. His employer just died. Is it possible he expected to get the sack, and he didn't want to deal with it?"

"I don't think Grimsby would have had a problem finding another position," Aunt Roz answered. She lifted her teacup and took it over to the table, where she sat down and crossed her ankles demurely. "He was with His Grace for a long time. And dear Henry might have provided for him in his last will, as well. It wouldn't surprise me."

Maybe not. In my admittedly limited view, the late duke hadn't had a sentimental bone in his body. He'd been a terrible old curmudgeon who had delighted in making things as difficult as possible for his family, and I couldn't imagine him willing anything to anyone beyond what was entailed in the estate. But it was possible that he had had warmer feelings towards a servant and confidant who had been with him for years. He certainly hadn't seemed particularly warm towards either of his grandchildren, and as for me, he had mostly pretended I didn't exist.

"I suppose we'll find out when it's time for the will to be read," I said. "Not that Grimsby is in any position to benefit now."

"Clearly," Aunt Roz said. "If there was a bequest for Grimsby, and it was sizeable, it will be interesting to see who gets the money now."

Ah. So Aunt Roz was thinking that someone might have killed Grimsby for the inheritance. It was a possibility I hadn't considered, but now that I did, I couldn't dismiss it outright. Whoever did it would have had to have known what was in the will, of course, but someone might have known that. Whoever had signed as a witness, for instance.

It was far more likely that Grimsby had been murdered because he was a blackmailer, of course. Because he knew something about someone that that someone didn't want to get out. That's the sort of thing someone kills over.

Although Aunt Roz might not have known about that. It didn't seem as if she had.

A chill passed through me when I remembered that when the shot rang out, I'd been by myself in the conservatory.

Now, Grimsby hadn't been blackmailing *me*, so I was hardly a suspect. But he had been blackmailing Christopher, and Christopher had also been alone in the garden.

But of course he hadn't been anywhere near the hedge maze, I told myself. Grimsby had arranged to meet him in the formal garden on the east side of the house.

Unless, a little voice in the back of my head said, he *had* been near the hedge maze. I couldn't prove that he hadn't. When Grimsby hadn't turned up in the formal garden by the predetermined time he was supposed to meet Christopher, Christopher might have taken it upon himself to go looking for the valet.

Did I think he had?

Of course not. I was sure he had done exactly what he told me he'd done: waited by the fountain. Christopher wasn't a murderer.

But could I prove he hadn't gone to the garden maze and shot Grimsby?

No. Not at all.

"This is bad," I said.

"You can certainly say that again," Aunt Roz agreed, and I came back to myself in time to see Christopher and Crispin come through the door, each with a bottle in each hand. It seemed we were to have a choice between libations in our tea this morning.

Aunt Roz gave them both a beaming smile. "There you are. Pippa just told me what has happened. I'll have a splash of whiskey, please."

"Our cups are over there," I added, pointing to the sideboard. "Doctor them however you like. But not too much for me, please. I'd rather not be insensible when the constables show up."

"Don't want to be careless with what we admit," Crispin nodded, without looking at me. I glanced sharply at him, but he either didn't notice, or simply didn't bother to acknowledge me. Instead, he busied himself with pouring liquor into one of the half-full teacups. "There you go, Darling." He held it out. "That'll put roses in your cheeks."

I rolled my eyes but took the cup. "Thank you, St George. Out of curiosity, where were you between eleven and eleven-thirty last night?"

"As I told you when I let you in last night," Crispin said, "I was having a drink to Grandfather's memory, before I retired upstairs to where every decent person ought to be at that time of night here in the pastoral tranquility of the countryside. My bedroom. Early to bed and early to rise. Isn't that right, Darling?"

I made a face, and he added, "You still haven't made that apology you promised, you know. You said you came outside to offer one, but in the hullaballoo of the discovery in the maze, I assume it must have slipped your mind."

Not quite. I'd referenced the apology, and we had been on semi-cordial speaking terms, so I had hoped that it might be enough and I could get away without actually having to make the promised *mea culpa*. But I guess such was too much to expect, at least when dealing with Crispin St George, who had no finer feelings to speak of, and who would insist on his pound of flesh.

"Of course." I fought back the grimace that threatened to overtake my countenance. "Although I did tell you I shouldn't have misjudged you based on the stories I have heard."

"You did," Crispin agreed with a grin, "and it was masterful, Darling, truly. Your way with words is astonishing. But you didn't really tell me you were wrong, did you?"

No, I hadn't. That was what I had hoped I'd be able to avoid. But since I clearly wasn't going to be...

I took a breath. "I'm sorry for accusing you of behaving badly with regard to the parlor maid, St George. I was wrong about you, and I'm sorry."

I steeled myself for whatever atrocious thing might come back my way, but then Aunt Roz tut-tutted and spared me from whatever Crispin's response was going to be. "Have you been misbehaving, Crispin, dear?"

"Not with the parlor maid," Crispin said. "That's just Darling's *idée fixe*." He slanted me a sideways look.

I sniffed. "I do not have an *idée fixe*. Don't be ridiculous, St George. I don't spend my time pondering what you get up to in your spare time. I have better things to worry about."

"I'm sure you do," Crispin said, and just like that, we were back to the dead body in the garden maze and the impending arrival of the authorities.

I turned to Christopher, who had been unusually silent throughout this whole exchange. "What's going on with you? You're being very quiet for someone who didn't even see the body."

"Crispin described it in quite enough detail," Christopher said with a grimace, "thank you, Pippa. And there's nothing going on with me. I'm just worried. Someone saw fit to murder someone else on the grounds last night. I guess I'm wondering who might be next."

That was a consideration that hadn't crossed my mind.

"Surely nobody else would be involved in this?" I said. "Grimsby—"

"There's no way to know who's involved until the police figure out why Grimsby was shot," Christopher answered, with quite a pointed look in my direction, to remind me that we weren't supposed to know anything about any blackmail attempts. Without that knowledge, Grimsby's murder could have been affected by any number of people for any number of reasons, none of which we would know anything about.

"Of course." It had been thirty minutes and I was already having trouble keeping things straight in my head. Better if I just didn't offer any unnecessary information, I told myself, so I didn't trip myself up. "At any rate, have some tea. Fortify yourself before the arrival of the constables. I'm sure we'll have to deal with an influx of all sorts of people today."

AND SUCH DID, in point of fact, turn out to be the case. Much more so than we expected at the time, even. Representatives for the local constabulary showed up in short order, spurred by

Tidwell's telephone call, and with all evidence of being excited about the opportunity to deal with a murder. I imagine it wasn't something they often got the chance to tackle in a small village like Little Sutherland.

That was only until someone figured out that Grimsby's death wasn't the only one to have taken place on the premises in the past twenty-four hours. Once the connection was made to the late duke's demise yesterday, even under vastly different circumstances, suddenly the Chief Constable got involved, and after that, it was a short step until Scotland Yard was called in.

And thus it was that we were faced, at around two-thirty that afternoon, with the arrival of four gentlemen in city suits, who had motored down from London for the express purpose of taking over the case.

At that point, Christopher and I were in the study, watching the happenings through the window. Francis was with us, too, and although Christopher and I had stopped fortifying ourselves with spiked tea some hours ago, Francis had taken the news of Grimsby's murder rather badly, and was clutching a glass of scotch. Not his first, either. His hands were shaking badly, and although we had both been tempted to ask him what he'd been up to last night, neither of us had quite had the courage to breach the subject.

Crispin had gone up to his rooms after lunch, perhaps in an effort to sober up in private, or perhaps just because he'd had enough of us by then. I had certainly had enough of him.

Aunt Roz, meanwhile, was in conference with Uncle Herbert, Uncle Harold, and Aunt Charlotte in the drawing room.

"Should have left while we had the chance," Christopher told me out of the corner of his mouth, as the official car pulled to a stop at the bottom of the steps.

I nodded agreement, even as I objected, verbally, to his

statement. "Unless we packed our things and left last night, I don't think there has been a time this morning when we've actually had the chance to go."

"Perhaps not," Christopher agreed, "but I can't help but wish we were miles and miles away from here."

He wasn't alone in that. In the background, Francis took a loud swallow of scotch, and I'm sure he felt the same. Outside the window, the doors to the car opened. From the passenger seat, a stocky man in a bowler hat, past the first glow of youth, emerged, and looked up to assess the Hall with sharp eyes in a stubborn, bulldog-like face. The driver was a younger man, perhaps a bit shy of thirty, weedy and fair, with a prominent nose and a rabbity look about him. From the back alighted a stocky brunet in tweed on one side, while from the other stepped an elderly gentleman in a black suit holding a doctor's bag.

I blinked. "Isn't that...?"

Christopher stared at the car, and at me, and at the car again. "Tom," he said eventually.

Over at the table, Francis raised his bloodshot eyes. "Garner?"

"Gardiner," Christopher corrected, which might in fairness have been what Francis was trying to say.

Francis nodded. "Works for Scotland Yard, does he?"

"So it appears," I told him. "Friend of yours?"

"Chap I knew at Eton," Francis said and drained the glass. "Guess I'd better go say hello."

He sat the glass on the table with a little more force than strictly necessary, and pushed to his feet. We both watched as he headed for the door, not quite as steady as maybe he should have been. He made it across the floor and through to the foyer in a mostly straight line, though, and without bumping into the door jamb, and that was really all we could hope for at this juncture, I thought.

I glanced at Christopher. "Do you want to go say hello, too?"

He shook his head. "I'd rather put it off as long as possible, if you don't mind."

"I don't mind at all," I told him, even though I was honestly quite interested in meeting—formally—the man who had taken the trouble to rescue Christopher from being arrested two nights ago. "I'm sure I'll get my chance to meet him later."

"I have no doubt whatsoever that you will," Christopher said resignedly.

NINE

The new arrivals split up before they even made it into the house.

Christopher's friend went with Francis and the old gent around the house and into the garden maze—a camera and the doctor's bag went with them—while the rabbit and the bulldog were admitted to the house by Francis, before Tidwell could even make it to the front door. His demeanor—Tidwell's—was noticeably put out by this, although it lessened when Francis left with the doctor and photographer to help them navigate the maze, thus leaving the inspector and, I assumed, another detective for Tidwell to manage.

He showed them into the drawing room. Christopher and I exchanged a look. "What do you want to do?" he asked. "Stay here? Go introduce ourselves? Listen at the door?"

"I think there's been enough listening at doors for the moment," I told him, "don't you? Besides, they're not likely to say anything interesting, are they? It's probably just introductions and getting the lay of the land."

Christopher shrugged. Now that he had left the window, he was pacing nervously back and forth in front of the fireplace, his face pale.

"You seem worried," I said, pointing out the obvious.

He glanced at me, but didn't stop the pacing. "Wouldn't you be?"

I took a seat on the arm of one of the chairs and put my hands together in my lap while he continued. "I was alone in the garden at the time when we heard the shot. If that was the shot that killed Grimsby—and while it might not have been, it was the only shot I heard..."

I nodded.

"I'd left you behind in the conservatory, but you couldn't see me. I could have run into the garden maze and shot him, and run back in time to find you in the conservatory."

Yes. There had been enough time for that.

"In that case I don't have an alibi either," I told him. "I could have run from the conservatory through the house and out the drawing room doors, into the maze, and back. The timing would have been tight, but I think I could have done it."

Christopher squinted at me. "You had no reason to kill Grimsby."

No. Not personally. But— "Maybe I killed him for you," I said.

"You wouldn't have done that."

It came out very certain. After a second he added, more hesitantly, "Would you?"

"If he came at you with a sword? Of course I would. Or I would have tried, at any rate."

"Well, he didn't," Christopher said. "This threat was a lot less direct than that. And anyway, that—what you said—would have been a big risk. You might have met someone as you ran through the house. Someone could have seen you."

That was true. "Tidwell was about. I saw him later, after we'd gone upstairs. He was turning out the lights in the foyer when I went past the top of the stairs. It was most likely him who opened the door to the conservatory while I was in there, too. And locked it for the night."

Christopher nodded.

"Although, you know, I wouldn't have had to go through the house. I could have gone out the conservatory door, too, after you'd gone into the garden. While you made your way into the formal garden, I could have stayed close to the side of the Hall until I got to the back, and from there I could have gone into the maze. That might have been even faster, and I wouldn't have had to worry that anyone would see me."

Christopher squinted at me. "I'm not sure I like the way you're talking, Pippa. You're making this seem reasonable."

I shrugged. "We both know I didn't. I stayed in the corner of the conservatory until you came back. But no one else knows that. And since we're both without proper alibis, perhaps we should consider remedying it."

He looked at me. "Lie, you mean?"

"Just a very small white lie. We went outside together for some fresh air before bed. Not because of Grimsby at all—I don't think we should mention being blackmailed by Grimsby; it just makes us look guilty for no reason."

"I don't know, Pippa..." Christopher said. "What if they find out?"

"How would they find out? Do you think someone else is going to admit to being blackmailed?"

I waited, but when he didn't say anything—because, after all, who would admit to having been blackmailed by a recent murder victim?—I continued. "It would solve the problem. I know you didn't shoot him, and I hope you know I didn't."

He nodded.

"This way, everyone else knows we can't have done it."

"Yes," Christopher agreed reluctantly. "But I don't want to drag you into it if I don't have to."

"I'm already in it, Christopher. When he decided to blackmail you, he blackmailed both of us. Besides, I was down there with you. I might as well have been outside as inside the conservatory."

I waited, but again he said nothing, just looked pensive.

"And," I added, "there's nothing you can do to stop me from saying I was with you, you know. You can't put your hand over my mouth to keep me from speaking. That would look very odd. So you could just say thank you and be grateful that I'm willing to lie for you."

"I just don't think you should have to do it," Christopher said.

I shrugged. "If it's between a small, white lie and the possibility that they'll try to pin this murder on you, I'd much rather tell the small, white lie. You had a very good reason for wanting him gone, you know. If they find out about it, and that you have no alibi, you'll be the prime suspect."

"But I wouldn't have killed him over it!" Christopher protested. "I'd find the money somewhere. Even if I'd had to beg my mother for help. Or eat beans on toast for a year. Or—God forbid—move back home. At least Grandfather can't throw his weight around anymore."

"I know you would have," I said. "But *I* know you. Scotland Yard doesn't."

"Tom does."

True. And he also seemed inclined to want to keep Christopher out of trouble, or at least out of jail, as far as it was possible.

"In that case," I said, "perhaps we don't have anything to worry about. But just in case this becomes an issue, I'd like you to have the strongest alibi possible. Because to be honest, Christopher, your motive is outstanding, too."

Christopher grimaced. "Thank you. I think."

"Don't mention it," I said. "Really."

We sat in silence for a few moments after that.

"I'm a bit worried about Francis," I admitted.

Christopher squinted at me. "How so?"

"Well, there's the dope. That's enough to worry anyone, I imagine. St George made it sound like it wasn't a big deal, but I don't like the idea of it."

"I'm sure Crispin has seen plenty of dope of his own," Christopher said, "but I agree with you. I don't like the idea of it, either."

"And the light in his room did go out while I was standing in the conservatory last night. Before we heard the gunshot."

"So Francis might have turned out his light, left his room, and gone to the garden maze," Christopher said. "Is that what you're saying?"

I nodded. "He knows how to use a gun." Something neither Christopher nor I did, as far as I knew. But Francis had been in the war, and the idea of settling things with a pistol might have come quite naturally to him.

"Ugh," Christopher said with a grimace. "I don't like this. I know we aren't as close as we used to be, but he's still my brother. I don't like to speculate on his viability as a murderer."

I didn't, either. "Perhaps we should just talk about something else entirely. I wonder how long we'll have to stay here before the police let us go home?"

"I imagine once they've arrested someone," Christopher said. "Just in case one of us did it, they wouldn't want us haring off to London and perhaps places further afield, where they might lose track of us."

"A good thing neither of us have plans for tomorrow, then."

Christopher nodded. "A very good thing."

ONCE THE CONTINGENT from the maze—Christopher's friend Tom and the old man I assumed was the police surgeon—made it back into the house, things started to move forward. We were all gathered together in the drawing room, from all different parts of the house—the above-stairs, I mean; the servants had their own gathering in the kitchen or staff room, I assumed—and everyone was introduced.

"Doctor Curtis," the bulldog-faced man said shortly, with a nod at the older gentleman. "The Yard's medical examiner. Detective Sergeants Gardiner and Finchley. And I'm Chief Inspector Pendennis. We've been called in by your local Chief Constable to investigate the deaths of Simon Grimsby and the late Duke of Sutherland."

A whisper of fabric ran around the room as we all shifted on our chairs.

"My father's death?" the new duke said blankly, and his wife added, "There's something to be investigated in my father-in-law's death?"

"When two deaths occur within a few hours of each other, in the same place and involving the same cast of characters, they both need to be investigated."

Pendennis folded his hands on top of the table, while we all processed being described as a cast of characters. Aunt Roz mouthed the words visibly, her brows creeping up her forehead.

I glanced at Christopher, who shrugged. Across the table, Crispin was looking unusually sober, while Francis looked sick. Physically so.

"We'll start the questions with everyone in the same room," Pendennis said. "Gardiner, take notes."

Tom Gardiner nodded, and pulled out a notebook and pencil. "Just ignore me," he said, with a flash of a boyish grin that wasn't directed at anyone at all. So far, he hadn't even glanced at Christopher, and Christopher hadn't looked at him, either.

"If you'll go around the table," Pendennis said, "and introduce yourselves for the record. Your name, your address—if it isn't here—your relationship to the deceased. We'll start with you."

He nodded to Aunt Roz, who drew a breath. "I'm Lady Roslyn Astley. Wife to Herbert, mother to Francis and Christopher. The late duke was my father-in-law. I had no relationship to his valet. I don't live here. My husband and I live at Beckwith Place, which was part of my inheritance from my late mother."

Pendennis nodded and turned to Uncle Herbert, who cleared his throat.

"Lord Herbert Astley. Roz's husband, Harold's younger brother. Francis's and Christopher's father..."

And so it went, around the table. When it was my turn, I said, "I'm Philippa Darling. Twenty-three years old. No relation to the late duke, or the current duke or viscount. Niece to Lady Roslyn through her sister, cousin to Christopher and Francis. I share a flat in London with Christopher."

The pencil that was scratching across the paper hesitated for a moment, or so I thought.

"We came down for the weekend at Christopher's grandfather's request," I added.

Pendennis looked up. "When was that decided?"

I glanced across the table at Crispin, and then away again. "Mr. Crispin Astley—Lord St George now—stopped by the flat on Friday evening to let us know that Christopher's presence had been requested for Saturday afternoon."

Crispin nodded.

"And you decided to come along?"

There was something sort of suggestive about the way he phrased it, and I felt my cheeks heat. "There wasn't really a question of anything else. I mean, we didn't discuss it. It was taken for granted, I guess, that we'd both go. We…"

I trailed off, not quite sure how to phrase it.

"They come as a set," Crispin muttered. I made a face, but didn't argue.

"Engaged?" Pendennis suggested.

Christopher and I exchanged a glance. "No."

"Things looked like they were headed that way last night," Crispin added, "but then my mother started screaming about dead bodies, so nothing was finalized."

Pendennis's bushy brows arched. "Dead bodies?"

"Just one dead body, I'm afraid," Aunt Charlotte said, with a quelling glance at her only son. "Crispin likes his little jokes."

Nobody seemed to find this one the least bit funny, and after a moment, Charlotte continued. "I took the duke—the late duke—his tea in his room yesterday afternoon, while everyone else gathered down here. That was when I discovered that he had passed."

"So you're the one who found the body?" Pendennis clarified.

Aunt Charlotte nodded. "When I went to take him his tea. He took most of his meals in bed these days."

"And what happened then? After you found him?"

"We called for the local doctor," Aunt Roz cut in. "Doctor Meadows, down in the village. He said it was most likely poor Henry's heart."

"He was an old man," Aunt Charlotte added, "and after the excitement of the afternoon…"

She trailed off while the rest of us did a sort of collective wince at the unfortunate choice of words. I can't imagine that anyone wanted to rehash the various conversations that had taken place in the Duke's Chamber yesterday, and with Scotland Yard of all people, but with those few words, Aunt Charlotte had opened the conversation up for just that.

And Pendennis wasn't the man to let it go unchallenged. "Excitement?"

Christopher was the one who took the bulldog by the... ears, I guess.

"He spent the afternoon yelling at some of us for various real and imagined peccadillos. In my case, it was that he wanted me to propose to Pippa, because I'd been stringing her along for a long time."

"I see." Pendennis glanced at me. "How long has it been, Miss Darling?"

"I've lived with the Astleys since I was eleven," I said. "But I don't know where the duke got the idea that I wanted to marry Christopher."

"You didn't? Don't?"

"Not particularly, no." I grinned at Christopher. "We're fine as we are. Aren't we, Kit?"

"Very much so," Christopher said.

Pendennis looked from him to me and back, with the helpless look of someone older who realizes he doesn't understand the younger generation. He even shot a look at Crispin, as if that would help. "So yesterday afternoon...?"

Christopher smiled, looking his best version of boyish and charming. "I figured it couldn't hurt to pretend for a bit. The old boy wasn't going to live much longer, given his age and the way he carried on, and I knew Pippa wouldn't be fussed. So..."

He shrugged. "I thought I'd propose and make him happy.

We could make it a long engagement that ultimately didn't go anywhere. But then my aunt came down the stairs and said that my grandfather was dead, and there was no point in going on with the charade."

"Interesting," Pendennis said. After a moment he added, "With that out of the way, who would like to go next?"

TEN

THE COMMUNITY CONVERSATION didn't last long after that. Nobody wanted to admit to their various sins, small or large, in mixed company, and Pendennis was forced to take us, one at a time, out of the drawing room and into the breakfast room for a private conversation. He took Finchley with him, presumably for note-taking, and left Tom Gardiner with us, presumably to do the same thing. Although with the situation what it was, there wasn't a lot of notation taking place. As soon as the door closed behind Finchley and Aunt Charlotte, Pendennis's first solo victim, Francis grinned. "So this is what you do all day, is it, Gardiner?"

The hour or two that had passed since the incident in the study had sobered him enough that Tom's name came out mostly unmangled. The latter also didn't seem to mind the familiarity, because he grinned back. "It's a lot of what I end up doing, yes. I follow Inspector Pendennis around, and take photographs and notes of what he thinks will be important."

"Enjoy it, do you?" Crispin wanted to know, and his query didn't sound quite as friendly. In fact, it had more than a hint of that patented St George condescension I was so used to hearing.

I had known both Crispin and Christopher during the time they went to Eton, of course. Christopher a bit better than Crispin, since I lived with Christopher and Crispin stayed with his parents at Sutherland Hall. But they had attended Eton from thirteen to eighteen, the same years I had been a student at the Godolphin School for Girls in Salisbury. (Which happened to have taught Dorothy L. Sayers, as well—"That Sayers woman," of Christopher's earlier mention—although sadly our years there hadn't overlapped. By the time I came along, she had moved on to Somerville College in Oxford. And at that time I'd also had no idea who she was, of course.)

At any rate, I didn't recall either Crispin or Christopher mentioning Thomas Gardiner during the time they'd been at Eton (and home for holidays), and now that I was able to see him more clearly than I had in London two nights ago, I put his age at around twenty-seven or so. Which would have meant his time there would have overlapped Francis's by a couple of years on one end, and Crispin's and Christopher's by a year at most on the other end. He would be closest in age to Robert, a fact which was borne out by the next thing he said, to Aunt Roz and Uncle Herbert. "I was so sorry to hear about Robbie. We weren't together in France, so I only learned of it afterwards."

"Thank you," Aunt Roz said, and even so many years later —almost a decade now—her voice turned froggy at the mention of her lost son.

"You served?" Francis asked.

"For a short while." Gardiner's face was sober. "By the time I made it to France, I only had to survive a couple of months before the armistice."

After a second he flashed another grin, but it didn't reach

his eyes. "Admittedly, there were times during those couple of months I didn't think I would. But I got lucky."

There were a few seconds' silence. Then Aunt Roz cleared her throat. "We were lucky, too. While we lost Robert, Francis survived. And Christopher was too young to serve. Had the war gone on longer…"

She trailed off, and then added, more strongly, "But as it were, Francis came back, and we didn't have to risk Christopher."

"Or Crispin," Uncle Herbert said.

His nephew looked up at him, and for a second there was a strange expression on his face. Surprise, that his uncle would have been concerned for his wellbeing? Or… it looked almost like anger, but why on earth would Crispin be angry that Uncle Herbert was happy he hadn't been old enough to die in the war?

I shook my head, because that didn't make any sense, and the movement caused Crispin to turn his attention to me instead. And yes, that was clearly anger I was looking at in his eyes; they were bright and hard, like silver. Perhaps he was offended that Uncle Herbert had lumped him in with Christopher. Perhaps he would prefer that his aunt and uncle didn't feel any care or concern towards him.

And then Tom Gardiner turned back to him to answer the question Crispin had asked before the exchange about the war made its mark on the conversation. "I do enjoy it. Killing people on the battlefield is one thing, and bad enough. Murdering them in peacetime is another."

He glanced around the table before he added, "No one had the right to point a gun at Simon Grimsby's chest and end his life. I don't care what he did or who he did it to. There's no excuse for that. And I want the person who shot him to pay."

Well, that was straight, anyway.

"Was that what happened?" Aunt Roz asked, with a swallow. "Someone shot him?"

Gardiner nodded. "We found the gun in the hedge maze. Whoever used it must have dropped it, or tossed it aside, after shooting Grimsby. But it was there. A Webley .455 Mk VI. The same type of pistol I used in France."

"Me, as well," Francis said. He looked a bit pale. Perhaps it was the memory of holding that pistol—or one like it—in his hand and pointing it at someone.

Not Grimsby, of course. Not last night, in the hedge maze. Ten years ago in France.

"Have you checked my father's collection?" Uncle Harold wanted to know. He'd been remarkably quiet until now, and I'd almost forgotten he was there, next to Uncle Herbert. "The gun room is down the hall in the west wing. Tidwell can show you."

Gardiner scratched something on his notepad. "We haven't done anything except process the crime scene yet. Finchley checked the pistol for fingerprints, of course."

"And?" Uncle Harold said.

"So far, we haven't taken anyone's prints, so we have nothing to compare them to."

There was a strange, humming, little moment of silence following his words.

"Dear me," Aunt Roz said, contemplating her fingertips as if she could already see the ink. "Fingerprints. How ignominious."

Gardiner's lips quirked. "Don't worry, Lady Herbert. Nobody thinks you had anything to do with it."

That was very nice and reassuring of him, although I wouldn't be too sure. Grimsby had been threatening one of her children, and if Aunt Roz knew that he had been trying to blackmail Christopher, I wouldn't have put it past her to shoot him stone dead.

Not that I thought she had. As far as I knew, Christopher hadn't brought the subject up to her. And if she hadn't known, she wouldn't have had a reason to do anything about it.

At any rate, Aunt Roz looked up at Gardiner with a warm smile. "You should call me Roslyn, dear. Everyone else does. Any friend of Robert's..." She trailed off.

Gardiner looked touched. "Of course, Lady Roslyn." He gave a brief bow from where he was seated at the head of the table.

"So he was shot," Uncle Herbert said. "With what might have been a gun from our father's collection."

Gardiner nodded. "Unless someone would like to claim ownership of the gun it's a good place to start."

"My service weapon is back at Beckwith Place," Francis said. "I didn't see any reason to bring it to this weekend's dressing down."

He smirked. "Under other circumstances I would make a joke about not wanting to be tempted to use it, but with the circumstances being as they are..."

Gardiner glanced at him. "Is that what this weekend was? A dressing down?"

Nobody answered for a moment, so I took it upon myself. "The late duke called everyone together so he could make his opinion of their behaviors clear. All the small ways in which everyone was falling short in bringing glory to the Sutherland name..."

There was a sound from across the table that sounded very Crispin-like, but when I looked up, it was Christopher's blue eyes that met mine with amusement.

"Well said, Pipsqueak," Francis nodded. He turned back to Gardiner. "We all fell short in Grandfather's eyes. Christopher hasn't proposed to Pippa yet. I should be married with an heir and a spare by now. Crispin's chasing women instead of settling down, although he isn't allowed to marry who he wants to marry, so I don't know that Grandfather could really complain about that one, although of course he did..."

Crispin shifted on his chair, but didn't say anything.

Francis continued, "Everyone's behavior was unacceptable in some way. Mother's and Father's, and I'm sure Aunt Charlotte's and Uncle Harold's. Nobody in the family was good enough for Grandfather."

"That's often the way it is," Tom Gardiner agreed, pleasantly. "My grandfather thinks I'm dishonoring the family name by doing what I do. Nothing the younger generation does is acceptable to these older folks. Although, of course, I am terribly sorry for your loss."

He looked up at Uncle Herbert and Uncle Harold, who sat like a united front at the end of the table, next to Aunt Roz.

I hadn't gotten the impression that anyone particularly mourned the old duke, but it was possible that Harold and Herbert, at least, were keeping a stiff upper lip. At some point, a very long time ago, he might have been the sort of father who interacted pleasantly with his young children, even if no evidence had remained of that into the time when I'd known him.

However, I didn't think Aunt Roz had ever had a close relationship with her father-in-law, and Christopher, along with the rest of the younger generation, seemed far from put out by his demise. Grimsby might have been one of the few inhabitants of the household who would have truly mourned the old man's death, and he hadn't had long to grieve.

And so we were back to where we'd started.

"Does anyone else want to claim ownership of a Webley pistol?" Tom Gardiner wanted to know. I shook my head, and watched Christopher and Crispin do the same.

"Didn't serve," Crispin said.

"Never felt the need for a gun," Christopher added.

"Wouldn't know how to use one if I had it," I said.

Tom looked at me carefully for a moment. "Point and shoot," he said. "Is there staff at Beckwith Place? If I were to ring there, would someone be able to let a constable in to determine that Mr. Astley's Webley is there?"

Aunt Roz nodded. Neither she nor Francis looked worried about the prospect, so Francis's service weapon must truly have been left behind at Beckwith.

Anything else would suggest that Francis had come to Sutherland Hall with the plan to kill Grimsby, anyway, and that wasn't likely at all. Even if Grimsby had been blackmailing him along with Christopher, chances were Francis wouldn't have known about it until he got here yesterday, much too late to make plans for Grimsby's demise by his own gun.

Besides, why bring your own pistol when Sutherland Hall had a room full of them, and everyone in the family knew it?

Tom Gardiner's thoughts clearly moved along the same path. "Who here had access to the gun room?"

"Everyone," Uncle Harold said, with a glance around the table. "The door is kept unlocked. The gun cabinets are locked, of course, but the family and staff would know that the keys are kept in my late father's desk in his study. Anyone could have taken them, gone to the gun room, unlocked a cabinet, taken a gun and ammunition, and replaced the keys. Or left them in the gun room. I don't think anyone's checked the desk to see if they're there. Until now, we didn't know that the gun came from my father's collection."

"We still don't know that," Gardiner reminded him, "but after we're done with the interviews, we'll have a look."

He contemplated his notes for a moment before he added, "Out of curiosity, was anyone in the gun room yesterday?"

We all shook our heads.

"Can anyone not account for their time at any point?"

There was a pause. I took the opportunity to fill it. "I was alone for a bit between tea and supper last night. I was in my room, but I can't prove it. Other than that, I've been with someone else pretty much every moment since I got here. For most of it, it's been Christopher. We took a walk around the grounds before tea, and again after supper..."

Christopher raised his head to look at me.

"You were outside last evening after supper?" Gardiner asked.

"Just for a short walk before bed. Around the formal garden. We wanted some fresh air. It had been a long day, between the traveling and the duke's temper tantrums, and then finding out about his death..."

There. I gave myself a mental pat on the back. I had gotten the fake alibi out, and made it sound reasonably convincing. And I had done it in front of Christopher, so now he knew I was committed to the lie and he could make use of it, too.

He was looking at me from across the table, and I gave him a reassuring smile. There was absolutely nobody around to say differently, after all. Crispin had seen us come in together, but he hadn't seen me while I was hiding in the conservatory, and as far as I knew, no one had seen Christopher while he was in the garden waiting for Grimsby to show himself, either. We could say we were together, and nobody would have any idea we were lying.

"St George let us in," I added, for verisimilitude. "Tidwell had already locked the door from the conservatory to the Hall by the time we got there. Around eleven-thirty, wasn't it, St George?"

Crispin looked at me across the table, his eyes still that hard silver color, almost accusing, but he nodded. "Yes. It was."

"Did you hear a shot while you were out there?"

Christopher and I both nodded, since we had, after all, both heard it. "We didn't think anything of it," Christopher said. "It sounded like it came from far away, and I thought maybe poachers in the wood behind the Hall..."

"The maze could have muffled the sound," I suggested, "maybe?"

"Where were you when you heard it?"

I looked at Christopher. I had been inside the conservatory with the door closed, so it would of necessity have sounded more distant to me. I had no idea where he'd been.

"On the east side of the house," he said, and if his voice was a bit tight, it wasn't very noticeable, at least not unless you knew him well. I hoped Tom didn't know him well enough to notice. "In the formal gardens near the fountain."

"The moonlight on the water was lovely," I added. That ought to establish that I'd been there and seen it.

"Romantic," Crispin commented blandly, but when I looked up, he was watching his hands, folded on the table, and not me. Tom Gardiner glanced at him, and then at me, and at Christopher, and back at Crispin.

"What about you, St George? You were downstairs when they came in? Did you hear the shot at all?"

Crispin shook his head. "I was having a drink in the parlor across from the conservatory when I heard the banging. The parlor is at the end of the east wing facing the courtyard, so pretty much as far as you can get from the garden maze. I didn't hear anything."

"Astley?" Tom looked at Francis.

"I'm also in the east wing, but facing the formal gardens," Francis said. "And I did hear the shot. But it..." He hesitated. "I didn't think it was anything I needed to investigate."

Tom nodded. "Out of curiosity, did you think it sounded closer than Kit did?"

Christopher shot him a look, maybe because of the diminutive, maybe because Tom seemed to question his recollection of the shot, but he didn't end up saying anything.

"I didn't think it was someone being murdered in the garden maze," Francis said, a bit belligerently, "if that's what you're suggesting."

"Of course not." Tom's voice was even and calm. "Kit said it sounded like it came from off the property. That it was poachers. Did you think so, too, or did you think it was closer than that?"

"I thought..." Francis stopped and looked off to the side, before he came back to the conversation. "I don't know what I thought, Gardiner. I was in bed. I'd had a bit too much to drink. It was the end of a difficult day. My grandfather died. And gunshots..."

He shook his head. "After the war, gunshots can be a tricky thing."

"Of course," Tom said, and said no more. "Lady Roslyn, Lord Herbert, did you hear this gunshot?"

Aunt Roz opened her mouth to answer—and their room faced the back garden, where the maze was, so I couldn't see how she could have avoided hearing it, unless she was dead asleep at the time—but before she could get a word out, there was a knock on the door, and then Finchley's face appeared in the gap between door and jamb.

"Pardon me. Chief Inspector Pendennis wonders if the Viscount St George would grace him with his presence."

"Of course." Crispin got to his feet and headed for the door, without looking at anyone. His father was looking at him, I saw, but Crispin either didn't notice or didn't care. He passed through into the hallway, and Finchley closed the door behind him.

Silence fell, until—

"Lady Roslyn?" Tom Gardiner prompted, and the conversation continued.

When Finchley came back, it was after another twenty minutes or so, during which it had been established that Aunt Roz had heard a shot, but hadn't thought anything of it—poachers—while Uncle Herbert hadn't heard anything. He had gone to sleep immediately, he said, while Aunt Roz read in bed. So at least they could alibi each other, to the degree that a sleeping person can alibi one who isn't asleep. Aunt Roz could alibi Uncle Herbert, but not vice versa.

Tom didn't look like he thought anything of it, but of course I realized that if Aunt Roz had slipped out and down the staircase and through the drawing room doors and into the maze, Uncle Herbert might have slept right through it.

Uncle Harold likewise pleaded the long day and his father's death for having succumbed to sleep almost immediately upon retiring. He hadn't heard the shot, either, he said, and of course Aunt Charlotte wasn't there to refute or confirm what he said. Pendennis must have told her to go elsewhere after their interview was over. Perhaps he didn't want her to share with the rest of us what his questions had been about.

And then it was my turn. "Miss Darling?" Finchley said. "Chief Inspector Pendennis would appreciate a moment of your time."

"Of course." I glanced at Christopher as I got to my feet, and tried to convey with that single look that he should relax, his alibi was well in hand. I don't know whether he caught on or not, but he smiled.

"Good luck, Pippa."

"I'll probably go to my room after," I told him. "Come find me when you're done."

He nodded, and I followed Finchley out of the room and down the hall to the breakfast room.

Pendennis was seated at the table, but he was gentleman enough to stand when I entered. "Miss Darling. Thank you for your time."

"Of course," I said politely, like I'd had a choice in the matter, like we don't all have to jump when Scotland Yard says to. "We all want you to figure out what happened."

"Have a seat, please. I just have a few questions for corroboration."

"Of course." I took a seat at the table and crossed my ankles demurely.

"Can you explain to me your relationship to the family? You're young Mr. Astley's intended, is that correct?"

"Not at all," I said. "That's Crispin's idea of a joke. I'm Christopher's cousin. My mother was Lady Roslyn's younger sister. She died in the influenza epidemic in 1919. I was taken in by the Astleys when the war broke out on the Continent and my mother sent me to England for my safety."

Pendennis nodded. If any of this was news, he didn't show it. "You came to Sutherland Hall with Mr. Astley yesterday afternoon?"

"With Christopher, yes. Crispin stopped by our flat in London on Friday evening to say that the late duke wanted to see Christopher here at the Hall yesterday afternoon. We traveled down together."

"The two of you and Lord St George?"

I shook my head. "He offered, but Christopher and I chose to take the train to Salisbury and get picked up there instead."

"Is there bad blood between the viscount and his cousin?"

"Not at all," I said. "I'm the one who finds Crispin annoying. He and Christopher get along quite well most of the time.

They had eleven years together before I ever came on the scene."

Finchley made a note. He had a notebook, too, just like the one Tom Gardiner was using in the other room, and he had placed himself sort of behind me, maybe so I wouldn't be so aware of what he was doing. I glanced over at the scratching of his pencil across the page, and then back at Inspector Pendennis, when he asked me, "Were you present for the duke's conversation with Mr. Astley?"

"Christopher, you mean?" I shook my head. "He wasn't *my* grandfather. I didn't hear any of the conversations, and I didn't have one of my own. Christopher told me his grandfather wanted him to propose to me, that it is unseemly that we're living together in our own flat without being married."

"How did Mr. Astley feel about that?"

"Irritated," I said. "It isn't... it wasn't the duke's place to tell him who he should or shouldn't marry. We're both adults. And we're more like brother and sister than cousins. I've lived with the Astleys since we were both eleven."

"But he came close to proposing marriage yesterday afternoon?"

"That was just for convenience," I said. "Christopher and I do not want to be married. But we decided we could pretend for a few months, if it would make things easier with the duke."

"There's no one else who would be upset if you became engaged to Mr. Astley? Or if he were to become engaged to you?"

"I can't speak for Christopher," I said, "although I can't think of anyone who would be upset if he got engaged." Apart from Flossie Schlomsky, I suppose, but she didn't really count, since her feelings towards Christopher were mostly mercenary. "As for myself, no. No one would care if I got engaged. To Christopher or anyone else."

"No gentleman friend waiting in the wings?" He smiled avuncularly. It sat strangely on his face.

I shook my head firmly. "No one like that."

Pendennis nodded, and went back to being the chief inspector from Scotland Yard. "When you arrived yesterday afternoon, you went upstairs with your cousin, and then spent the time while he was talking to his grandfather doing what?"

I thought about claiming that I'd gone to my room by myself, but then I decided I might as well tell the truth, especially since there was someone who could gainsay me if he chose. Perhaps he already had. "I argued with St George. I found him eavesdropping in the passage between the Duke's and Duchess's Chambers, and dragged him out of there so he wouldn't hear what the duke had to say to Christopher."

Pendennis nodded, so Crispin must have confessed about that particular encounter. And about the eavesdropping. "And after that?"

I went through the events of the afternoon, leaving out the blackmail and suggesting simply that Grimsby had come to Christopher's room to unpack his—Christopher's—weekender bag. Then we arrived at tea, and the interrupted proposal.

"So you were in the drawing room when Lady Charlotte came down the stairs to announce that His Grace, the Duke, had died? Can you tell me how everyone reacted?"

"It was just the four of us," I said, "and we reacted the way you would assume. We've all gotten a bit too used to death, since the war and the influenza epidemic. Everyone knows someone who died. But I didn't notice anything out of the ordinary. Surprise. Maybe shock, but not much of that. He was old and unwell and his family knew it."

Pendennis nodded. "Then what happened?"

"Christopher got Aunt Charlotte a glass of brandy. Aunt

Roz stayed with her. Crispin, Christopher, and I went upstairs to make sure Aunt Charlotte hadn't made a mistake."

"Describe the Duke's Chamber to me," Pendennis said, which I did, in all the detail I could remember, while Finchley's pencil scratched across the notebook behind me.

Then we went through the wait in the drawing room, what everyone said, the doctor's visit, supper, and finally Christopher's and my trip downstairs before bed, when we heard the gunshot. I told it to Pendennis the same way I'd told it to Tom earlier, with Christopher and me arm in arm in the east wing formal garden when we heard the shot. If Pendennis doubted me, I saw no indication of it.

Then it was time for this morning.

"You followed Lord St George into the garden maze?"

I nodded.

"How did you know he would be there?"

"I didn't," I said. "First, I looked for him in the courtyard, because he'd gone out through the front door. Then I went to the carriage house, in case he'd decided to take the Hispano-Suiza out for a drive. He likes to go fast, and I thought perhaps he might fancy a jaunt to get over his bad mood."

"But he wasn't there."

I shook my head. "The car was, but he wasn't. So I went to the maze. We used to play in it when we were children. And it had come up in conversation that morning."

"Why was that?"

"I saw someone move through it last night," I said. "After we came upstairs and I was getting ready for bed. I caught a movement out of the corner of my eye when I went to pull the curtains in my room."

"Tell me what you saw."

"It was just a glimpse of the top of someone's head above the closest hedge. Moving towards the exit. I ran into the duchess's room, but by the time I got there, they must have already left, because I didn't see anyone come out."

"Can you describe the person you saw?"

"Fair hair," I said. "Combed back. All I saw was the very top of the head, so that's literally it. Fair hair slicked back. And it could have been anyone. Every man in the Astley family has fair hair that they slick back. So does one of the footmen, and at least one of the grooms." And Detective Finchley. Of the family, the only ones of us with brown hair was Aunt Roz and myself.

"This morning?" Pendennis prompted.

"I brought it up to Christopher over breakfast. Crispin overheard and decided to contribute something cheeky. We got into a row, and he stormed out, and Christopher told me I owed him an apology. So when he wasn't in the courtyard and hadn't taken out the motorcar, I went to the maze."

"And he was there," Pendennis said. "With the body."

I nodded.

"Can you describe the scene?"

I described the scene and did my best to downplay the fact that I had behaved like a Victorian maiden, not at all like the thoroughly modern girl from the new century I liked to think myself.

"Thank you, Miss Darling," Inspector Pendennis said when I was done. "Did you get the impression that the Viscount St George was in shock when you found him in the maze?"

He'd been pale, certainly. And a bit shaky. Although I hadn't honestly paid a whole lot of attention to anything but my own reaction.

Pendennis made a humming sound. "And neither of you noticed the pistol?"

I hadn't. I couldn't say what Crispin might have noticed,

only what he had drawn my attention to. And the pistol hadn't been among those things.

"And then you came inside," Pendennis said. "Together?"

I nodded. "I didn't want to stay there alone with the body, and it must have been there since the previous night anyway, so there was really no point in standing guard over it. If anything was going to happen to it, it would have already happened, we assumed."

Pendennis nodded. "Thank you, Miss Darling. Anything else you would like to add?"

I told him there was nothing. "May I go to my room now?"

"After you allow Detective Sergeant Finchley to take your fingerprints."

I looked at Finchley, who nodded towards the sideboard where the orange juice usually sits. Now it was a fingerprint station with ink and pieces of paper. I let him roll each of my fingers on an ink pad and then on a piece of paper, and signed the corner of the paper where he told me to sign.

"Just one more question, Miss Darling," Inspector Pendennis intoned as I made my way towards the door afterward, rubbing at my fingers.

I stopped. "Of course, Inspector."

"You said you caught a glimpse of someone moving through the garden maze last night, and immediately ran down the hall and into the duchess chamber to see who it was."

I nodded. It hadn't been a question, but as far as it went, it was correct. "That's right."

"Was there a particular reason that someone moving through the garden maze might have been of interest to you? Was there a reason you wanted to know who it was? You said you thought the shot had come from farther afield, so it couldn't have been concern about that."

Oh.

The reason I'd been interested was because Grimsby hadn't shown up to the appointment he'd set with Christopher, and I'd thought it was strange. I'd been further wound up by my time alone in the conservatory, and the gunshot, and the snake—or perhaps mouse or lizard—that had slithered across my foot, and being locked in and having to ask Crispin for help in getting out. But I couldn't say any of those things to the inspector.

"No," I said instead. "It was late and I was curious. I had thought everyone else was already in bed. There was no other reason."

He nodded. "Thank you, Miss Darling. That will be all."

"Thank you, Inspector," I said, and headed for the door again, and closed it firmly behind me. Neither of them said anything until I was outside in the hallway, and by then, all I could hear was the murmur of voices through the wood, and not the actual words they said.

I glanced down the hall at the door to the drawing room, but instead of heading that way, I did what I'd said I'd do, and made my way to the foyer and the staircase to the first floor, where my room was.

ELEVEN

I was still rubbing at my fingertips, trying to get rid of some of the ink, when I reached the top of the staircase. That must have been why I didn't realize what was happening until it was too late.

As such, it came as a surprise when a hand shot out of nowhere and wrapped itself around my wrist and yanked. I stumbled to the left with a shriek, and found myself towed behind Crispin towards the door to the Duchess's Chamber. He pushed it open, hauled me over the threshold, and kicked it shut behind us. I twitched my arm out of his grip and rounded on him.

"What on earth do you think you're doing?"

"I should be asking you the same thing," Crispin said, eyes narrowed. "What was that, down there?"

"What do you mean?" So many things had happened downstairs that you'll excuse me for having no idea to which of them he was referring.

"You're giving Kit an alibi for murder when you have no idea whether he did it or not?"

"Of course he didn't do it!" I said, and added, when I realized what I'd just admitted, "And how do you know that's what I was doing? You can't possibly know that!"

"If I didn't before, I do now," Crispin said coolly. "But actually I did know. Remember when you and Kit were alone in the study earlier, after Francis had left to take Kit's boyfriend and the doctor into the maze?"

"I don't think he's Christopher's boyfriend," I said, "and I think it would be a very good idea if you didn't use that word." About either of them, actually. "I think he's just an old friend from Eton who happened to know about the raid on Friday night, and who made sure..."

Crispin's eyebrows rose, and I caught myself before I volunteered any more information he didn't already know. "Never mind. We were alone in the study. You said so yourself. How would you know what we were talking about?" Or that Francis had taken Tom Gardiner and the surgeon into the maze?

He smirked. "You know what's in the corner of the study, don't you?"

Of course I did. "The secret staircase. Eavesdropping again, St George?"

"One learns such fascinating things," Crispin drawled. "Although that wasn't the gist of what I was trying to do. I was just coming down to join you. I took the staircase because I thought it would be faster. But then, when I heard you talking..."

He trailed off.

"What did you hear?"

The smirk widened. "Oh, all sorts of things. Like the fact that Kit's on a first-name basis with Detective Sergeant Thomas Gardiner, and that Grimsby was blackmailing him over it."

"That's not—"

"Of course not, Darling. I'm sure what Grimsby was

holding over Kit's head was the whole gown-and-wig thing that I happened to see when I was in London Friday evening."

That had, in fact, been exactly what Grimsby had been holding over Christopher's head, and I absolutely hated the fact that Crispin knew it.

"What do you want?" I asked flatly. "Why are you telling me this, and how much would it cost for you to keep your mouth shut?"

The smirk turned into a grin. "More than you could afford, Darling. However, I wouldn't expect you to pay anything at all. That would be blackmail, wouldn't it, and we both know what happens to blackmailers."

The implication was clear, and I fought back a chill that threatened to creep down my spine like a cold drop of rain. Yes, we did both know what happened to blackmailers. Unlike Christopher, who had missed that pleasure, Crispin and I had both seen the results of blackmail up close and personally this morning.

"What is it you want, then? Why tell me, if you don't want something from me?"

"Who said I don't want something from you?" Crispin retorted, and I had to physically clench my hand into a fist to keep from slapping the annoying expression off his face.

"You know, St George, you are without a doubt the most frustrating person on the face of the earth."

"Thank you, Darling," Crispin said.

"That wasn't a compliment. So what is it you want me to do in this friendly exchange of favors?"

"I want you to forget every single word you heard my father say to me yesterday afternoon," Crispin said. "And any words you may have heard me say to him."

"So the whole conversation."

"That's correct. Whatever part of it you heard while you

were lurking in the hallway outside my door yesterday, I want you to forget it."

I smirked. "You're a fine one to talk about eavesdropping, you know. It's not so enjoyable when it happens to you, is it?"

"That's different," Crispin said.

"Oh, is it really? Because it's you, I suppose?"

He didn't answer, and I added, "It's easier said than done, you know. It's not like I can actually unhear what I know I heard."

"You can put it out of your mind," Crispin said. "And if you know what's good for you, you will."

I stuck my hands on my hips and narrowed my eyes. "Are you threatening me, St George?"

He did the same. "I don't know, Darling. Am I?"

He might be, actually. As usual when I got into it with Crispin, I had forgotten everything else in the effort to win the current disagreement. But now that I had been recalled to myself, I remembered that he did, in fact, know things, about both Christopher and myself, that I didn't want to get around. So yes, he might be threatening me. Or at least he was reminding me of the trouble he could cause, if he chose to.

"Fine," I said. "I'll do my best to forget everything I heard you and your father say yesterday afternoon. Although I fail to see what the big deal is. If you've fallen in love with someone, it's hardly something to be ashamed of. I honestly didn't think you had it in you, so—"

"That!" He pointed at me, or more accurately came within an inch of poking me in the nose with the tip of his index finger. "*That* is what I don't want to happen. It's none of your business what feelings I'm capable of, or for whom, and I don't want you to stick your nose into them. My feelings are my own, and absolutely none of your concern. You are a menace,

Darling, and always have been, and if you find out anything about this—"

He seemed to recall himself, and took a few seconds to get his breathing and voice back under control before he added, much more calmly. "I would take it as a very great favor if you would keep your pointy little nose out of my private affairs, and for that to happen, I need you to forget everything you heard. And if you can't do that for me, then perhaps I'll just happen to accidentally let it slip that I know you and Kit weren't together last night."

"Blackmail!"

"Not at all," Crispin said. "A simple case of one good turn deserves another. I don't want your nose in my private business, and you don't want my nose in yours. This way, we both get what we want."

He was right, of course. However—

"I don't know why you're making such a big thing out of this, St George. It's not like I'm going to go find your girlfriend and tell her what I really think of you. She probably wouldn't believe me, anyway. She probably thinks you're the bee's knees and the fly's thighs, everything that's lovely, although I can't imagine how anyone who knows you could have gotten that impression..."

"Just because you bring out the worst in me," Crispin said, "doesn't mean that other women don't see my value—"

"Your title and your money, you mean."

"Just because that's all *you* can see, Darling—"

"Oh, will you stop calling me that? It's the most annoying thing in the world, and you keep doing it."

"It's your name, Darling, and besides, it's not like you'd appreciate it if I—"

"No, I definitely would not. You're right about that. Nor would I want to—"

"Exactly. So—"

"I'm going to my room." I yanked the door to the hallway open and kept talking to him over my shoulder—and over his words—as I crossed the threshold. "I don't want to see you again for the rest of the day. If you see me coming, I want you to turn around and walk the other way, and I'll do the same. Or I swear to God, St George, Grimsby's won't be the only murder here this weekend."

"I don't think Grimsby's *was* the only murder here this weekend," Crispin said with a smirk, "but I get your point, Darling. I'll stay out of your way if you'll stay out of mine."

"Deal."

He nodded. "All right, then. Have a lovely afternoon, Darling."

"Oh, for..." I shook my head. "Goodbye, St George."

I desperately wished I could have appended a 'forever,' to that sentence, but since I'd have to see him again for supper or there'd be questions, I simply left the door open and took off down the hallway towards the west wing. Behind me, Crispin shut the door to the Duchess's Chamber with exaggerated care, and wandered off in the other direction. When I turned to look back just as I reached the end of the central wing, it was to see him disappear around the opposite corner towards his suite of rooms. He was not looking back at me.

"You CHANGED," Christopher said when he was finally released from downstairs and arrived in my room. His fingertips were still black from ink, and I waved him towards the basin in the corner before I ran my hands down the blue and white dress I was wearing, again.

"I had to. Your cousin left ink on my sleeve."

"Crispin?" Christopher dipped his fingertips into the water and held them there.

"Do you have any other cousins?"

"I have you. And any other little bye-blows Uncle Harold might have sired along the way."

"I didn't ink my own sleeve, Christopher. I was careful. And if I had, I would have admitted it."

I sat down on the edge of the bed and crossed my ankles. "Do you think your uncle has other children out there? Wouldn't they be banging down the door for consideration when he's a future duke? Or present duke now?"

"Depends," Christopher said, wiggling his fingers in the water. "I would hope he had better sense. But he's older than my father, and my parents had Francis and Robert before they had me. Crispin is younger than I am, if not by much. So there were ten years there, when Uncle Harold could have been sowing his wild oats before Crispin was born."

"Wasn't he married to your aunt for those years?"

"Some of them," Christopher said, looking around for a towel. There was one there, next to the basin, with fresh ink smears from my fingers, and he picked it up. "Uncle Harold and Aunt Charlotte married later than my parents. She's younger than him by a few years, too."

"More than a few."

Christopher nodded. "And it took them a while to have Crispin after they were married, as well. All of which leads me to think that there might be bye-blows. But it's not something I know anything about. So Crispin grabbed you? What did he want?"

He plopped his posterior down on the edge of the bed next to me and crossed one knee over the other.

I made a face. "To tell me he knows that I lied to the police about being outside in the garden with you last night."

"Wonderful," Christopher said, in a tone which indicated, clearly, that it was anything but. "I knew you shouldn't have lied. Now he'll tell them you did—"

"He won't. We made a deal."

He slanted me a look. "What kind of deal?"

"He'll keep quiet about that if I forget what I heard—what *we* heard—through the door to his room yesterday."

Christopher's forehead wrinkled. "The conversation with his father? Why would he care?"

"I have no idea," I said, "but he was adamant about it. Told me his affairs were none of my business—yours, either, I assume —and that I'd forget the whole thing if I knew what was good for me."

Christopher's eyes widened. "He threatened you?"

"Just enough to make sure I knew he meant it."

Christopher didn't say anything in response to that, and I added, "For some reason, he really doesn't want anyone to know anything about it. I'm not sure what the problem is. Or rather, there must be something I'm not seeing, because from where I'm sitting, the problem is obvious. He has fallen in love with some actress or *danseuse* or something, and his father won't approve of him marrying her..."

Christopher nodded. "But there's no reason you or I, or anyone else, can't know about that. We don't care who he's in love with, and I would be delighted to see my cousin marry for love instead of duty."

He made a face. "Of course, Uncle Harold has a rather different view of that whole thing. He wants Crispin to marry an heiress with a title of her own. If it had been him who was murdered, that would have been a different story. But since it wasn't..."

I widened my eyes until they felt as if they might roll right out of my head. "Surely you're not suggesting that St George would have shot his father over this... this..."

Chit? Trollop?

I couldn't come up with a word that was bad enough, so I settled for, "—affair?"

"With Grandfather and Uncle Harold dead, he'd be Duke of Sutherland," Christopher said, "so it's not like he would have lacked incentive. With both of them gone, he could marry anyone he wanted."

I suppose he could. "Good thing it was Grimsby, then, and not your Uncle Harold who ended up dead."

And then I thought about what I'd said. "Wait a moment. You don't think...?"

"I don't see how that makes any sense at all," Christopher said. "Grimsby is probably the one who found out about Crispin's love affair, and he clearly told both Uncle Harold and Grandfather about it. Remember what Uncle Harold said? 'Your grandfather won't approve, and neither will your mother and I'? And if the secret was already out, Crispin had no reason to kill Grimsby."

"Unless he was angry about it being found out. And he killed Grimsby in revenge."

"There would be nothing to gain from that," Christopher said firmly. "And he's not stupid, you know, in spite of you not liking him very much."

No, he wasn't. "I guess we're back where we were, then. Someone else killed Grimsby."

"Someone did," Christopher nodded. "It wasn't me. And I don't think it was you."

I shook my head. "I had no reason to. Unless I did it for you."

"Please tell me you didn't."

"Of course I didn't," I said. "I stood in the conservatory, just as I told you, and watched the light go out in Francis's room, and the door from the hallway open and close. I heard the shot, the same as you did. But I didn't move from the corner of the conservatory, not even when something slithered—slithered, Christopher!—across my foot, and I didn't shoot anyone."

Christopher nodded. "I didn't, either. I don't know how I'd be able to prove it, because I didn't see anyone, and no one saw me. How did my cousin know you were lying, by the way?"

I grimaced. "When you and I were talking in the study earlier? He was tucked away in the secret staircase, like the sneak he is."

Christopher rolled his eyes. "Of course he was."

"And another thing. He called Detective Gardiner your boyfriend at one point."

Christopher stared at me, while red flooded his face all the way to the tips of his ears.

"I told him not to do it again," I said, "and I got the impression he understood—"

"That's not true," Christopher stammered. "He's not... we're not..."

"—but he didn't promise. So..."

"Damn him," Christopher managed, his voice hoarse. "If the police weren't here right now, I'd kill him myself. Just go over there, wrap my hands around this throat, and choke the life right out of him."

I could understand the impulse—St George made me feel that way pretty much every time he opened his mouth.

"I don't care about myself," Christopher added. "He can say whatever he wants about me. But Tom... it's not like that. I told you the truth, Pippa. He's a chap I knew at Eton. Older than me by several years. Robbie's age. He and my brother were friends, and when he recognized me last month at Lady

Austin's, he warned me that a raid was coming soon and it would be better for me if I didn't come back."

"But you went anyway."

"And he must have guessed I would, because he got there first and pulled me out. We were a block away when we heard the whistle."

"That was nice of him," I said.

Christopher nodded. "But the point is, it wasn't for me. I'm sure it was for Robbie, and for Mum and Dad. They've had enough to deal with, with losing Robbie, and are still dealing with it, with Francis. If Tom could keep them from dealing with me being arrested, I figure he thought that would be a help."

"He sounds like a nice man," I said.

"He's a very nice man," Christopher answered, "but the point is, we're not together in any way. Today was literally the third time I've seen him since I left Eton five years ago. And I didn't see him much before that, either, since he was only there for the first year that I was. We're not friends. Merely acquaintances. And after this, I'm not sure we'll be that. If there's a raid on Lady Austin's next month, I'm sure he'll leave me to hang. If I'm not in prison for murder already by then."

"Don't say that!" I exclaimed. "There's no reason why anyone would want to arrest you."

"Two people are dead," Christopher said. "One of them, at least, was definitely murdered. They're going to want to arrest someone."

Of course they were. "But it doesn't have to be you!"

"Let's look at the evidence," Christopher said. "Someone shot him dead. Someone who had access to the gun room, and who knew where the keys to the display cabinets were kept."

Yes. There was no way around that, it seemed.

"I was one of those people."

I opened my mouth, and he waved me to silence. "I wasn't the only one. There's the rest of the family and the staff. But while I could see one of the staff murdering Grimsby—he might have been blackmailing one of them, too, or at least might have known something about someone they didn't want him to know..."

I nodded.

"—I don't see one of the staff killing Grandfather. Most of them have been with him a long time. They were well paid. They seemed to like him well enough. And it wasn't like he was long for this world, anyway. He was almost ninety, with a bad heart."

"Are we sure he was murdered, though? Did the police ask you about it?"

Christopher shook his head. "Just where I was and what I was doing between the time I saw him in his room and the time Aunt Charlotte came screaming into the drawing room that he was dead."

"We were together during that time," I said, "so if anything happened, we couldn't have done it."

"Unless we're lying for each other."

"Well, we're—" *Not*, I was going to say, until I remembered that actually, we were.

Not about that, though.

"Do you think someone killed him?" I asked.

Christopher shrugged helplessly. "I have no idea what to think. It didn't cross my mind until Scotland Yard brought it up —why kill a man who's going to die in a few months or a year anyway?—but it seems like they think someone might have. Or at least they're looking into whether it was possible. I'm guessing Doctor Curtis will take him in for autopsy."

We both grimaced at the thought.

"If you're going to write a murder mystery," Christopher

said, "you definitely know what to write about now. You've seen two dead bodies, one of which was violently murdered."

"Funny enough," I answered, "the appeal has somewhat left me, to be honest."

Christopher nodded. "I can quite see that."

After a moment, he added, "I'm not sure, Pippa. Maybe if we treat this like a crime novel? The old duke is dead, by what's maybe a fatal dose of heart medicine, and his valet and confidant has been shot. The suspects are his sons, his daughters-in-law, his grandchildren, and his staff. Who did it?"

"Someone without an obvious motive," I said. "Me, probably."

He snorted. "You weren't even on the list."

"I should be on the list," I said. "I was here. I had access to the gun room and the duke's—your grandfather's—medication. As much as anyone else did."

"But you were with me when he was poisoned."

"If he was poisoned." I shook my head. "This isn't working. If we all had means—access to the gun and the medication—and opportunity—access to your grandfather's room and the maze—then motive is what matters. Who had motive?"

"Me," Christopher said. "For Grimsby, at least. And what's more, I'm the only one we know for certain had a motive for killing Grimsby. We're theorizing about everyone else."

Yes, we were. But if Christopher hadn't done it, then someone else must have. And they must have had a motive, too.

"He might have blackmailed someone else, as well. Most likely he did. Why stop with one?"

Christopher shook his head. "In novels, it's usually about money, isn't it? Inheritances and such?"

It was. Often enough that 'usually' probably qualified.

"The estate is entailed," Christopher said. "The title goes to Uncle Harold and then to Crispin, along with the Sutherland properties. The Hall and the House in London. But Grandfather owned things that weren't entailed, too. And he could threaten to withdraw those from someone who misbehaved."

Yes, he could have. "Like he could have threatened your father into not bankrolling you and me and our flat in London."

Christopher nodded. "Which we would have hated, but we wouldn't have committed murder over it. Someone else, for whom the stakes were higher, though..."

"Like Francis and his drug habit. Or Crispin and whatever is going on with this girl he thinks he's in love with."

"If he says he's in love with her, he probably is," Christopher said. "But yes. Uncle Harold clearly didn't approve, and since it came up this weekend, it's likely that Grimsby brought it to Grandfather's attention this weekend, and then Grandfather brought it to Uncle Harold's attention. And Uncle Harold yelled at Crispin about it. And if Crispin feels strongly enough..."

I made a face. Crispin St George in love. *Ugh.* "So there's Crispin and Francis. There's your mother and her sideline, although I don't see her murdering your grandfather because he found out that she's been selling gossip to the weekly tabloids. That's hardly a killing offense."

"None of them are killing offenses," Christopher said. "At least not to you and me. I wouldn't kill anyone over Kitty, and you wouldn't, either. So what if we'd have to move back to Beckwith Place, or even Sutherland Hall? We'd survive."

I nodded.

"But who's to say what someone else believes is worth killing over? Grimsby was a blackmailer, and Grandfather wasn't going to live much longer anyway. It's quite easy to justify murder under those conditions."

Perhaps it was.

"My head hurts," I said. "How about we get some fresh air before tea? And find something else to talk about?"

"We can try," Christopher said darkly, "but I think it's going to be a while before I can think about anything else, honestly."

After a moment, he added, "At least until someone's been arrested, who isn't me."

"You're not going to be arrested." I stood up and held out my hand to him. "I won't let them arrest you."

"I don't think there's a lot you can do about it if they do," Christopher said, but he got to his feet and put his hand in mine.

TWELVE

By supper, Doctor Curtis had withdrawn from Sutherland Hall with both bodies. The local mortuary had sent two motorcars for their conveyance, and Doctor Curtis had gone along, presumably to do the autopsy on the late duke. I imagined no autopsy would be necessary for Grimsby, as it was hardly a secret how he had died. A gunshot wound at close range straight into the heart tends to be immediately fatal, and surely no autopsy was required to confirm it.

Inside the Hall, Scotland Yard had taken over the breakfast room as their domain, but only Chief Inspector Pendennis had spent much time there. After the interviews, both Finchley and Tom Gardiner had gone to work plying their trades throughout the house. The duke's bedchamber was photographed and dusted for fingerprints on every available surface, and so was the gun room as well as the late duke's study, presumably to see who might have accessed the drawer where the keys to the gun cabinets were kept.

I hadn't been in the duke's study and hadn't touched the

keys, so I wasn't worried—not on my own behalf, at least—but on the other hand, it's extremely difficult to prove a negative, and I could have easily accessed the study and opened the drawer with my traveling gloves still on, and nobody would have been any the wiser.

As a result of everything, we all became quite jumpy as the evening wore on. The police took their cold supper in the breakfast room—cold, because things were topsy-turvy below-stairs as well as above. Aunt Charlotte, in a fit of socialism, had invited the detectives to sup with the rest of us, but Pendennis had declined, either out of finer feelings or because he didn't want his underlings to mingle too comfortably with the suspects.

He must have known of Thomas Gardiner's relationship to the younger Astleys. Francis wasn't known for being reticent, and I assumed he had greeted Tom with all due excitement upon his arrival. Nor was it likely, really, that Tom would have kept the information from his superior.

It occurred to me—quite belatedly, and I felt stupid for not realizing it sooner—that when Pendennis had left Tom in the dining room with the rest of us, it might not have been because he thought Tom would put us at ease, but rather because he thought that some of us might feel so comfortable with Tom that we'd speak about things in front of him that we would not have brought up in front of Finchley or Pendennis himself.

And Tom would, of course, share those things with his colleagues. Because, as Christopher had so eloquently pointed out, he and Tom weren't friends. They had seen each other a handful of times over the past ten years, and Tom owed Christopher very little. He certainly didn't owe him loyalty over and above the loyalty to his job and his superior.

At any rate, they supped alone. And so did we. And it was grim, and silent, and featured occasional bursts of awkward conversation that had no bearing on what was going on across the hall. I guess none of us felt that we could really talk about what we were all thinking, which I'm sure was that one of us was a murderer.

At least that's what I was thinking, as I sat there quietly between Francis and Christopher and poked at my cold roast beef with skinned cherry tomatoes in horseradish sauce and cold asparagus.

One of us was a murderer.

Or, to put it a bit more charitably, it was possible that one of us was a murderer. It was also possible that the autopsy would show that the late duke had died a natural death, and it was quite possible, perhaps even likely, that the person who had shot Grimsby was below-stairs instead of up here with us.

But one of us might be a murderer.

It wasn't me. I knew at least that much.

And it wasn't Christopher. He'd been quite close to proposing to me when the news about the duke's demise came, so clearly Christopher would go to great lengths so as not to have to murder his grandfather, and I refused to believe he had it in him to shoot Grimsby.

Besides, Christopher wouldn't have known that Grimsby was going to be in the garden maze. They had arranged to meet in the formal garden. I had heard them. When Grimsby didn't show up there, Christopher wouldn't have known where to find him. And the center of the hedge maze isn't the type of place you simply stumble on.

So not Christopher. Not that I'd believed it anyway.

I slanted a look to my left. Francis's hands were shaking enough that he had a hard time cutting up his roast beef. While that could be due to nerves, it could equally well be due to withdrawal from his drug of choice. For all I knew, Scotland

Yard might have found and confiscated it. It surely wasn't legal to be in possession of.

Or perhaps it was, and Francis was simply abusing the amount he was taking of a perfectly legal narcotic.

At any rate, he was shaking. He certainly had reason to be upset with Grimsby, if the valet was the one who had told the late duke about Francis's drug habit. And if the duke had threatened to cut Francis off—from the drugs he needed to get through his days and nights, or from the money he needed to acquire them—then Francis would have had a strong reason to want the duke dead, as well.

He knew where the guns were kept. And more importantly, he knew how to use them.

Last night, while I'd been hiding in the corner of the conservatory, the light in Francis's room had gone out. He could have gone to bed at that point, of course. That's what he had told Tom he'd done, and his explanation had certainly made sense.

Or he might have been lying, and had turned out the light prior to coming downstairs. He could have taken the main staircase down, gone directly through the drawing room, across the terrasse, and into the maze.

Francis has the same fair hair as the rest of the men in the family, and he knew the twists and turns of the maze as well as any of us. It could have been him I'd seen out of the corner of my eye later.

So motive, means, and opportunity for Francis.

Next to Francis on the other side sat Crispin, and I would have loved to be able to pin the murder—both murders —on him.

As a preference, I would have liked for it to be no one in the family, of course. A natural death for the old duke, and some unsavory associate of Grimsby's from outside the house altogether for the valet. But with the pistol having come from the gun room—and that seemed to be a determined fact by now—the killer was someone who had access to the inside of the house. If it wasn't one of the staff, then Crispin was the one I would most like to throw to the wolves.

But to be fair, since I knew I had a tendency not to be when it came to St George: aside from my own personal dislike of him, was there any reason to think he was guilty?

Like all of us, he knew where the guns and keys were kept.

He had left his room during the pertinent time period last night, and had been close enough to hear us knocking on the conservatory door to let us back in. The story about toasting his grandfather in the parlor was at the same time logical—why wouldn't he do that?—and illogical, because didn't he have liquor of his own upstairs in his own sitting room?

He had the fair Sutherland hair, and I hadn't gotten a good enough look at the head bobbing along the maze to determine whether it was more silver than gold. Here in the dining room, Crispin's hair was definitely a shade closer to platinum than either Francis's or Christopher's—I glanced at them both to make sure—but out there, in the darkness and the moonlight, it could have been any one of them.

Uncle Harold obviously knew about Crispin's romantic entanglements, and so had the late duke. Killing Grimsby wouldn't have helped him at all on that score. But Crispin might also have other secrets, ones we knew nothing about. Secrets Grimsby might have discovered and shared with the late duke. His Grace, Duke Henry, might have threatened to cut Crispin off from his friends in London, including the girl he loved. He might have threatened to cut off the money, or access to the car, or he might have threatened to do worse. Interfere with the girl somehow? Pay her off, so she'd go away and leave Crispin alone?

Some women would have snatched at an opportunity like that, assuming the amount was big enough. Perhaps Crispin had been afraid to lose his ladylove, and so he had decided to eliminate his grandfather before the latter could put such a plan into action. As Christopher had pointed out, Crispin had benefitted from his grandfather's death in multiple ways. He was the Viscount St George now, one step closer to the dukedom, and an even better prospect on the marriage market.

So yes, I could definitely make a very good case for Crispin being guilty, and that was apart from my inclination to believe the worst of him.

Aunt Roz cleared her throat, and I jumped. Several of the others must have been equally deep in thought, because they startled visibly, as well. Aunt Charlotte had a grip around her knife that boded ill for someone.

"Everyone finished with dinner?" Aunt Roz wanted to know, her voice rusty, like it had been a long time since she'd used it.

We all murmured acquiescence—appetites were clearly at an all-time low—and Aunt Roz nodded to Tidwell. "My compliments to Cook, and you can start to serve pudding, if you will, Tidwell."

"Very well, Lady Herbert." Tidwell bowed himself out. We heard the sound of his shoes disappear down the hallway, hard soles slapping against the floor.

"Have the representatives for Scotland Yard indicated where they'll be spending the night?" Aunt Roz asked Aunt Charlotte, her tone determinedly normal.

Charlotte looked alarmed, as if the question hadn't crossed her mind.

"It's getting late," Aunt Roz added, "and I can't imagine they'll want to carry on through the night. If we're to provide accommodations for them, it might be a good idea to let the staff know."

Lady Charlotte's face congealed, either at the idea of hosting police detectives in her house—and it *was* her house now—or because Aunt Roz had been the one to take charge and suggest it.

Aunt Roz must have noticed, because she added, blandly, "Of course it's up to you, Charlotte, dear. Sutherland Hall is your domain now. I'm just suggesting that it might be easier to let Mrs. Mason know now rather than later."

Mrs. Mason was the housekeeper, who would be in charge of airing out the necessary linens and getting them on the beds for any unexpected guests.

"Couldn't hurt to put'em up for the night," Uncle Herbert grunted, and Aunt Charlotte rested her eyes on him for a moment. "Creates some goodwill, doesn't it? And there are plenty of bedrooms to choose from, after all."

"And young Tom Gardiner *is* a friend of the boys from Eton," Aunt Roz added.

Aunt Charlotte looked from her over to Crispin, and then to Francis and Christopher. Her eyes, the same glacial gray as Crispin's, glanced off me like I wasn't even there.

"Of course," she said after what felt like an eternity, and pushed her chair back from the table. Everyone except Aunt Roz and myself shot to their feet. "I'll go talk to Mrs. Mason right now. Excuse me."

She swept from the room after Tidwell, curls bouncing and skirts flying.

Unlike Aunt Roz, who took to bobbed hair and drop-waist dresses like a duck to water—all the better to hide the slight affluence around her waist now that she's in her fifties and has given birth to three boys—Aunt Charlotte likes to remind everyone that she's a decade younger than her husband. She has kept not just her trim hourglass figure, but her ash-blond curls, too. "If it's good enough for Mary Pickford," I heard her say the one time Aunt Roz dared to suggest that she might want to make a change.

Aunt Charlotte vanished through the door into the foyer, and all the men dropped back into their seats again. I patted my bobbed hair and was grateful that it didn't take me an hour to give my hair the prerequisite hundred strokes with a brush every night.

I went back to my cogitation.

Aunt Roz was next. Her secret didn't seem to be the sort someone commits murder over. She might end up snubbed by society if word got out that she'd benefitted financially from things told her in confidence. But once everyone learned of Francis's situation, it would mitigate the scandal. People understand the motives of a desperate mother, and Aunt Roz is well liked.

On the other hand, she would definitely commit murder for Francis. Or for Christopher. Or for that matter—I thought —for me.

So yes, Aunt Roz might have shot Grimsby. Not over me, of course. But over Francis, or—if she learned that Grimsby was blackmailing him—over Christopher. There had been a lot of eavesdropping going on over the past day and a half. Who's to say that Aunt Roz hadn't overheard Christopher and me, or Christopher and Grimsby, talk? Her light had also been on when I'd made my way past her and Uncle Herbert's room on my way to the east wing last night. And the light had been out when I came back. If Uncle Herbert had been asleep, there had been nothing to keep Aunt Roz from flitting down the main staircase and out the drawing room doors to the maze.

Unlike the rest of the family, her hair was not fair, however. Then again, could I be a hundred percent certain of what I'd seen? It had only been a glimpse, out of the corner of my eye, in the dark. With the moonlight gleaming on it, perhaps Aunt Roz's brown hair might have looked more gold than dark for a moment?

I didn't think it had been her, was fairly certain it hadn't been, but I couldn't completely disregard the possibility, either.

Uncle Herbert…

He was sitting next to Aunt Roz, and was fiddling with his flatware. Occasionally, he would look up and across the table, and then look down again, with a sort of pained expression on his face.

Uncle Herbert probably knew what was going on with Francis. I'm sure it pained him. How could it not? We had all watched Francis struggle since the war. I hadn't realized he was self-medicating to the degree that he was, but I had known about the shell-shock, the nightmares, the nerve elixirs, and the drinking. And there was Robert's death, and the survivor's guilt that had surely come with it.

So yes, Uncle Herbert had to be aware of what Francis was dealing with. He might have known what his wife was doing to help pay for it, as well. Unlike Uncle Harold and Aunt Charlotte, Uncle Herbert and Aunt Roz had always seemed to have a good relationship.

He had never struck me as someone who would lash out with violence, though. He didn't like to discipline his children; certainly not corporally. It was Aunt Roz who was the disciplinarian, and she did it by withholding privileges, not by wielding the switch or cane. Going into his father's gun room, removing a pistol, and proceeding to shoot dead the man who had blackmailed his younger child, or might have threatened his older one, didn't seem like something Uncle Herbert would do.

Besides, if he and Aunt Roz shared a room, and she was

awake, there was absolutely no way he could have removed himself without letting her know about it.

On the other hand, they might have been in it together. Uncle Herbert might have run out to the maze while Aunt Roz read in bed and gave him an alibi. There was no reason it couldn't have happened that way.

Next to Uncle Herbert was the empty seat where Aunt Charlotte had sat. The napkin she had left on the table looked like she might have been clutching it in her hand with the same death grip she'd had on her fork. It was all crumpled and lined with wrinkles. Then there was Uncle Harold. I watched him out of the corner of my eye, since it would be quite noticeable to turn my head to look at him.

Like Uncle Herbert, he's fair-haired, although they were both starting to turn silver at the temples now that they were into their mid- to late fifties. And they have the same fair complexion, with blue eyes and slightly pointed noses.

Which reminded me...

"Would you say my nose is pointy?" I whispered to Christopher.

He looked at me. And then at my nose. And then he whispered back, "Not particularly. More turned-up, isn't it?"

"That's what I've always thought."

"So?"

I made a face. "Crispin told me earlier to keep my pointy nose out of his business."

On the other side of me, Francis smothered a laugh.

"I was speaking metaphorically, Darling," Crispin said from down the table. He didn't even bother to turn and look at me, just offered the remark to his plate.

His father's eyes narrowed. "Don't be familiar, St George."

Crispin's lips compressed for a second, whether at the admonition itself or because his father had addressed him by his title and not his given name. Then he said, blandly, "It's her name, Father."

"Her last name, even," Aunt Roz added. "He's hardly presuming, Harold."

Uncle Harold grunted something.

"It's all right," I said, with a glance down the table that ought, rightly, have made the bane of my existence drop dead where he sat. "I have no need to be any more familiar with St George than I already am. He can keep his formal form of address, and I'll keep mine."

"That works for me, Darling," Crispin said.

I nodded. "Good. As you were, then."

"Yes, Darling."

He smirked. I sneered. Francis chuckled, and Aunt Roz shook her head, but smiled fondly. Uncle Harold didn't. He glared at his only son and then turned his attention back to his own hands. They were folded very tightly on the edge of the table. I wondered who he fantasized about strangling. If it was Crispin, I could certainly relate.

Aunt Charlotte returned shortly after this exchange, and took her seat between her husband and Uncle Harold. Then there was Tidwell with the puddings, before we were given leave to retire for the rest of the evening. Christopher offered me his arm, and I tucked my hand through his elbow and let him escort me towards the door. "Where to?"

"I have no idea," Christopher said. "I don't know which rooms are off-limits and which are in use by the police. Can we sit in the library if we want? Or the billiards room? Anyone for a game of whist?"

Crispin, who was oozing along behind us, scoffed. "How terribly old-fashioned of you, Kit. Couldn't we at least make it a rousing game of mah-jongg or gin rummy?"

"There's the gramophone," I said. "We could dance. Or listen to something, at least."

"Not tonight, Pippa." Aunt Roz spoke from behind me, where she was being escorted into the foyer by Uncle Herbert. "Not quite the thing, you know, with two people murdered and a police investigation going on."

Of course not. "My apologies. I wasn't thinking."

"Bridge, then?" Christopher said.

"I could play a game of bridge," Aunt Roz said. "Charlotte?"

Aunt Charlotte murmured that she'd be delighted. Three minutes later, the members of the older generation were settled around one of the tables in the billiards room, watched over by a dozen mounted heads of deer, antelope, and the like. Crispin and Francis had gravitated towards an open window on the far wall, where they were smoking a cigarette each. Crispin had his dangling between elegant fingers, only occasionally lifting it to his lips, while Francis was taking frequent, short drags that made him look angry, like a puffing dragon.

"Fancy joining them?" Christopher wanted to know with a glance in that direction.

I shook my head. "You go ahead. I've had about all I can stand of St George for one evening."

"He wouldn't constantly needle you if you didn't constantly snipe at him, you know," Christopher said.

I snorted. "Yes, he would. Besides, I don't constantly snipe at him."

"You snipe at him enough."

"Enough for what?"

Christopher rolled his eyes, and I grinned. "You go on over there. I think I'm going to head up to my room. I have some thinking to do."

He lowered his voice. "About this mess?"

"What else?"

"Then I'd rather go with you. We can think together."

That suited me very well. Christopher might have some additional insight about his various family members and what they were capable of. "Let's go, then."

"After you." He bowed me towards the door.

THIRTEEN

At the top of the stairs we went left. It was quieter in the west wing, with me as the only guest, and that made it less likely that we'd be overheard.

Or at least that was how I had reasoned it out when I told Christopher, "This way," at the top of the staircase. It wasn't until we had turned the corner from the central wing into the west wing that I realized how wrong I had been.

A door halfway down the hallway was standing open. Light was spilling out, and from inside we could hear the rustling of fabric and a voice.

"—no problem at all, Mrs. Mason."

The voice was masculine, a pleasant baritone, and next to me, Christopher stiffened. The reason became clear a moment later, with the next sentence from Mrs. Mason. "Very kind of you, Mr. Gardiner."

Tom must have been smiling. I could hear it in his voice. Very friendly and approachable. I wondered whether he'd been born with it, or whether it was something they taught you when you joined Scotland Yard. "It seems the least I can do, when we're putting you to all this trouble."

I deduced they were making the bed, and that Tom was helping Mrs. Mason get the rooms for the unexpected guests ready. Normally, one of the housemaids would be doing that duty, but with two handsome, young men involved, Mrs. Mason might have found it safer to take on the task herself.

And she probably wasn't afraid that one of the maids would let herself be tumbled onto the fresh sheets. I'm sure it was more a concern that someone would be loose-lipped around the handsome young detectives, and might articulate some secret about the household that Tidwell and Mrs. Mason wouldn't want articulated.

"It's no trouble," Mrs. Mason said firmly. And added, after a moment, "Lady Roz says you went to school with some of her boys."

Aunt Roz is popular with the servants, both at the Hall, at Beckwith Place, and in Town, and they use her informal title rather than her formal one around the house.

"All of them," Tom corrected, over the rustling of fabric. "Two years with Francis, one year with Kit, and all of them with Robert."

"God rest his soul."

"Amen," Tom said.

Silence reigned for a minute, only filled by the sounds of sheets and blankets being fitted to the bed. Christopher and I stood like statues in the middle of the hallway, afraid to make a noise for fear they'd hear us and stop talking.

But now Mrs. Mason must have taken her courage in her hands. It wasn't something a devoted servant should do—they're supposed to be seen but not heard—but I guess under the circumstances, family friend and all, she decided to make an exception. "Tidwell says it's possible His Grace, the old duke, was murdered."

The rustling stopped. Either the bed was made, or they'd stopped trying and were facing one another across the expanse of the mattress.

"It's possible," Tom said guardedly. "That's all we know right now. The police surgeon took him to the mortuary in Little Sutherland. He'll find out."

There was a pause. "It wasn't Lady Roz," Mrs. Mason said.

I arched my brows. So did Christopher.

"I'm sure it wasn't," Tom Gardiner replied, and sounded like he meant it. "Is there a reason you want me to know that?"

"I just wouldn't want anything bad to happen to Lady Roz."

"I see," Tom said, but didn't say anything more. I wondered whether Mrs. Mason realized that she was making Aunt Roz sound rather more guilty than not by bringing it up, but from her tone of voice, I would guess not. She sounded sincerely concerned that the police, in the person of Detective Sergeant Thomas Gardiner, should understand that Aunt Roz wouldn't do such a thing.

Nothing else was said, until Tom changed the subject. "I guess we're done in here?"

"This is it," Mrs. Mason confirmed. "All three rooms are ready. There's no one else in this wing except young Miss Darling, and she's quiet as a mouse. You won't hear hide nor hair from her."

"It seems curious," Tom remarked, "that Miss Darling's room is here, in a separate wing from everyone else."

"Oh, Lady Roz and Lord Herbert's rooms are up there at the end of the central wing, so she isn't all alone. But Her Grace— Lady Charlotte, that was—was adamant that it was improper for the young lady's room to be so close to her son and the other young gentlemen. So Miss Darling is in the west wing, and Master Francis, Master Christopher, and Master Crispin are in the east wing."

"I see," Tom said. "Her Grace doesn't have a problem with Miss Darling sharing this wing with Inspector Pendennis, Detective Sergeant Finchley, and myself?"

Clearly she hadn't, or they wouldn't be making up rooms directly across the hall from me. I glanced at Christopher, who made a face. It was obvious that Aunt Charlotte's sense of decorum only extended to her own family, of which I was not considered a member.

By now there was the sound of footsteps inside the room, and Christopher and I looked from one another to the door to my room, which was still farther down the corridor. We could attempt to reach it, but would most likely be seen as we moved past the open door to the room that currently held Tom and Mrs. Mason.

Or we could back up, silently, and pretend we'd just now arrived in the west wing, and hadn't heard any of the foregoing conversation.

Or we could stand, frozen, like deer outlined in the headlights of a motorcar, when Mrs. Mason and Tom came out of the room. And that's what we ended up doing, since our silent exchange of options hadn't given us consensus. Instead of moving forward or back, we stayed where we were, and got caught in the middle of the hallway, no doubt looking very guilty indeed.

Tom Gardiner's brows arched when he saw us. Mrs. Mason is too well trained to show surprise, so she merely skirted us with a murmured apology and headed towards the servants staircase at the end of the wing, the one that matched the one in the east wing that Christopher and I had scurried up and down so many times over the past day and a half.

The two of them—Tom and Christopher—stared at each other for a moment. Then—

"In here." Tom turned on his heel and disappeared back into the room he'd just came out of. It hadn't been made clear whether I was included in the invitation, but I hadn't been excluded either, and until I was, I wasn't going to miss out on an opportunity to learn something new. So I put my hand in the middle of Christopher's back and gave him a push towards the door. He looked down at me, but stepped forward.

"Shut the door behind you," Tom said. By the time I had nudged Christopher across the threshold ahead of me, Tom had moved away from the door and over to the window. I shoved Christopher a few feet further into the room and shut the door carefully at my back. Then I leaned on it, and surveyed the room.

Tom, meanwhile, looked from Christopher to me and back. "How much did you hear?"

Christopher seemed to have lost his ability to speak, so when he didn't answer, I took it upon myself to provide the requested information. "Nothing we didn't know already. You're staying the night. All of you. Across the hall from me. Which apparently doesn't bother Aunt Charlotte as much as me sharing a corridor with her son and her nephews."

And perhaps her husband, but who knew? If Uncle Harold had a habit of chasing women his son's age, I hadn't seen any signs of it, but that didn't mean the habit wasn't there, just that he'd never exposed me to it.

Meanwhile, Crispin's reputation with women was legendary, and Aunt Charlotte had probably heard about it. Hard to say whether she was protecting him from me, or me from him, I supposed—either was equally ridiculous, of course —but no doubt it had been in her mind that it would be a good idea to keep us apart. As if I would have touched Crispin with a barge pole, other than to whack him over the head with it if he came anywhere near me.

When Tom didn't answer, merely nodded, I continued. "Christopher's grandfather may or may not have been murdered. Aunt Roz is popular with the staff, so they don't want her to be guilty."

Tom's lips quirked. "So I gathered."

"If you discussed anything else of interest, we didn't hear it."

"We didn't," Tom said. "The more interesting conversation took place in the staffroom between tea and supper. Any questions we had were answered then."

Of course. "Are you..." I hesitated. "Do you know who shot Grimsby?"

Tom looked at me for a moment. It was quite a curious look, as if he were trying to read my mind, an attempt to turn my brain inside out to discover what I already knew, or perhaps what he thought I suspected.

"I know a few people who didn't," he said eventually. "If the shot you heard between eleven and eleven-thirty was the fatal shot, the maids are all alibied. They share rooms, and were together at the time. The same goes for the footmen. Mrs. Mason has her own room, and so does Cook and the butler."

"But surely nobody thinks that Tidwell or Mrs. Mason or—God forbid!—Mrs. Sloane ran out into the maze with a pistol to shoot Grimsby?"

Not that Cook would be able to run if you prodded her with a horsewhip. She must be in her sixties, if not seventies, by now, and would make two of Mrs. Mason. Cook is, not to put too fine a point on it, a big woman.

Besides, what kind of secret could she possibly have, that Grimsby could blackmail her over?

"Nobody thinks so," Tom confirmed, "but as long as they're

not alibied, they stay on the suspect list. It's the only way it works."

"Good thing you and I were together," I told Christopher brightly, "or we'd be on the suspect list, too."

He looked at me. So did Tom. After a moment, Tom turned back to Christopher. "What sort of mess have you gotten yourself into, old chap?"

"Don't know what you mean," Christopher muttered, and if ever someone looked guilty, it was my cousin facing Detective Sergeant Thomas Gardiner.

I sighed. "Christopher—"

But... "Kit," Tom said, and the familiarity brought Christopher's head up in a way my addressing him hadn't done. "I don't know what you're trying to do here, but I know very well that you and Miss Darling weren't having a romantic stroll to the fountain and back at eleven o'clock last night."

He glanced at me, and then turned his attention back to Christopher. "Not only because it only takes a few minutes to walk from the conservatory to the fountain, and because the weather wasn't conducive to strolling around after dark, but because unlike some people, I know that you didn't stop to canoodle along the way."

Christopher's face twisted automatically, and so did mine. He glanced my way, gauging the expression on my face. When he saw that the suggestion caused the same revulsion in me that it did in him, he smirked, and looked for a second disconcertingly like his cousin.

"Fine," he told Tom. "We didn't just walk to the fountain, and we didn't stop anywhere to canoodle."

"And please don't make that suggestion again," I added.

Tom glanced at me, and then at Christopher. He had obviously identified the weak link here. "Were you even together?"

"Of course we were together," I said. At the rate this was

going, with the way Tom was practically wrapping Christopher around his finger, we'd both end up without alibis if we weren't careful.

Tom ignored me, just kept his eyes on Christopher's face. "I can't help you if you don't tell me the truth, you know."

"That *is* the truth," I said.

Tom's eyebrows rose, and he shot me another look before he turned back to Christopher. "Kit?"

Christopher squirmed. There's no other word for it. He wriggled like a worm on a hook, or like a little boy who had been caught with his hand inside the biscuit jar. When he glanced at me, guilty conscience was written plainly all over his countenance. I threw my hands up, literally and figuratively. "Fine. It's your funeral."

"Hopefully not literally," Tom said dryly. "Spill, Kit."

"We went out together," Christopher said. "But Pippa stayed in the conservatory. Both because the weather wasn't great—there wasn't any point in us both being wet and cold—and because I thought it would be easier to negotiate with Grimsby on my own."

"So you had an assignation with Grimsby?"

"You don't have to make it sound like that," I interjected. "That wasn't romantic, either."

Tom looked like he wanted to smile but knew he shouldn't. "I assumed as much. What was it, then?"

"Blackmail," Christopher said flatly, and Tom's eyebrows rose.

"You lost me. Can you go back to the beginning and start from there?"

"That would be me," I said, lifting a hand. "On Friday night, after St George showed up at the flat and told us Kit had to come here tomorrow—yesterday—for a visit with his grandfather, he—Christopher—left. You know all about that, I'm aware."

Tom nodded.

"After he left, Grimsby showed up. He wanted to talk to Christopher. When I told him Christopher wasn't home but that I could take a message, he said he'd speak to him, Christopher, tomorrow—yesterday—here at Sutherland Hall."

Tom nodded.

"When we arrived, the duke was talking to Francis, so we went into the parlor to wait. Then Grimsby came and said it was Christopher's turn. On the way up, they made an assignation—" I grimaced, "—to take place in Christopher's room after his dressing down by the duke. It was indicated that I could be there if Christopher wanted me to be, so I was."

Tom nodded.

"He had been subtly threatening all along, and I didn't want Christopher to deal with him alone. So—"

"I'll take it, Pippa," Christopher interrupted, and turned to Tom. "He had figured out about Kitty, and what I've been doing in London. He said he hadn't told Grandfather about it— and I believe him, because Grandfather didn't bring it up, and he absolutely would have had he known; instead it was all about how I needed to get off my duff and propose to Pippa, and he wouldn't have suggested that if he'd known—"

He swallowed. "Well, that might not be true. It might be even more likely, actually..."

He trailed off, caught up in the tangent, and I decided I might as well take over again. Christopher was clearly preoccupied with his not entirely pleasant train of thought.

"So," I said, "Grimsby didn't seem to have spilled the beans about Kitty to his employer, and he said if Christopher would pay him—Grimsby—a thousand pounds, he wouldn't tell the duke then, either."

Tom whistled. "That's a lot of money."

"You're telling me," Christopher said, recalled to himself. "And that's what I told him. I said I needed time to figure out how to get it. So we arranged to meet in the formal garden, by the fountain, at eleven. He went on his merry way, and Pippa and I tried to come up with a solution."

I nodded. "Neither of us has that kind of money lying around, though. We could get it, but it would take asking Aunt Roz or else living on beans on toast for a while, and we discussed those options. We even decided that perhaps getting engaged would be a good idea, just in case it might make everyone—or someone, like the duke—more inclined to be generous. Engagement gifts and whatnot."

"Hence the truncated proposal before tea," Tom said, looking amused.

Christopher nodded. "It's not like we want to get married, you know. Or like we actually would have. We would have waited a decent period of time and broken it off. It was never more than a hoax."

"I'm sure," Tom said blandly. "So that takes us through tea and to dinner, I assume. The local doctor showed up, diagnosed natural death, and departed."

"And we didn't return to the proposal," I confirmed. "Christopher's grandfather was the one who had been pushing for it, and he was dead. It didn't seem worthwhile."

"But you still had Grimsby and his extortion to deal with."

I nodded. "After dinner, we both went downstairs together. I stayed in a corner of the conservatory to make sure Christopher could get back inside. He went outside to meet Grimsby."

"By the fountain." It was impossible to tell from Tom's tone whether it was a statement or a question, and whether he believed it or not.

"That was the agreement," Christopher nodded. "Pippa

was there, she knows it, too. I waited by the fountain, and he never showed up."

"But at one point you heard a shot. When was that?"

Christopher and I looked at each other. "Maybe a quarter after eleven? Maybe a bit later?"

"It was after the light went out in Francis's room," I said. "He might be able to tell you more specifically when that was."

Tom nodded. "What did Grimsby have on you, Miss Darling?"

"Pippa," I said, "please. Any friend of Christopher's is a friend of mine."

He didn't respond, just arched his brows, and I added, "He didn't have anything on me. Or nothing he mentioned. I wasn't related to Christopher's grandfather—I'm Roslyn's niece through her sister—so I can't imagine he found it worthwhile to dig into my indiscretions."

"What sorts of indiscretions would he find if he did?"

Christopher smirked, and again looked like Crispin for a disconcerting moment. "Nothing at all. She's as pure as the driven snow. Other than living with me, she's not doing much of anything."

"I can't find a job," I told Tom. "Nobody wants to hire me."

He nodded. "Lots of young women up from the country looking for jobs these days."

Yes, indeed. "Other than that, I don't really do much of anything. I read a lot. I spend time with Christopher. I have a couple of friends, or friendly acquaintances, from Godolphin I take tea with once in a while. I try to avoid being roped into shopping with Flossie Schlomsky."

"Who?"

"A neighbor," Christopher said. "The American woman down the hall. I've told you about her."

Tom nodded. "But nothing Simon Grimsby was holding over your head?"

"Nothing he saw fit to mention," I said. "Why?"

He hesitated. Glanced at Christopher, glanced at me.

"What is it?" Christopher asked. "You can tell us."

"I shouldn't." Tom ran a hand over his hair.

"But you can. And we won't tell anyone. Will we, Pippa?"

I shook my head. Tom sighed.

"When we went through Grimsby's room earlier, we found a notebook. It was full of information he must have discovered about everyone in the household."

"Grandfather had him do the legwork," Christopher said, "obviously. Grandfather was old and infirm, stuck in bed. There wasn't much for a valet to do. So Grandfather sent him out on little errands. I'm sure he'd dug up dirt on everyone."

Tom didn't confirm or deny that. "What do you know about the rest of your family?"

I knew nothing about Uncle Herbert, but Crispin had passed the information about Aunt Roz and Francis on to me, so I figured I might as well share it. If Tom had Grimsby's notebook, he'd know about it, anyway. And he might have already asked Crispin, who wasn't the type to keep something like that to himself. In fact, he might have mentioned telling me, and if I didn't tell Tom, then I'd look like I was keeping things back.

It was all quite confusing and circular. Now I understood why, in novels, the police always advised everyone to tell the truth. Once you start lying, outright or by omission, it's awfully hard to remember what you've said or not said and to whom.

"Francis has a drug habit," I said, "and Aunt Roz has been selling information to the gossip rags to help pay for it."

Tom nodded. "Have you seen the notebook?"

I shook my head. "The late duke brought both of those

things up in conversation yesterday afternoon. I heard it second-hand."

Tom's brows arched. "Who heard it first-hand?"

I grimaced. "Crispin. The new Viscount St George. He was hiding in the passage between the Duke's and Duchess's Chamber, listening in."

"And he told you?"

I nodded, even while I registered the fact that I had apparently underestimated Crispin's sense of family duty. It seemed as if he hadn't shared these juicy tidbits with Scotland Yard after all. Tom must have read it in the notebook instead.

"Father probably has some gambling debts," Christopher added. "Or if not actual debt, he's losing a bit more than he should on the horses, I think."

"What about your aunt and uncle? Anything you know or have heard about them?"

"Not from Crispin," I said. "If he heard anything about his parents, he didn't see fit to share it with me. But they lived here with the duke, so he could have spoken to them at any time. It wasn't like it had to happen yesterday."

"And St George himself?"

I hesitated. It wasn't like I owed Crispin anything, but I had promised him I'd forget about the conversation I'd heard him have with his father yesterday. And I had told Christopher as much, but of course Crispin hadn't extracted the same promise from him.

Or if he had, Christopher seemed willing to break it. "He's in love with some woman my aunt and uncle don't approve of. That's the only thing I've learned about him this weekend that I didn't already know. His other escapades are hardly a secret. He runs with a very fast crowd when he's in London."

Tom nodded. "Any idea who the woman is?"

"I could guess," Christopher said, with a guilty look at me, "but that's all it would be. Guessing. And I could be wrong. His name has been associated with Lady Violet Cummings, and the Honorable Cecily Fletcher, and Millicent Tremayne, the actress, and that's just in the last few months."

My face twisted. "He's a cad."

"He gets around," Christopher agreed. "They're all good old English girls, though, and supposedly that's one of the things that makes this girl unacceptable to the family. She's foreign. So there has to be someone else."

I squinted at Tom. "Are you telling me that Grimsby failed to find out? He nosed out Christopher's secret identity and Francis's drug use and Aunt Roz's financial sideline, but he wasn't able to figure out who Crispin supposedly fell in love with? How is that possible?"

"I don't know whether he found out or not," Tom said, and he sounded frustrated by it. "There are a few pages missing from the notebook—three or four, we think—and if there was something about the Viscount St George's love affairs in there, they must have been on one of those pages."

All of them, more likely. Given the rumors that floated around, I had no problem imagining three or four notebook pages filled with names of women Crispin had wronged.

"Well, that's convenient," I said.

"You're telling me," Tom answered.

"Why would Grimsby tear out the pages that applied to Crispin?"

"He wouldn't," Christopher said. "Someone else did it. That's what you think, isn't it?"

He pinned Tom with a look. I turned from one to the other of them. "Wait. You're saying whoever killed Grimsby tore out the pages? Why not just take the whole notebook? It seems easier."

"Is that what you would have done?" Tom asked.

"I wouldn't have torn out the pages pertaining to myself and left the pages pertaining to everyone else, certainly. That would make me look very guilty, wouldn't it?"

Tom nodded. "And yet, that's just what someone did."

My eyes widened. "Tore out the pages about me?"

"If there were pages about you," Tom said. "They're gone, so we have no idea what was on them. It could have been information about you, or it could have been information about someone else."

"But there are pages missing."

He nodded.

"And there's nothing in the notebook about me?"

He shook his head.

"What about Christopher? Francis? Aunt Roz?"

"The information we discussed, about Francis and Lady Roslyn, is there," Tom said. "There's some information about Lord Herbert's gambling. Some losses, some wins. Nothing remarkable either way. Certainly no debt."

Christopher looked relieved.

"There's nothing about Kit," Tom added. "Or St George. Tidwell the butler has a lady friend in Salisbury he sees on his days off. One of the chambermaids is carrying on with one of the footmen, and the kitchen maid is sneaking food out of the kitchen to her sister in the village on her weekly afternoons off. One of the grooms gambles worse than Lord Herbert, albeit for much smaller sums, but given their respective positions in society, the groom is in hock up to his eyeballs and is about to find himself afoul one of the local bookies."

"Lovely."

"Cook had a child out of wedlock once upon a time, before any of us here were born. There's no Mr. Sloane, since she's not been married. The chauffeur occasionally uses the Crossley to visit family in Southampton when no one else needs it. They're all petty crimes and small infractions, nothing you'd think would turn into murder. But we have to look at it all."

"But there's nothing about me or Pippa?" Christopher said. "Not even the things we've just told you?"

Tom shook his head.

"I don't know what to think about that," I said. "We know he had information about Christopher. And there must have been something about me, if the duke—the late duke—wanted Christopher to propose to me. We know there's plenty of dirt available on Crispin."

"But Grandfather might not have wanted Grimsby to unearth information about that part of the family. There wasn't anything about Uncle Harold or Aunt Charlotte, was there?"

Tom shook his head.

"There should be something about you and me, though," I told Christopher. "We know that Grimsby looked into us. He said as much. The fact that those pages aren't there, seems very suspect."

"Maybe someone is trying to make us look guilty," Christopher suggested. "As if we'd be stupid enough to tear out the pages about ourselves while we left everything else."

I nodded. "You'll be looking for the pages, I assume? Going through everyone's rooms? All the common areas?"

Like the books in the library, every one of which could have a couple of sheets of notebook paper tucked inside, and nobody would ever know.

"Tomorrow," Tom confirmed

..

.. "Whoever has those pages goes to the top of the suspect list. Although I don't expect to find them anywhere. Whoever took them has surely set fire to them by now."

"Hopefully not." I glanced at Christopher. "I think I'll go to my room now."

He nodded. "I'll see you tomorrow, Pippa."

I waited, but when he made no move towards the door, I headed off on my own and left them there. One of them had something to say to the other, it seemed, and it was probably none of my business what it was.

FOURTEEN

The west wing was deserted when I came through the door
into the hallway, so it was easy to scurry the few yards to my
own door and duck inside without being seen by anyone. I shut
the door behind me before I flicked on the light on the night
table and went to the window. There was no movement in the
maze tonight. I looked.

It didn't matter anyway, because the next second I had
yanked the drapes across the window, and whoever might have
been out there couldn't see what I was doing through the thick
fabric even with the lights on.

But even so, I made sure to move away from the window
before I lifted the dinner dress I'd brought to wear yesterday,
and had ended up wearing tonight instead, over my head and
onto a hanger. Then I divested myself of my undergarments
and slipped into the pale blue silk pyjamas Aunt Roz had given
me for Christmas last year, and a pair of quilted slippers.

All that done, I positioned myself in the middle of the floor
and surveyed my room.

Like all the rooms in Sutherland Hall, it was big and

opulent and full of old furniture, expensive rugs, and heirlooms. The wallpaper was damask. The bed was a canopy-style with velvet draperies and intricately carved posts. Everything was heavy and dark and ornate.

What I really wanted to do, was crawl into that bed, pull the draperies down around me, and forget that this weekend had happened. It had been a very long Sunday, full of a lot of upsetting incidents, from the quarrel with St George over breakfast and then seeing Grimsby dead in the maze, to the conversation we'd just had with Tom Gardiner across the hall. Sleep—oblivion—beckoned, but I resisted the call. If Tom was right that several pages had been ripped out of Grimsby's notebook, and Christopher was right that whoever had ripped them out was the killer, and Tom had told the truth when he said that whoever was found with the pages in their possession would be of interest to the police... well, I thought I had better make sure that the pages hadn't somehow found their way into my room.

I knew, of course, that it hadn't been me who ripped them from the notebook. I hadn't known that the notebook existed until Tom told us about it. It hadn't crossed my mind to go looking for something like that in Grimsby's room, although in retrospect, perhaps it should have. It had obviously occurred to someone else.

There were, to my mind, only two reasons why someone might have taken those pages. As I had told Tom myself, it was much more logical for the killer to take the whole notebook. If he or she had, who would have known that Grimsby had even had a notebook in the first place? And taking the pages pertaining to oneself while leaving the rest of the notes would only draw attention to the fact that they weren't there.

No, whoever tore the pages out, those specific pages, must have done it to make someone else look guilty. Specifically, the people mentioned in the missing pages. And so it was that I had determined to search my room, every nook and cranny, to make sure they weren't here. I sincerely hoped Christopher had the wherewithal to do the same when he made it back to his own room.

I started with the most obvious places: the drawers in the night tables, the little escritoire over by the wall, and the wardrobe.

There was nothing in the night tables, nothing taped to the back or underside of the night tables, and nothing taped to the underside of the night table drawers. Since I was close to the bed anyway, I checked under the pillows—nothing—and ran my hands under the edges of the mattress as far as I could reach. There was nothing there either.

The escritoire was next. It boasted writing paper and pens, ink, a dictionary, blotting paper, all the usual things you can find in an escritoire. None of it looked like notebook paper. I riffled the papers and shook the dictionary before I checked under the piece of furniture and under each drawer there too, to be thorough. That done, I moved on to the wardrobe into which I had decanted my weekender bag yesterday afternoon.

I started with the outside, and felt my way around the bottom and back of the wardrobe as far as I could reach.

It was a large and unwieldy piece of furniture, and it didn't look as if it had been moved away from the wall in recent memory. There were no scratches on the floor in front of it, which I thought there would have to be, if Grimsby's killer had been at it. We weren't dealing with a syndicate, but a single person, and a single person couldn't have moved the wardrobe out from the wall without dragging it across the floor, which would have left marks.

I pulled the desk chair over to the front of the wardrobe and climbed up on it. There was nothing on top of the wardrobe except a lot of dust. Whichever of the Hall's chambermaids was in charge of this room, obviously hadn't been as thorough as she should have been when she readied the room for occupancy this weekend.

Inside the wardrobe, I checked the toes of the three pairs of shoes I had brought with me to Wiltshire: the brogues, the blue strap-shoes I wore with the blue-and-white afternoon dress, and the gray T-straps that went with the butter-yellow evening dress I had just taken off and hung in the wardrobe. (It had an uneven hem and was covered with little metal spangles, so the gray shoes looked very well with it, especially when I paired them with a pair of silvery gray silk stockings.)

There was nothing crumpled up and shoved into the toes of any of my shoes. There was nothing hidden among my unmentionables, and nothing tucked into the pocket of any of my garments. The cloche hat I had worn for the trip down was likewise empty.

I was just about to throw in the towel and rejoice in the fact that I didn't seem to be on the receiving end of the killer's attention when my eyes fell on the weekender bag itself. It was neatly folded and eased onto the top shelf of the wardrobe, where I had shoved it after I had finished emptying it, but something about it didn't look quite right.

Let me say first of all that I'm not usually careless about my belongings. I do perhaps keep my stockings in a bit of a jumble, when I should treat them with more respect, but I take quite good care of my clothes and shoes overall. And I'm rather fond of my weekender bag, if it comes to that. Trips are always fun. I just don't usually make sure it's quite so carefully folded before I put it away. In fact, I could distinctly remember having shoved it onto the shelf above the clothes in a bit of a hurry yesterday afternoon, because it was time to go down to tea.

I hesitated before I reached for it, almost like it might suddenly lurch out and bite me when I least expected it. Of course I knew it wouldn't. Whoever folded it up so neatly and stuck it up there, hadn't nestled a viper inside the bag. That was ridiculous. But nonetheless, I found myself not really wanting to touch it. And yes, I knew I was being silly. The chambermaid might simply have seen the condition of the bag and decided to do me a favor by folding it more properly, and that was all there was to it.

I told myself I was being ridiculous, grabbed the corner of it, and dragged it down. I moved out of the way of it, though, so it landed on the rug in front of the wardrobe with a sort of *flump*. I stood back and watched it for a moment, to make absolutely certain that nothing venomous was about to slither out, before I got to my knees in front of the bag and started poking at it.

It didn't take long, obviously, since the bag was empty, or was supposed to be.

I found what I was looking for—and frankly, hoping not to find—tucked under the piece of stiff leather that served as the inside bottom of the bag. Someone had reached in and slipped a couple of folded pieces of paper underneath, out of sight, clearly hoping I'd not realize they were there whenever I opened the bag next.

That was if I was supposed to be opening the bag at all, and the papers weren't intended to be found by the police during their search tomorrow morning. They were well-hidden, but probably not well enough that Scotland Yard would have overlooked them.

I pulled them out and then thought better of what I was doing, and went to the escritoire for a letter opener, which I used to unfold the sheets of paper. By then, I had moved over to the bed, where I had more room to spread out across the counterpane, and I figured the fewer of my fingerprints on the sheets, the better for me.

There were three sheets altogether, lined front and back, and covered with cramped, very dark, somehow rushed handwriting. The words ran together. If there's anything to the noble art of graphology, I would have said that Grimsby was modest and unassuming, repressed, and probably not terribly well educated—there were errors in spelling. Of course, the truth might just have been that he'd been in a hurry, and good notebooks cost money, so he was trying to squeeze as many words as possible onto each page.

None of it mattered, anyway. He was dead, and what was important was the information in front of me.

That, and the fact that someone had hidden it in my room. Someone who was trying to frame me for murder.

I squinted at the first page. *Christopher Nicholas Henry Astley*, it said.

It was followed by Christopher's birthdate—March 21st, 1903—and the address of our flat in London. There was the name of Evans the doorman. Florence Schlomsky was mentioned, with a question mark next to her name. There was a day of following Christopher around London last month: shopping at Marks & Spencer, tea at the Savoy, the purchase of a pink evening gown with tassels that Grimsby surmised had been bought for me.

The inference, of course, was that I was a kept woman, something which Grimsby clearly planned to convey to His Grace.

He figured out differently when he saw Christopher wearing the dress, exiting our building the following week. I'd walked out with him, wearing something different, so there'd really been no question whatsoever about the dress being mine.

Then it was tailing Christopher to the location where last month's drag ball had been held. I made a mental note of the address, although I assumed that after this month's ball—and the raid by the police that Christopher had so narrowly escaped —next month's ball, if there was one, would take place somewhere else.

Grimsby hadn't been able to make it inside the venue, but had loitered outside—in what I hoped was a rubbish-filled alley, in miserable weather, for hours—until Christopher appeared again, this time accompanied by a young man. Grimsby had jotted down a description that could have applied to Tom Gardiner—brown hair, tweed suit—but that could equally well have applied to any number of other men.

They'd gone off in a cab, and by the time Grimsby caught up, Christopher was going inside the lobby of our building, while Tom had disappeared. Grimsby had asked Evans who Tom was, and Evans had been unable to provide the answer, beyond telling Grimsby that he'd never seen the young man before, and no, he hadn't visited Christopher previously.

After that, there were a few more instances of Grimsby tailing Christopher through London, shopping and taking tea and doing various other, normal things, but there were no more mentions of young men, and Tom had not made another appearance. Grimsby had been in London on the evening of the next drag ball, too, of course, but on that occasion he had called at the flat rather than follow Christopher, and we should probably be grateful for it.

I moved on to the next sheet. *Philippa Marie Schatz Darling*, it said, followed by my birthdate. I was born some four months before Christopher, for your information, in November of 1902.

The first line below my name said, <u>GERMAN!!</u> in capital letters, with several exclamation points and a heavy underline. I made a face when I saw it, since it's still not a great time to be German in England, and I don't appreciate the reminder.

It's not as difficult as it was a decade ago, in the middle of the Great War, but it could be easier. Especially considering everything that's stirring over in Germany these days—Herr Hitler and his book and all the unpleasantness surrounding the failed *coup d'état* and all that—and I'd really rather forget that part of my heritage altogether, now that I have embraced my mother's homeland and been embraced in turn.

I tore my attention, with a little bit of difficulty, away from that single word, and continued down the page.

Grimsby had followed me around, too, but not as assiduously as he had followed Christopher. There were quite a few mentions of me and Christopher together: alone in the flat in the evenings, having tea somewhere, shopping at Fortnum & Mason for food we were planning to consume for dinner together. There was a mention or two of me having run interference when some girl, Flossie Schlomsky or someone we'd met while shopping, had batted her eyes at Christopher, and I had stuck my hand through his arm and tugged him away.

Of course, Christopher knew, and I knew, that it wasn't because I wanted him for myself. But it was quite clear where the late duke had gotten the idea that there was more between us than actually existed. It must have looked to Grimsby very much like I had interfered out of jealousy, or at least out of my own designs on Christopher.

I rolled my eyes and moved on. If anyone thought I would have murdered Grimsby over this, they had to have a screw loose somewhere.

Crispin Henry Jonathan Astley, the last sheet said, and I hesitated. I had promised Crispin that I would forget the conversation he'd had with his father. Reading the notes Grimsby had taken veered into territory I had mostly agreed I would stay out of.

On the other hand, Tom had said that whoever ripped the

pages out of the notebook might be the murderer. I knew it hadn't been me or Christopher who did it. That left Crispin.

Although if he'd killed Grimsby over what was in the notes, it made absolutely no sense that he'd leave them with me, even in an effort to make me look guilty. My own notes, sure. Christopher's, yes, because if I'd killed Grimsby, it would have been over what he did to Christopher, not over anything he did to me. But why would Crispin share his own offenses with me?

It made no sense.

And all that aside, the notes were here. Was I really principled enough not to read them, when I had them in front of me and they might be full of ammunition I could use against St George later?

Clearly I wasn't. I leaned forward and began to decipher Grimsby's cramped writing. Due to the overabundance of information, it was even smaller and more crabbed than on Christopher's sheet.

Below the affluence of names, and Crispin's birthday—June 5th, 1903, which was circled, and the circle had the initials L.M. with a question mark next to it—the gossip went on for the entire back and front of the sheet. There was even scribbles vertically in the margins.

And it made sense, I realized, since, when Crispin came up to London, he stayed at Sutherland House, where the staff was loyal to His Grace and thus to Grimsby. It was abundantly clear that they had had no compunctions whatsoever about sharing what they had seen and heard over the past couple of years. There were stories of Crispin staggering in at nine in the morning, still sozzled to the gills, with his wallet and all his money gone. There were stories of Crispin, clearly under the influence of alcohol or something else, wrapping a Ballot 2 LTS racing car around a light pole somewhere in the West End and walking away with nothing worse than a bump on the head, laughing. There were stories of Crispin coming home drunk and angry, destroying the duke's sitting room when he wasn't served more alcohol fast enough. Stories of Crispin coming home half dressed, with his shirt half buttoned, his emerald cufflinks missing, and with lipstick stains on his collar and neck. Stories of Crispin not coming home at all, but spending the night in jail, sobering up.

A story of a woman coming to the door of Sutherland House carrying a baby, looking for the baby's father.

I hadn't heard anything about that, so Crispin—or someone else—must have managed to hush it up. I wondered whether he truly was the father of the baby, or whether it was just a ploy to get money from him. When you're young and handsome and the heir to a title and a massive fortune, it could equally well be either. I had watched women pursue Christopher with a single-mindedness that was disturbing, and he wasn't the heir to the dukedom and the bulk of the money. It was worse for Crispin, I was quite sure. And given the way he was carrying on, it wasn't outside the realm of possibility that someone would try to snag him with an illegitimate child ploy.

Not that I would put it past him to dally with a girl who ended up with child, either. It seemed very much in character for him to look to his own pleasure first, and her future second. But I would have expected him to deal with it honorably if he did. Since I hadn't heard anything about this, I was inclined to believe it might have been a lie.

Her name had not made it into the narrative, but there were plenty of other women mentioned by name, including the three Christopher had told Tom Gardiner about earlier. All were part of the set of very fast Bright Young Things Crispin hung around with while in London. A couple of heiresses, the granddaughter of a famous painter, and another actress of the burlesque variety had names I recognized.

There were so many of them, it was hard to believe he'd had time to woo them all. Then again, maybe there wasn't a lot of wooing involved. Maybe their morals—Crispin's included—were so loose that they all just fell into bed with one another willy-nilly, whenever the desire struck.

My face puckered. It wasn't a pleasant thought. I may be modern, but I'm not promiscuous. And much as I abhor Crispin—and I'm sure I've made it clear just how very much I do—it was difficult to look at this list of... they weren't even peccadillos, were they? They were honest to goodness vices, or big, whopping sins, at least if you're of the persuasion that such things exist. Drunkenness, debauchery, fornication...

Or alternatively, if I wanted to be kind and understanding, which doesn't come naturally to me on the subject of Crispin St George, they were cries for help.

At any rate, it was difficult to look at the list and not feel a little bit sorry for him. Not to mention a bit angry with Uncle Harold, who had to have known that this was going on. Surely the staff at the house in Town would have reported all these happenings to the Hall? How could Uncle Harold look at this behavior and justify telling Crispin the things we'd overheard yesterday? Why not just let him marry the girl he thought he was in love with, even if she was unsuitable? At least that way, the rest of the family wouldn't have to watch him distract himself with alcohol and women and motorcar accidents because his life didn't seem worth living.

My face twisted, halfway appalled at what I had read, and equally appalled that I felt sincere pity for Crispin, who surely would not want that, especially from me.

Back to business, I told myself. Was there anything here to indicate that Crispin had killed Grimsby, taken the notebook pages, and hidden them in my room?

None of what I had read about him, I had to assume, was

secret. The staff at Sutherland House had given Grimsby all this information; there was nothing here about following Crispin around, the way Grimsby had stolen after Christopher across London. Unless Grimsby had discovered something about Crispin that wasn't in the notes, I could see no motive for murder.

And how likely was it that Grimsby had kept some of Crispin's sins out of the notebook when he had detailed Christopher's and mine, the ones he had shared with the duke as well as the ones he had kept to himself?

From what Tom had told us, I had to assume that the same had been true for what Grimsby had known about Francis and Aunt Roz.

So in spite of having been the person to find the body, always a suspicious position, Crispin didn't seem to have had much of a motive for killing Grimsby.

Unless the blackmail was not the reason for Grimsby's murder, of course. I had assumed it was, because it made for such a nice, tidy motive. But what if it was, instead, in detective novel parlance, a red herring? What if Grimsby had been killed because he knew something about the late duke's death, instead?

Crispin had motive there, if the duke hadn't been willing to let him marry the girl he wanted. But even without that, he was now the Viscount St George, one step closer to the dukedom, and a single death away from being duke himself.

And if Grimsby had known—suspected, even guessed—that Crispin had killed the duke, then Crispin had reason to want Grimsby out of the way, too.

Perhaps Grimsby had decided to blackmail Crispin over that, and now here we were, full circle. Grimsby had been killed because he was a blackmailer after all. It was just over something much, much more dangerous than the few closely guarded personal failings in Grimsby's notebook.

And what's more, it would also explain why Crispin might have left his own dossier in with mine and Christopher's when he hid the sheets in my weekender bag. (Assuming he did, of course. It doesn't do to get too enamored with one's own theories.) He would have read them first, and would have realized that they included nothing compromising, and so he might have felt safe in including them. Making me feel sorry for him might have struck him as a humorous side benefit. Something else I wouldn't put past him.

I wondered whether Tom had gone downstairs to the incident room yet, or whether he was still across the hall talking to Christopher. The sooner I passed these papers off to the proper authorities, the better it would look for me, I imagined. And perhaps for Christopher, too.

I used the letter opener to gather and fold the sheets again, and then I slid them carefully into an unused envelope I found in the escritoire. That done, I headed out into the hallway, envelope in hand.

The west wing was deserted. The door to the room where I had left Christopher with Tom earlier was open now, and no one was inside. The other two rooms put to use for Scotland Yard were equally empty, their doors open and lamps lit to make it easy for the detectives to make their way there later. I assumed this meant the representatives of law and order were still hard at work downstairs.

The light was on under Aunt Roz's door again, the way it had been last night, and I skirted it carefully. There was a murmur of voices from within tonight, so Uncle Herbert must be there, too, and awake. Unless Aunt Roz was reading out loud to herself, I suppose.

I thought about sweeping down the main staircase, but of

course I was in my pyjamas, and besides, I wanted to share what I had found with Christopher before I handed the evidence over to the police. So instead, I continued past the top of the staircase towards the east wing.

The light was on in Aunt Charlotte's room, too, but Uncle Harold's was dark. And then, as I turned the corner, I saw what looked like a party down at the other end of the corridor.

That's a slight exaggeration, of course. But Christopher was there, leaning against the wall next to his own open door, and Tom Gardiner was there, and Francis, as well as Crispin, who looked a bit rough, with his cheeks pink, his hair mussed, and his eyes dilated. Given the list of his conquests currently in my hand, I wondered who he had found to run her fingers through his hair here at Sutherland Hall.

As I moved closer to them, Christopher straightened from his slouch against the wall and unfolded the arms that had been crossed over his chest. Crispin looked me up and down, from the toes of my slippers over the silk of my pyjamas up to my head and back, and his mouth twisted. Francis giggled, his pupils like pinpricks in his pale face, and Tom's eyes went immediately to the envelope in my hand before he looked at my face, while somehow managing to circumvent entirely the pyjamas that were the first and last thing Crispin had noticed.

"Passing love notes, Darling?" the latter sneered when I extended the envelope to Tom, who took it with what I can only describe as a look of delight on his face.

"Is this—?"

I nodded.

"Where did you find it?"

"Bottom of my weekender bag," I said, since, if Crispin was the one who had put the sheets there, he already knew that, anyway.

Tom tilted his head consideringly. "And is it—?"

"All three of us," I confirmed. "There isn't much there, though." Or not much that would be of help to Scotland Yard, at least not if I were any judge.

"What is it?" Francis wanted to know, and Tom turned to him with a pleasant smile.

"Just an account of movements that Miss Darling promised to write down for me."

He turned the smile on me, as blandly as you please. "Thank you. I'll make sure Inspector Pendennis gets it."

"No problem at all," I told him, equally politely, and looked around. "What are the four of you doing, standing around in the hallway at this time of night? Plotting murder and mayhem?"

"I was just on my way in," Christopher said, "when Francis and Crispin came up the stairs."

And they had stopped for a chat, I assumed. No mention was made of Tom, but it seemed he must have walked Christopher to his door, to be caught there along with the other three.

"Well, I just wanted to hand off the account of my movements," I said. "I should—"

"How did you know Detective Sergeant Gardiner was going to be here?" Crispin wanted to know. Clearly, being inebriated did nothing to impair his cognitive ability, even if his delivery wasn't quite as sharply edged as usual.

Because, of course, I hadn't known that Tom would be here. I had assumed that Tom would have gone back downstairs to join his colleagues, not be standing in the hallway outside Christopher's room.

"Lucky guess?" I ventured. And since I didn't feel like explaining it in any more detail, I added, "I'm going back to my room. Good night, gentlemen."

"I'll walk you," Tom said, with a nod at Christopher. "I'll be staying across the hall from you anyway."

"How perfectly lovely for you both," Crispin drawled.

I rolled my eyes. "Mind your own, St George. Considering the string of broken hearts you've left in your wake, you really have no cause to comment on anyone else's love life."

Not that there was anything like a love life between me and Tom Gardiner. But Crispin didn't need to know that.

And anyway, it was the wrong thing to say, because the corners of his mouth turned up in a malicious smirk. "Is that jealousy I hear, Darling?"

"You wish," I said and turned on my heel. "Good night, Christopher, Francis. I'll see you in the morning."

"Sleep well, Darling," Crispin's voice said behind me, oozing... something. "Sweet dreams."

I didn't dignify the comment with a response, just shot Tom Gardiner a look of mingled frustration and frustrated violence when he came up on the side of me and we continued up the hallway together.

FIFTEEN

I wasn't able to share the details of my find with Christopher until the next morning after breakfast. I couldn't go back to the east wing after Tom walked me to my door, just in case Crispin lay in wait, ready to pounce as soon as I showed my face again. He clearly suspected that the envelope I had handed over to Tom didn't hold what I had claimed it held.

And then when I made it down to the dining room—Scotland Yard was still using the breakfast room—Aunt Roz was there, and I didn't want to discuss the matter in front of her.

She looked rather worse for wear, and I mean that in the kindest way possible. Like the rest of us, she had planned to come to Sutherland Hall for tea and perhaps an overnight stay. Now, like the rest of us, she was stuck here until the police decided to let us leave, with only what she had packed into a weekend bag that was surely no bigger than mine, and with the concern that her father-in-law had been murdered and one of her relatives might hang for it.

And yes, I was in that position, too. But I wasn't in my fifties, they weren't my husband and my children, and I was still sleeping reasonably well. Aunt Roz had dark circles under her eyes, and the grooves running from her nose to the sides of her mouth were dug deeper than I was used to seeing them. There was a tiny divot in the middle of her forehead, where she was drawing her brows together in a worried frown.

When I sailed through the door, in the same skirt and blouse for the third day in a row, she greeted me with what was undoubtedly intended to be a welcoming smile. "Pippa! Good morning!"

"Morning!" I said, equally brightly. "Lovely day out there."

Aunt Roz glanced at the window, which was mostly covered with the heavy drapes befitting a room that's mostly used at night. "If you say so."

"Well, I haven't been out in it. But it looks nice from the windows."

I picked a plate from the sideboard and started filling it. A spoonful of eggs, a sausage, a piece of ham, tomatoes...

When I sat down at the table, after adding toast, a glass of orange juice, and a cup of coffee, Aunt Roz's eyes fell on my arm. "Dear me. What happened there?"

"Oh." I gave the regularly spaced blotches of ink on my sleeve a disgruntled look. "I forgot to give my blouse to the maids to clean yesterday. Your nephew got fingerprint ink on my sleeve."

"Crispin?" She contemplated the evenly spaced marks with her head tilted. "Why would Crispin grab your wrist like that?"

"He wanted my attention," I said, just as Her Grace, Charlotte, Duchess of Sutherland, rounded the corner into the dining room.

She must have heard the last few sentences, because she came in with her eyes on my sleeve and her mouth twisted into a moue of displeasure. "Crispin did that? I'll talk to him."

"There's no need," I said, as she made her way towards the sideboard. "I've already let him know I didn't appreciate it."

I might have been mistaken, because it wasn't easy to tell, but I rather think I saw the corners of her lips turn up. As if she were pleased I'd put her son in his place. She probably knew all about his shenanigans in Town, and perhaps it made her happy that there was one woman, among all the others, who didn't fall for Crispin's dubious charms.

"I wouldn't even be wearing it," I added, "but I didn't bring enough clothes for an extended stay. We thought we'd be back in London yesterday afternoon."

Aunt Roz nodded. "I'm wearing the same skirt for the third day in a row, too. I doubt we'd be able to find anything worth having in the village, but Salisbury isn't far. Not if we take the motorcar. Do you suppose the police would let us go shopping if we asked nicely?"

Tom might. "It couldn't hurt to ask," I said. "Would you like me to go across the hall?"

"Finish your breakfast first, Pippa." She forked up a bit of sausage of her own and conveyed it to her mouth. I'm sure it tasted just fine—with the exception of the roast duck on the evening the old duke died, and that was understandable, all the food from the Hall kitchen tastes good—but from her expression, it might as well have been sawdust. "Would you like to come with us, Charlotte?"

"I don't know—" Aunt Charlotte said, but before she could finish, her son had interrupted her.

"Come with you where?"

He looked better than last night, so perhaps he was so used to getting sozzled at night that waking up in the morning doesn't present a problem. Aside from some faintly purple shadows under his eyes—which we all had, to be fair, and they were nowhere near as dark as Aunt Roz's—he looked just as usual. Completely and properly dressed, shaved, hair immaculate, sneer in place. "Good morning, Mother. Aunt Roslyn. Darling." He gave me a nod.

Aunt Charlotte had her mouth open to speak, but before she could, Aunt Roz got in first. "We're hoping to take the motorcar to Salisbury to do some shopping. None of us brought enough to wear, and Pippa's blouse is beyond repair."

Crispin nodded, with an almost imperceptible flicker of his eyes to my sleeve. "I'll drive you."

"That's not necessary," Aunt Roz assured him. "I'm sure Wilkins—" The chauffeur. The one with the habit of taking the duke's Crossley to Southampton, "would be happy to oblige."

"It would be my pleasure," Crispin told her formally, and without so much as a smug twinkle in his eyes. "It's the least I can do, after befouling Darling's blouse."

"Crispin, dear—" his mother began, wincing, but was drowned out again by Crispin's talking over her.

"I'll buy you a new one, Darling."

"I'm not having you buy me clothes, St George," I told him. "I don't care if you were the one who ruined it in the first place. You're not buying me a new one. I can buy my own clothes."

"Of course, Darling." He made a mock bow, full of all the smugness he had left after the assurance to Aunt Roz.

I huffed, and pushed my chair back. "I'll go ask Tom if it's all right if we go off for a couple of hours."

"Your breakfast—" Aunt Charlotte began, looking at my still-full plate.

"I lost my appetite." Damn Crispin. "I'll let you know what the police say. And then I'll go wake Christopher. I'm sure he'll want to come along. He loves to shop."

Crispin murmured something, and took my chair for himself. I gave him a sharp look, but he didn't look at me as I turned on my heel and swept from the room.

. . .

An hour later, we were piled into the Hispano-Suiza on our way to Salisbury. The representatives for Scotland Yard hadn't minded at all what we were doing.

"Not planning to make for the coast, are you?" Pendennis had grunted, and when I said no, we were just driving to Salisbury, he had waved his hand in a dismissive gesture. Tom had winked at me, while Finchley had stayed busy with whatever he was doing over by the sideboard. More fingerprints, most likely. Perhaps he was testing the notebook pages.

It ended up being five of us in the car. Francis was still abed, and neither Uncle Herbert nor Uncle Harold seemed inclined towards a shopping trip. They planned to spend some time together discussing the estate, now that their father was out of the picture. I had no idea why Crispin wanted to go to Salisbury, honestly, since Aunt Roz had been right: Wilkins was available, as was the Crossley, and this was precisely the sort of outing they were meant for.

However, Crispin insisted, so the rest of us piled in: Christopher in the backseat, with me and his mother on either side of him, and Aunt Charlotte in pride of place next to Crispin in the front seat. No one disputed the seating arrangements, but really, Christopher's legs were longer than Aunt Charlotte's, so he might have been more comfortable up front, while Aunt Charlotte would have fit better into the back seat with me and Aunt Roz. Aside from size, Aunt Roz surely had seniority of age and dignity, and should have been up front for that reason.

Then again, I didn't imagine either of them really wanted to sit next to Crispin—I certainly didn't—so the arrangements served as well as any others. Besides, Aunt Charlotte *was* his mother, so he couldn't very well snub her by not offering her the place of honor.

We arrived in Salisbury some forty minutes after we left, having taken our lives in our hands multiple times between Sutherland Hall and town. Crispin's desire for fast living clearly extended to the motorcar, even with passengers in it, because he drove like the hounds of hell were nipping at his heels. Perhaps he just really wanted to get away from the Hall for a bit, and that was why he had offered so insistently to drive us.

Once we had parked the H6 outside the Style & Gerrish department store on Blue Boar Row, Aunt Charlotte—who had plenty of clothes; she lived at the Hall, after all—took hold of her son's arm and towed him away to the stationary department. He looked disinclined to follow—perhaps he hadn't given up hope of causing an uncomfortable scene by insisting on buying me a new blouse—but he'd been properly brought up, so he went with his mother. Aunt Roz, Christopher, and I headed into the ready-made ladies' fashions department.

I won't bore you with a detailed description of our shopping. I'm not averse to pretty clothes, nor is Aunt Roz, and Christopher, of course, has his own reasons for being interested. We spent a pleasant hour combing the racks, and ended up with a twill skirt and blouse for Aunt Roz, a pleated skirt and two blouses for me: one to replace the one Crispin had, as he said, befouled, and the other to match the new skirt I bought. Christopher refrained from indulging himself in front of his mother, but I could tell he admired a lovely cloche hat with a cluster of felt violets pinned to the brim. It would certainly bring out the blue of his eyes, so I threw it in with my other purchases, and had the dubious pleasure of having Aunt Roz tell me, "The green would look better with your complexion, Pippa, dear."

When we gathered back at the Hispano-Suiza with our purchases, Crispin was sullen and silent, which led me to believe that he might have gotten a talking-to from his mother during our absence. He handed her into the front seat with less than his usual overblown charm, and let Christopher deal with getting Aunt Roz and me situated in the backseat. Not a single "Darling," fell from his lips on the entire drive back, which made me wonder whether Aunt Charlotte had finally managed to impress upon him the impertinence of his addressing me thusly, even if it was, in actuality, my name. We all knew that Crispin did it because he thought it was funny to make me squirm.

Although Aunt Charlotte probably didn't care at all about what did or didn't make me squirm, so it was more likely that she had reproached her only son for having had too much to drink last night, and for insisting on making a nuisance of himself this morning.

Either way, he clearly didn't appreciate it, whatever form the chastisement had taken, and the drive home was even less pleasant than the one to Salisbury. I spent it hanging onto the door on my side of the Hispano-Suiza so I wouldn't accidentally get thrown out of the motorcar on one of the turns, and die.

Back at the Hall, we gathered in the library to wait for luncheon to be served. Aunt Charlotte excused herself to carry her parcels to the back of the house, while Aunt Roz and I loaded up one of the footmen with our packages, and asked him to convey them to our rooms. Christopher's cloche, by necessity, ended up going to my room, of course.

Crispin, who had bought nothing and had nowhere else to

be, threw himself into a chair with a sulky expression, and kicked his legs out.

"Why so glum, St George?" I asked. "Did your mother tell you that you're not allowed to call me Darling anymore?"

He looked at me. "As a matter of fact she did—" He waited a long, breathless moment before he curled his tongue around my name, "Pippa."

Each P was pronounced with deliberation. I winced.

"Please," I had to take a breath in order to force the word out, "Crispin—"

And that was as far as I got, because my face literally puckered around the taste. He knew it, too, because his lips twitched, while Christopher let out a laugh.

"Don't make her do it, St George. You can tell it's literally painful."

"That seems to me to be an excellent reason for making her do it," Crispin said piously, but he relented with a smirk. "Yes, yes, Darling. I know it hurts. You can continue to call me St George, and I'll keep calling you Darling. Agreed?"

"Agreed," I said, because anything was better than having to use his first name. Forcing my mouth to shape the syllables had made me feel like I was sucking on a lime. "Just perhaps be a little more careful when your mother's around? You don't want to give her the wrong idea."

"No, we wouldn't want that," Crispin nodded pleasantly. "I'll endeavor not to sound like I'm flirting when my mother's apt to hear, Darling."

"Oh, is that what you think you're doing?" Because there was certainly nothing flirtatious about that last sentence.

"Of course." He sounded surprised that I'd even question it. "You're the light of my life, Darling. I thought you knew that."

"Funny way you have of showing it," I said, and rolled my

eyes. Crispin smirked and opened his mouth for another volley, but—

"I wonder how the police did on their room search this morning?" Christopher mused, probably in an effort to change the subject. What it did, was cause Crispin to abandon me in favor of Christopher, and make Aunt Roz take an interest in the conversation, which she had hitherto watched with mild amusement.

"Room search? Whatever do you mean, Christopher?"

"Oh," Christopher said, with a guilty sort of wriggle, "I forgot you didn't know. Tom told me yesterday—Detective Sergeant Gardiner—that they were going to search all our rooms this morning."

Aunt Roz pulled her brows together, while Crispin arched his. "Surely that was before Darling here handed Tom," his voice lingered on the name, "her love note last night?"

Aunt Roz's brows arched this time, too. "Pippa? Something you'd like to tell me?"

"St George," I said, with emphasis, "is making a joke. It wasn't a love note."

"Of course it wasn't," Crispin scoffed. "Nor was it your movements for any given time. You would have told those to Pendennis during the interview yesterday, and the other detective would have taken them down. Fletcher. Fletchley. Whatever his name is."

"Finchley," Christopher said, from where he had fallen into another chair and was looking quite as boneless as Crispin had earlier. "And you're a bit too smart for your own good, Crispin. What do you think it was, if not a love note or Pippa's movements?"

Crispin glanced at him, and then at me. "I have no idea. But if I were to guess, something you found in the bottom of your weekender bag, that someone else had put there, and that would help the police in their duty. Something like, say, the notes Simon Grimsby took while he was digging up dirt on all and sundry?"

Christopher was right: Crispin really was too smart for his own good, or at least for mine. "Fine. It might have been something very much like that."

"Pertaining to," his voice made quotes around the words as he repeated what I'd said last night, "—'all three of you.' Who would the third be, I wonder? Perhaps Cousin Francis?"

"Or perhaps you," I said sourly. And added, before he could question whether it really had been him, "It doesn't matter. Scotland Yard has the information now, and from what I could tell, there was nothing there to implicate any of us in either murder."

He looked at me for a second. Then— "I wasn't aware that Grandfather's death had been ruled a murder."

"It hasn't," Aunt Roz said, "as far as I know. For now, we can hope that he died naturally, in his sleep, of old age and too much excitement."

It was a lovely thought, but personally I figured it was probably too much to hope for. And given the look that passed between Christopher and his cousin, I rather thought that they both felt the same way about it that I did.

You will have noticed, I'm sure, that no one present questioned Crispin's assertion that Grimsby had been digging up dirt on everyone in the family. No one questioned the idea that he might have had notes about us all, either. As for the fact that Scotland Yard was now in possession of the notes, it didn't seem to inordinately discomfit anyone present. I wondered whether that meant that none of us was guilty, or whether Crispin had simply taken my word for it that the notes had been harmless.

"I guess I'll go wash up before luncheon," he said, and unwound himself from the armchair.

"Capital idea," Christopher told him, and did the same. "Care to accompany me upstairs, Pippa?"

"I would be delighted," I said, and took the hand he offered, and let him pull me to my feet. "Aunt Roslyn?"

"I'll stay down here, dear. I'll see you all for lunch."

The boys bowed, and I dropped a curtsey, and we headed out and up, leaving Aunt Roz in the library to ponder the brevity of life, much like Hamlet with Yorick's skull.

AT THE TOP of the stairs, we sent Crispin off to the east wing to effect his toilette, while Christopher came with me. He didn't say it, but I knew it was so that he could try on the cloche hat Hugh the footman had taken up to my room. Christopher hadn't been able to try on a lady's hat in the middle of the millinery department of Style & Gerrish, of course, so this was the first time he'd have a chance to see how it looked on him. While he preened in front of the mirror, turning this way and that, I slipped out of the stained blouse I'd been wearing since breakfast, and into the new one we'd bought in Salisbury to match my existing skirt. The entirely new outfit could wait until tomorrow.

"Very becoming," Christopher said, meeting my eyes in the mirror when I stepped up next to him to see how I looked.

I nodded. "The violets really bring out your eyes. Of course, I'm sure you knew they would."

He smirked. "I was talking about your new blouse, Pippa, but thank you."

"Oh." I examined myself in the mirror. "You don't think it's a bit too demure?"

It was yellow with small green dots, with a bow at the neck, pleats on the shoulders, and long sleeves that ended in narrow cuffs. I could imagine myself having worn something very much like it when I was twelve or fourteen.

But Christopher shook his head. "It's very becoming. And the cut is elegant. You look lovely."

"If you say so." I turned away from the mirror again. "I suppose I'd better keep your cloche in my room until we get back to London." And there as well, actually. "It wouldn't be good for the police to find it in your room when they do their search."

"The police already know," Christopher said, plucking the cloche from his head. "Or at least Tom does, so I assume the rest of them do, as well. I'm more concerned with the servants."

And so, perhaps, he should be, given how easily the Sutherland House servants had gossiped with Grimsby. "Just leave it on the stand," I said. "Would you like me to come with you to your room, or are you just going to wash your hands in the basin and go downstairs as you are?"

"Is there something wrong with the way I am?"

"Nothing at all," I assured him. "Everything about you is exactly as it should be."

There were no ink stains on his sleeves, and he looked perfectly like a young gentleman at his leisure in the countryside, in plus fours and a belted sports coat and a perfectly knotted tie.

"I'm sorry I didn't get the chance to tell you about Grimsby's notes last night," I added. "I came to your room to show them to you, but then Tom Gardiner was still there, and I couldn't not hand them over when he realized I had them..."

"Of course not, Pippa." Christopher poured water from the jug into the basin and dipped his hands in. "I would have liked to have seen what you found, but I agree. With the situation you walked in on, there was nothing else you could do."

"What kind of situation was it?"

We hadn't had a chance to confer at all, all morning long. Aunt Roz and Aunt Charlotte and Crispin, or some combination of the three of them, had been dogging our steps every minute of today so far.

Until now, but at this point we hadn't the time to cover it all before the meal gong.

"Tom and I were standing at the top of the stairs," Christopher said, drying his hands on the towel that hung next to the basin, "when Francis and Crispin started up, looking like either one of them could tip over backwards and fall to his death at any moment. Crispin was drunk as a lord, and Francis..." He hesitated.

"Francis had indulged in something that wasn't alcohol," I agreed. "Did you see his eyes? His pupils were no bigger than pinpricks."

Christopher nodded. "Tom was supposed to be on his way down, and I was going to my room, but he came with me to help me get them both to their doors. Crispin had drunk enough that he was unsteady on his feet, and I guess Tom recognizes illegal intoxication when he sees it, because he was trying to get Francis to talk to him about what was going on."

"At least Crispin only had to make it up the stairs and down the hall to find his bed," I said. "Grimsby's notes included a story about him wrapping a Ballot 2 LTS—that must have been the car before the Hispano-Suiza?"

I've never had more than a passing interest in motorcars. They're fine as transportation, but I don't notice them otherwise. Christopher nodded.

"—around a light pole in the West End."

"Good Lord." He looked at me, wide-eyed. "How did I miss hearing about that?"

"He walked away in one piece and with barely any injuries.

The consequence of being so drunk his body was limp upon impact, I assume." I shrugged. "The staff at Sutherland House didn't hold back when it came time to telling Grimsby anecdotes about St George. If you have a couple of hours, I'll share them with you."

He arched his brows. "It'll take that long?"

"At least." Or perhaps not. But if we wanted time to discuss everything properly, then yes.

"Some other time, then," Christopher said. "Maybe on the train home. We'll need something to talk about."

"If we ever get out of here."

"We'll get out of here," Christopher said. "Surely it can't take that long to find out who of a very limited cast of characters could have shot the valet?"

"You wouldn't think so." I headed for the door. "Luncheon, then?"

"After you," Christopher said, and held the door.

SIXTEEN

"How about a walk?" I asked Christopher after luncheon was concluded.

We had made polite conversation over cold meats and salads in the dining room. Crispin had complimented my new blouse, still using the name his mother didn't want him to use, and she had frowned at him when he did it, but without saying anything.

"You're born in June, St George," I had asked, "aren't you?"

He nodded. "Yes, Darling. Are you planning to throw me a party?" He smirked.

"I hardly think any party I would throw could compare to what you're used to," I answered, which I admit wasn't a very good answer, even if it was true. By that point, I regretted asking and wasn't sure why I had.

Part of my mind had been on Grimsby's notes, and how Crispin's birth date, unlike mine or Christopher's, had been circled, with an LM? next to it. Clearly there was something about the date, or about Crispin's birth, that had caught Grimsby's attention, but I had no idea what it was, or even how to form the question to find out.

"Can you think of anyone with the initials L.M.?" I asked Christopher.

He thought about it. "Maybe Langston Mariner? A chap I knew at Eton? You wouldn't know him, though, I don't think."

"Laetitia Marsden," Crispin said with a smirk. It was a sort of self-satisfied smirk, and when I recognized the name from Grimsby's dossier, I realized why. "You know Laetitia, don't you, Darling?"

"Not the way you do, I'm quite sure," I answered. He had a point, though. Both in that I knew her, or knew of her—her reputation was quite as fast as his was—and that she might be a viable owner of the initials. She was clearly associated with Crispin in some way. Hard to say what his birth or birth date might have had to do with it, but there was at least a connection there.

"There's Doctor Meadows down in the village," Aunt Roz said. "His first name is Lionel, I believe."

"The old gentleman who was here Saturday night?"

She nodded. "He's been the local doctor for thirty years or more, I'd say."

"The late duke didn't want a specialist from Harley Street?" That seemed like something I would have expected from the Duke of Sutherland. Only the best.

"Henry trusted Doctor Meadows," Aunt Charlotte said distantly. "He'd known Doctor Meadows's father back in the day, and continued to rely on the son when the father passed on the practice."

"So Doctor Meadows's father was a doctor, too?"

Aunt Charlotte nodded. "There has been a Doctor Meadows in Little Sutherland for a very long time. Lionel

Meadows delivered Crispin, and his father delivered Harold and Herbert. Before that, the Meadows women were midwives, I believe."

"Interesting," I said, with a look at Crispin. He made a face. I guess the idea of having been delivered didn't appeal to him. "Thank you."

"If you need to talk to Laetitia, Darling," Crispin said with a smirk, "let me know and I'll be happy to get in touch."

No doubt. "Don't put yourself out, St George. Although, of course, far be it from me to stand in your way if you'd like to see any of your previous conquests again."

"I don't know that I'd call Laetitia Marsden a conquest, Darling. It was more that she conquered me, really—"

"Enough!" Aunt Charlotte's voice snapped like a whip, and the look she directed at her only son could have pinned his ears to the wall. "This is totally inappropriate conversation for the luncheon table, and in front of your mother and your aunt, not to mention an unmarried female relative. Keep it to the changing rooms at the Club, Crispin!"

Crispin flushed, a wave of hot pink staining his cheeks and the tips of his ears. "Yes, Mother."

It was a quiet meal after that. Aunt Charlotte engaged Aunt Roz in discussion about the funeral arrangements for the late duke, and then Crispin excused himself a minute later. He didn't wait for permission to leave, just pushed his chair back, tossed his napkin on the table, said, "Excuse me," in a half-choked voice, and strode out. Nobody responded. I kept my eyes on my plate, and so did Christopher. I think Aunt Charlotte might have given a sort of regal nod, but I didn't lift my head far enough to see. Crispin kept his composure out of the room and up the stairs, but after about thirty seconds, we could hear a slam that reverberated from above, heavy enough that a couple of the lighter pictures on the wall did a shimmy. I deduced Crispin had closed his door with enough force to rattle the windows.

"Temper," I murmured to Christopher.

He nodded. "Always has. Comes from being the youngest and smallest, I imagine."

"He isn't any smaller than you."

"Not now. But until you came, and we all grew up, he was always the smallest. And he's still the youngest."

He was. Not that there was anything any of us could do about that. You're born when you're born, after all.

Anyway, thus it was that after luncheon I asked whether Christopher would like to get out of the house for a bit, and we set off down the driveway towards the village.

I had an ulterior motive, of course. In fact, I had several. I wanted to get out of the Hall, because for all its size, Crispin's bad humor hung like a storm-cloud over all of it, creeping down my spine and making me jumpy, waiting for the next bout of thunder and lightning. I wanted time to tell Christopher about Grimsby's notes. And I wanted an opportunity to talk to Doctor Meadows, if I could finagle one.

Langston Mariner from Eton wasn't likely to have had anything to do with Grimsby and the notes. If Christopher had known him, Crispin probably had, too, but I hadn't heard his name before today, so he wasn't likely to be significant in any way. And while Laetitia Marsden might have been significant to Crispin—or not—I doubted she had anything to do with his birthday, or birth date, or birth.

The use of initials did make a little more sense in her case, admittedly. She was already mentioned in the dossier with her full name, so it was reasonable that Grimsby might refer to her again by her initials. But beyond that, I couldn't fit her logically into the narrative.

But Lionel Meadows, the doctor who had delivered Crispin on June 5th almost twenty-three years ago, he might be important. And so I had orchestrated the walk to the village partly for fresh air, partly for private conversation, and partly because I thought there was a chance we might be able to beard Doctor Meadows in his den.

On the way there, I regaled Christopher with the information from the notebook. "He followed you around London for days, Christopher! Watched you shop and take tea and buy food and clothes. He followed you to Lady Austin's drag ball last month, and watched you leave with Tom Gardiner. I assume it was Tom Gardiner you left with?"

Christopher nodded, his cheeks almost as pink as his cousin's had been after Aunt Charlotte's reprimand earlier.

"Grimsby didn't seem to have figured out who he was. Or if he did, he didn't mention it. Maybe it wasn't important. Your grandfather wanted information about you, after all."

"And got it," Christopher growled. "I can't believe the old man sent his valet to spy on all of us. Not just that he'd do it in the first place, but that he'd give the job to one of the servants! Didn't he know how they talk?"

"I'm sure he did," I said, tucking my hand a little tighter through his arm as we made our way down along the edge of the road to the village. The road was narrow, and bordered by ditches, and the surface was uneven. "But I imagine he didn't feel like he had a choice. He couldn't get around to do it himself, and I can't imagine he'd ask a family member. You can't tell me St George, if he'd been tasked with it, wouldn't have made up horrible things about both of us. Even if only for the fun of the thing."

"I can't imagine he could have come up with anything worse than Grimsby did," Christopher said, and I shook my head.

"About you, perhaps. The truth is already damning enough there, I suppose. Although Grimsby didn't share that part with your grandfather, did he?"

"Only because he was hoping to profit from it," Christopher said darkly, which of course was true.

"At any rate, I'm sure St George would have delighted in making up horror-stories about me. If it had been up to him, I would be hiding horns under my hair and a forked tail under my skirt. Cloven hooves in my shoes, too, probably." I glanced down at them, scuffing along the dirt road.

"He's just jealous," Christopher said, and I turned to him, my eyes wide.

He gave me the same wide-eyed look back. "You didn't realize that? Of course he is, Pippa. Until you came along, he and I were playmates. You can't imagine that Aunt Charlotte would have let him play with the village children?"

Well, no. Of course not. That would be far beneath the dignity of the heir to the Sutherlands.

"Francis and Robert were older and had gone off to school, so it was just him and me left. Until you came along, and suddenly I had a sister who lived with me and went with me everywhere. You took his place."

"I had no idea," I said, as our shared history realigned itself in my head. "Now I feel terrible."

"Don't." He glanced at me. "You didn't do anything wrong, Pippa. You were perfectly happy to include him. You just wanted to be accepted. He was mean to you almost from the start. None of it was your fault."

"Still. If I had realized it was because he felt left out, I would have endeavored to include him more."

"That's kind," Christopher said, "but it was a long time ago. We're adults now, and he still takes every opportunity to annoy you."

He did. And speaking of— "That was almost painful at lunch, wasn't it? I know he was being his usual boorish self, but his mother didn't have to slap him down like that."

"He deserved it," Christopher said.

"He deserved something. But maybe not that. Actually striking him across the face might have been less upsetting. And anyway, *I* should have been the one to do it. I was the one he was trying to get a rise out of."

"As usual," Christopher said. "He does a beautiful job of getting under your skin."

"I know he does." I grimaced. "I wish I could stop rising to the bait. He just seems to know exactly what to say to annoy me the most. Especially now, when I'm at my limit after having to deal with him for three days straight. I'm usually better at keeping my temper."

Christopher, wisely, refrained from confirming or denying that.

"It'll be over soon," he said instead, soothingly. "I guess Laetitia Marsden was one of the girls Grimsby found in his research?"

I nodded. "Along with the three you told Tom about the other night, and half a dozen others. Including one who showed up at Sutherland House holding a baby."

His eyes widened. "Not really?"

"Really. She isn't Mrs. Crispin Astley, or more accurately, Viscountess St George, at this point, though, so I assume the claim was dubious. But that happened."

"Good Lord," Christopher said. "Any idea who she was?"

"The dossier didn't say. Not an heiress, socialite, or Bright Young Person, I assume, or we'd probably have heard."

"So he'd been slumming," Christopher said, and I winced.

"I'm not sure you ought to put it like that."

He glanced at me. "How else would you put it? He's Lord

St George. And she must have been a shop-girl or a waitress or —God forbid—a prostitute. The sort of woman who can be hushed up."

"Surely he wouldn't frequent prostitutes? Not if he can have any socialite he wants?"

"Can he, though?"

Couldn't he? There was the girl he wanted to marry, I suppose, but she couldn't be an heiress or socialite, or his parents would surely have approved of her. And other than that...

"There was a long list of women in the dossier that he's had some sort of relations with. He shouldn't have to visit brothels to have his needs met."

Christopher shrugged. "Was there anything in Grimsby's notes other than women? You mentioned a car accident?"

"Drunk in charge," I nodded. "He crashed a car into a light pole somewhere in the West End. And walked away laughing, apparently. He destroyed one of the rooms in Sutherland House when he came home drunk and angry. He's showed up without his wallet, and without his cufflinks, and without all his clothes on. I assume he must have brought some of these women to Sutherland House, too, for the staff to know about them."

"So he's a cad and a bounder and a few other of those old-fashioned words."

I nodded. "Other than that—" And it was plenty, really, "the only interesting thing was the circle and the initials around his birthdate."

"So we're walking to the village to see if Doctor Meadows is available."

"Among other things," I said, rather pleased that he'd figured it out on his own. "I also wanted to get out of the house for a bit, and to have a chance to talk to you about Grimsby's notes."

"And now we've done both."

Indeed. "As I told Tom Gardiner last night, there really wasn't much in the notes that's likely to be helpful. A lot of information about St George's misdeeds. You and me going about life in London, shopping and taking tea and things like that. Nothing very damning in any of it. Tom already knew about Kitty, and it's not like St George is keeping it a secret, how thoroughly wicked his behavior is."

Christopher shook his head, just as the village came into view below us. The vista of Wiltshire opened up, with rolling fields to the left and right. We had made it to the other side of the copse of trees we could see from the Hall, and now the Hall was visible in its turn from the bend in the road. The afternoon sun shone on the warm stone of the walls and made the many windows reflect glints of light. A small figure in black moved across the courtyard past the fountain, perhaps Tidwell or one of the footmen or, if they'd taken to dressing in mourning for the late duke, Francis or Crispin.

The next second there was a loud sound, and something slapped hard against my arm.

"Ow," I said, putting my hand to it.

The second after that, Christopher had tackled me, and I was rolling down the incline into the ditch on the side of the road, shrieking.

"Sorry," Christopher said a minute later, when we had taken stock of ourselves and each other. "So sorry."

We were still sitting at the bottom of the ditch, and he was apologizing profusely. "Sorry. I thought you'd been hit."

"I'm not sure I wasn't hit," I told him, eyeing the blood seeping out of my arm and into the tweed of my jacket. For a second, before my head started swimming and I had to look away. "That was a gunshot, wasn't it?"

"It sounded like one," Christopher said grimly. "Then, when you said *Ow* and grabbed your arm, I thought you'd been hit. Or I didn't think at all, I guess. I just wanted you out of the way. So I pitched you into the ditch."

"I appreciate the quick thinking." Even if there hadn't been another shot. There might have been one if we'd stayed on the road, visible.

"Someone shot at us," Christopher said.

"I think you're right."

"Do you suppose they'll come to see whether we're dead?"

They might. Although— "There was only one shot, so I'm sure they—whoever they are—realize that at most, one of us is dead. But it might be a good idea if we move from here."

"Where do you want to go?" Christopher asked. "Back to the Hall? Or down to the village?"

Back to the Hall held very little appeal, when there was someone there taking potshots at people. Although eventually it couldn't be avoided, I assumed. We lived there for now.

But also for now— "The village. It's a perfect opportunity to visit Doctor Meadows. And while I talk to him and have my wound bandaged, you can ring up the Hall and arrange to have someone fetch us."

"Can you make it to the village?" Christopher sounded concerned.

"I'm fine," I said. "It's just a scratch."

It smarted quite a bit, to be honest, and bled more than I liked, but I didn't think I was in any danger of succumbing to the vapors between here and the village. It was my arm that had been hit, not my leg, which made everything easier. I'd had childhood injuries—scraped knees and the like—that had been almost as bad as this. "We could try to wrap it with something, I suppose."

"I'm fresh out of bandages," Christopher said, and reached for his collar, "but I'll sacrifice my tie, if that'll suit."

"I'm sure it'll be fine. And you have a clean handkerchief, I'm sure."

"Naturally." He whipped it out, fashioned it into a pad, and wrapped the tie around my upper arm twice to hold the folded square of cotton in place. "It would be easier without the jacket, but since we still have a bit of walking to do, it'll be better if you keep it on."

I nodded. "Let's follow the ditch for a while before we climb back up on the road. I don't fancy another bullet, to the chest this time."

"Suits me," Christopher said. "I'm dressed for it."

He was, in plus fours and sturdy walking shoes. I was a bit less so, but I managed to muddle along just fine until the road began to descend and we were no longer in the direct line of fire from the Hall. At that point, Christopher boosted me back up onto the road, and we descended into the village in the approved way.

I kept an ear out for the sound of an engine from behind us, in the event someone from the Hall—the shooter, or someone else—had decided to take one of the motorcars out to see what the shot was about. But we made it all the way into Little Sutherland without being overtaken by anyone, and Christopher nudged me down the High Street to the right. "The doctor is this way, if I recall."

"You've been here before?"

"To the village, many times. To the infirmary, once that I can recall." He led me along the street with my (good) arm in a gentle grip. "I broke my arm when I was seven or eight, falling out of one of the apple trees in the orchard. We were playing Robin Hood, as I recall, and the Sheriff of Nottingham was throwing these hard, little winter apples at me. It was before your time."

"Let me guess. St George was the Sheriff of Nottingham and it was his fault?"

"Obviously," Christopher said. "We played together rather a lot before you came along."

"Poor Crispin." Who had lost his playmate on my arrival.

"Poor me, rather. It was my arm that broke." Christopher shot me a look. "Why is it that you can say his name to me but you can't bear to say it to him?"

I shrugged, and immediately regretted it when my arm throbbed. "Too familiar, I suppose. He seems to have a problem wrapping his tongue around mine, too. At least without making a mockery of it."

Christopher made a face.

"And I don't use it often," I added. "I've been calling him St George for years, long before it became his title, just so I could avoid using his first name. But I think..."

I hesitated. But then Christopher gave me an encouraging nod, so I continued. "I think, after this weekend—between the information in the dossier, and that fight with his father we overheard, and what happened over luncheon, and now what you told me about growing up together—I feel bad for him. So it's easier to think of him as a poor little boy and use his first name."

"He'd hate that," Christopher said, which was undoubtedly true, and came to a halt outside one of the many pretty little stone cottages that lined the High Street. "Here we are." He indicated the bright red door of the village surgery. "Are you ready?"

"The sooner, the better," I answered. "This wound isn't going to suture itself."

"I suppose not." Christopher knocked, and then turned the knob. The door opened into a dim waiting room. He nudged me over the threshold and followed me in, shutting the door behind us.

SEVENTEEN

FIVE MINUTES LATER, I was stripped to just my skirt and camisole, sitting in the doctor's surgery while he treated the wound on my arm. Christopher was left to cool his heels in the waiting room, not because he hadn't seen me in my camisole before, but because we didn't want to shock the doctor unduly by insisting that he be let in. Doctor Meadows was already concerned enough over the wound itself. "And you say you think it was a bullet?" he asked worriedly as he wiped at it.

"I'm fairly certain it was a bullet," I answered. "We heard what sounded like a shot, and then something slapped my arm. Doesn't it look like a bullet wound?"

I peered down at it, and felt my head swim, so I looked away again.

"It looks like something came close enough to gouge a furrow through your upper arm," the doctor said. "It could very well have been a bullet."

He finished cleaning it—I unclenched my teeth—and began applying salve to it. After the initial sting, the liniment spread a soothing kind of coolness across the wound.

"Quite a lot of things going on up at the Hall this weekend," Doctor Meadows commented.

"Quite a lot," I agreed. "Grimsby's murder, of course, and I suppose you heard that Scotland Yard suspects the old duke may have been killed, too?"

I wasn't trying to rub salt in the wound—pun totally intended—by bringing up Doctor Meadows's failure to accurately diagnose the late duke's cause of death, but a shadow crossed his face nonetheless. "I did hear that that might be the case. Doctor Curtis, the police surgeon, did the autopsy yesterday evening, while I was present—he was my patient, after all—and it looks like it might have been an overdose of his heart medication. Of course, the results of that are indistinguishable from any other heart event..."

He looked into the air for a moment before he recalled himself to the task at hand, "—but analysis of the stomach content showed that such may have been the case."

"That's terrible," I said warmly. "It must be very difficult for you. I know you were the Sutherland family doctor for a long time."

"Many years." He wandered to the cabinet by the wall for the supplies he'd need for the next part of the process.

"And your father before you, I hear."

He nodded. "Many years."

"Aunt Charlotte—the new Duchess of Sutherland—said that you were the one who delivered Crispin when he was born twenty-three years ago."

"Indeed." He turned, hands full of gauze and bandages, and more lively now that he had been reminded of something he had done right. "Lady Charlotte—Her Grace now—went into labor several weeks earlier than expected. We were all very worried that there would be something wrong with the baby."

I weighed the (clearly God-given) opportunity to point out

all the things that were wrong with Crispin, but since he wasn't present to hear them, I decided there was no reason to exert myself. Of course, I still gave myself a mental pat on the back for having the strength to abstain.

Instead, I asked, "You mean Crispin was—" I made quotation marks in the air, "premature?"

In case you're unaware of the connotations, 'premature' in a certain tone of voice is a euphemism for a baby born seven or eight months after a wedding, when the family doesn't want there to be any question about the baby's legitimacy or the fact that its parents were legally wed when it was conceived. It's code for two people having created a baby outside of wedlock, but lying about it when the baby's born.

But the doctor shook his head. "Oh, no. Nothing like that. Lady Charlotte and Lord Harold—His and Her Grace—had been married for several years by the time young Crispin came along. In fact, they'd been married for long enough that there had been some speculation about an issue on his or her part. It's usually her part, of course, at least according to the husband's family, but in this case I rather fancy..."

He trailed off again, before he recalled himself. "At any rate, there was no question about the baby being the legitimate offspring of the Duke and Duchess. He's very clearly a Sutherland down to his bones."

Yes, he was. He had his mother's hair and eyes, but Crispin's face was all Sutherland, from the pointed chin and high cheekbones to the exaggerated cupid's bow of his mouth.

"So there was nothing unusual about it?"

The doctor looked up from where he was winding bandages around my arm. "What do you mean, unusual?"

Well... what I meant was something unusual in the sense that it would have caught Grimsby's attention enough to have him make a note of it in his blackmail log. But of course I couldn't say that. It wouldn't make sense, for one thing, and for another, we probably wanted to keep Grimsby's blackmail attempts secret.

So I said, "Nothing in particular. Just... unusual."

"No," Doctor Meadows said. "Not aside from the fact that he came about three weeks earlier than he should have. Lady Charlotte went into labor on a Friday afternoon. The baby was born by late evening. It didn't take long. Being premature, he was small."

"Of course. So nothing unusual happened?"

"Nothing out of the ordinary." Doctor Meadows fastened the last of the bandage. "There you are. Good as new."

Not quite that, but at least good enough to go on with. "How much do I owe you?"

"I'll settle the bill with the Hall," Doctor Meadows said.

"I don't live at Sutherland Hall full time."

"If the Hall has a problem, I'll contact Lady Roslyn," Doctor Meadows said.

There didn't seem any point in arguing, so I thanked him and put my blouse and jacket back on before I went out to the waiting room where Christopher, as it turned out, was pacing. When I came through the door, he stopped, turned, and stared. "Are you all right?"

"Fine," I said. "It was really not a very big wound."

"It bled a lot."

It had bled a lot. "The doctor said it should heal just fine. You'll have to carry my bag when we go back to London, though. I'm not supposed to lift anything heavy for the next week, to keep it from opening back up."

"Hopefully we'll be back in London sometime in the next week," Christopher said grimly.

"I'm sure we will be. You said it yourself. How long can it

take to determine who of a fairly small group of people committed two murders?"

"After this afternoon, I'm more worried about being murdered before I can get there," Christopher said.

Ah. Yes, that was a consideration now. Or had become one.

"Did you call for one of the motorcars to pick us up?"

Christopher nodded. "Someone should be here shortly."

"Who did you speak to? Did you tell whoever it was what had happened?"

"It was Tidwell," Christopher said, "and I didn't. I asked him to fetch Tom Gardiner to the phone, and I told *him* what had happened."

Wonderful. "Hopefully he'll have the rifle found and the shooter apprehended before we get back up there."

"I wouldn't count on it," Christopher said. He was remarkably grim this afternoon, but then it isn't every day someone takes potshots at us. "Whoever is doing all this, has gotten away with it so far."

True. "Let's go outside and wait." I took his arm and led him towards the door. "It smells like antiseptic in here."

And blood, although that might have been in my imagination. My arm smarted, and by now the events of earlier had caught up with me, too, and I had realized just how close I'd come to a much more serious injury.

Not to mention the possibility of a fatal one, although there are quite a few inches between the outer edge of my arm and the middle of my chest, or for that matter my forehead. So maybe whoever it was hadn't meant to fatally injure. Perhaps it had just been a warning. Albeit for what, I had no idea.

"Have you been doing anything you haven't told me about?" Christopher asked when I floated this idea past him. He squinted suspiciously at me when he asked. It could have been the bright afternoon sun on the High Street, but more likely it was his state of mind.

I shook my head. "Truly not. You know everything I've done since I got here."

"Then I can't think of any reason why anyone would want to kill you. You don't know who the murderer is, do you?"

"Absolutely not."

"You've thought about it, of course."

I nodded. "Of course. Haven't you?"

"Of course."

"Who do you think it is?"

"I can't imagine," Christopher said. And added, pensively, "Or I don't want to."

I nodded, since I could understand that. "I'll tell you what I'm thinking, if you'd like. If you promise you won't get upset."

He squinted at me. "If there's something you think I might be upset about, perhaps it would be better if you didn't tell me?"

"I imagine it would be hard for you not to be upset," I said honestly. "They're all your relatives. Every last one of them."

"And Grandfather was my family, too, even if I didn't like him very much. It was fine for as long we thought he had died a natural death. When no one had to be guilty of his murder. Now..." He shook his head. "Are you sure it couldn't be one of the servants?"

"Of course I'm not sure," I said, shading my eyes with my good hand. I thought I had seen the sun glint off a piece of metal up the road, but when I looked, there was no motorcar coming. "From what Tom said, all the maids and footmen are alibied, but it could have been Tidwell or Mrs. Mason or Cook or, I assume, Wilkins, or maybe one of the grooms..."

Christopher nodded. "But?"

"But I wouldn't know about them. I've been thinking about the above-stairs."

He huffed out a breath. "Fine. Tell me."

"Well, of all of us, you have a pretty good motive for killing Grimsby, but as far as I know, you had no motive whatsoever for killing your grandfather. Of course, it's possible they're wrong and he wasn't murdered…"

"Did the doctor say that?"

"He said that the effects of too much heart medication looks like heart failure. But apparently there was too much heart medication in his stomach. Then again, I suppose that could have been an honest mistake. He might have felt poorly after all the excitement and decided to dose himself."

"Not impossible," Christopher agreed.

"But for the sake of argument… Francis had a good motive for killing both of them, if your grandfather threatened to withhold the drugs Francis relies on. He doesn't have an alibi, at least not for the shooting."

Christopher nodded, his jaw tight.

"Of course, we don't know that your grandfather did that, so Francis might have had no motive whatsoever. Your mother would kill for either you or Francis—"

"Or you," Christopher said.

"—but I don't think she would have killed your grandfather. Then again, I feel like there's still a question of whether or not he was murdered."

Christopher nodded.

"She has no alibi for Grimsby's murder. Not if your father was asleep by then. Or if they were in it together."

"My mother wouldn't try to shoot you, though," Christopher said.

No, she wouldn't. And just in case the aim had been off and Christopher was the intended victim, it was even less likely that Aunt Roz was behind it. So this was either someone else, not the murderer of the other two, or the reason was different.

"I have no idea what your father's motive would be, but if he and your mother were in it together, it was likely because of Francis."

Christopher nodded.

"I have no idea about Aunt Charlotte or Uncle Harold. Crispin didn't mention them, nor did Tom. We could ask him, and see if there was anything in Grimsby's notes he'd be willing to share. But without that, there's nothing I can come up with but wild guesses."

Christopher nodded.

"They don't share a bedchamber, though, so either of them could have gone down to the hedge maze and shot Grimsby, I think. Even if I have no idea why they would."

I took a breath. "And then there's St George."

"Tell me," Christopher said.

"He had opportunity to kill both of them. He was alone in his room when we went down to the conservatory Saturday night—or at least I assume he was—and he could have gone out to the maze after we left. Or could already be there, I suppose, if he'd gone out and left his light on. We didn't hear any noises from inside his room that night. Or at least I didn't. Did you?"

"I don't think so," Christopher said. "The argument with Uncle Harold was earlier in the evening."

And we both clearly remembered that. "Like everyone else in the house, he knew where to find the gun and ammunition. And on Saturday afternoon, he was in the duchess's passage, listening to everyone's conversations. It would have been easy for him to go through the hidden door into his grandfather's room and kill him. He wouldn't even have to venture into the hallway to do it."

Christopher nodded thoughtfully. "That's true, of course. But why would he?"

"Well," I said apologetically, "he's the Viscount St George now, isn't he?"

Christopher's eyes widened. "You think he killed Grandfather for the title? But..." He shook his head. "No, Pippa. Grandfather was on his way out already, surely? He was almost ninety. Crispin would have become viscount in a year or two anyway."

"Yes," I said, "but the girl he wants to marry might have married someone else by then. With your grandfather dead, he's one step closer to the title, and maybe a step closer to getting what he wants, as well."

Christopher was silent for a few seconds. "It's possible, I suppose," he said reluctantly.

"Of course it's possible. Maybe that was one of the conversations he overheard while he was lurking in the passage. His father and grandfather discussing how they're not going to let him marry the woman he wants. So he waits until his father leaves the room, and then he pops through the hidden door and kills his grandfather. But Grimsby comes in and sees him. He puts Grimsby off, offers him money, probably—he'll have more of it now that he's the Viscount St George—and then he arranges to meet him in the garden maze at eleven."

Christopher opened his mouth, and I held up a hand to silence the objection I knew was coming. "This would have been after Grimsby arranged to meet you, but there would be more money in meeting Crispin, so it makes sense that Grimsby would ditch the meeting with you over the meeting with him. And it's not like he could come to you and reschedule. How would he explain it?"

"Ye-e-e-s," Christopher said, although he didn't sound overjoyed.

"Problem?"

"Not with the timeline." He shook his head slowly. "No, it all makes sense. He's just not very bloodthirsty, you know?"

"Crispin? He broke your arm when you were eight."

"That was an accident. I'm not sure whether he or I cried more when it happened."

"Perhaps he was just afraid he was going to get in trouble?"

Christopher shrugged, and turned towards the road from the Hall. This time, there was definitely the roar of an engine. A few seconds later, the Hispano-Suiza screeched to a stop in front of the surgery.

Given the car, not to mention the driving style, I had expected to see St George behind the wheel. I was wrong, nor was the figure in the passenger seat the new viscount. Tom Gardiner shot from behind the wheel, and Aunt Roz launched herself from beside him, hurtling across the cobblestones towards us. "Pippa! Pippa, dear! Are you all right?"

I braced myself for impact, but she stopped short of embracing me, which was probably a good thing, as it would have hurt. Instead, she rocked to a stop a foot in front of me and gave my arm an anxious look. "How is it?"

"The doctor says it'll be fine in a week or two," I said. "I might have a scar, but it wasn't a deep wound, so maybe not."

She nodded. Meanwhile, Tom (who had been on the other side of the car, and who had taken the trip across the street a bit slower) had stopped beside Christopher. I sharpened my ears for their conversation, but unfortunately, it turned out to be not much of one.

"Are you all right?" Tom asked.

Christopher nodded.

A moment passed in silence, then Tom gave him a pat on the shoulder and turned to me. "Miss Darling."

"Pippa," I said, "please."

He nodded and looked at my arm. "We'll need a complete statement from both of you once we get you back to the Hall. Kit wasn't terribly coherent on the phone."

He gave Christopher a sort of rueful look. I was glad to hear it, actually, because who wants their best friend to be calm and collected after one's almost been shot?

"But I'll take the broad strokes now," Tom added, "once we get you into the car."

He offered me his arm, which I took, and let him lead me across the cobblestones to the Hispano-Suiza. "Back or front?"

"I'll sit in the back with her," Aunt Roz said, and slipped into the backseat ahead of me, away from my bandaged arm. "Christopher, dear, you go up front."

Christopher nodded and slipped into the front seat. Tom, meanwhile, made sure the door was shut safely behind me before he walked to the other side of the motorcar and slid back behind the wheel.

"Talk," he said, after throwing the vehicle into gear so we could roll off down the street.

The High Street was too narrow to turn the motorcar around, so we ended up driving almost to the other end of the village and back before we could head back out of Little Sutherland in the direction of the Hall. Meanwhile, the story was quite easy to tell.

"We were on our way down to the village. We had just come out from behind the copse of trees to where we could see the Hall again—"

"And be seen," I interjected.

Christopher nodded. "There was the sound of a shot, and Pippa clapped a hand to her arm and said *Ow!* I looked at her and saw the blood on her arm, and realized what had happened —or at least what I thought had happened—so I pushed her into the ditch and followed myself, just in case there were more shots."

"Quick thinking," Tom said with approval, which turned Christopher faintly pink over the cheekbones.

"Well, it turned out to be useless. There were no more shots. And when we started to talk about it, it turned out that Pippa didn't have a bullet in her arm, after all."

"It was just up here," I said, as the motorcar climbed the hill at a much faster pace than we had come down. "Look, Christopher. There's the Hall. We were... over there somewhere, weren't we?"

Christopher nodded. "See the weeds over there? And how the dirt is stirred up on the edge? That's where we went over."

Tom nodded, slowing the motorcar almost to a crawl. He peered through the windshield and over the side of the car at the road, up at the Hall, and then over his shoulder.

"What are you looking for?" I asked curiously when he seemed to look straight through me.

His eyes focused back on my face. "Every projectile has to go somewhere. If it didn't end up in your arm, it's somewhere else."

Of course. He was looking for the bullet.

"Finch and I'll have to come back and hunt for it." He put his foot down on the gas and the motorcar picked up speed again as the Hall disappeared behind the trees.

"I'll come with you," Christopher said.

Tom shot him a look and seemed to contemplate telling him he couldn't. But instead he simply nodded. "That would be helpful. Thank you."

"It would be my pleasure," Christopher informed him. "I want to find whoever did this just as much as you do."

Beside me, Aunt Roz nodded agreement.

• • •

We drove into the courtyard two minutes later, and burst past Tidwell and into the foyer. "I'll go fetch Finch and talk to Pendennis," Tom told Christopher. "Wait here."

Christopher nodded. Meanwhile, Aunt Roz turned to me. "Let me help you upstairs, Pippa. I'm sure you'd like to change."

I absolutely would. The sleeve of my beautiful new blouse was shredded, and so was the sleeve of my jacket. And while the tweed jacket could perhaps be mended—once the blood had been washed out of it—the blouse was a lost cause. I was pretty sure I had blood in other places, too—I could see it on my hands, and suspected there was some on my face, perhaps even in my hair—and there were the grass stains and dust from the road ground into my skirt and stockings.

I must look a fright, an assessment that was borne out by— who else?—St George, who appeared on top of the stairs like the ghoul he was, just when I looked my worst.

"Goodness, Darling," he drawled, as he descended the staircase with all the regalness of a royal, "don't you look rather the worse for wear? Did you have a tumble somewhere along the way?"

The gaze he flicked onto Christopher and Thomas Gardiner made it clear that he'd used the word 'tumble' in its most suggestive way. That was only until he'd descended far enough to get a look at my arm—or more accurately the blood and the bandage. At that point, all the amused maliciousness dropped off his face like it had been wiped clean with a rag, and his eyes widened.

"What happened?"

"I got shot," I said callously—and a bit inaccurately—and had the pleasure of seeing his face lose whatever color it had had left.

"Shot?"

His eyes flicked from me to Aunt Roz, to Christopher, to Tidwell, and finally to Aunt Charlotte, who had come out of one of the rooms off the foyer, probably at the sound of our voices. I hadn't even realized she was there, until Crispin's eyes fell on something behind me, and I turned my head and saw her standing there.

"Dear me," she said, "that's terrible, Miss Darling. Is there anything I can do?"

"I was just going to take Pippa to her room," Aunt Roz said, snaking an arm around my waist, "and help her clean up and change. Christopher?"

Christopher nodded and fell in behind as Aunt Roz guided me towards the bottom of the stairs. I assume his task was to make sure I didn't topple over on my way up.

"I'm fine," I said irritably—which was probably a sign that I wasn't fine, actually. I'm usually not irritable. But my arm hurt, and I felt grimy, and all the fussing played on my nerves, and St George's expression rubbed me wrong, the way it usually did, even though he actually looked more concerned than happy right now.

"Of course you are, darling." Aunt Roz didn't pay my grumbling any mind whatsoever, just kept pushing me towards the staircase. "Excuse us, Crispin, dear."

She nudged him out of the way, just far enough that we could pass each other without touching. I glanced up as we moved past, expecting some sort of snide remark, but his eyes were fastened on my arm, on the bandage and blood on my sleeve, and his lips were tight. He didn't say a word while we walked by, and then he gave himself a sort of shake and glanced over at Aunt Charlotte. "A libation, Mother?"

Aunt Charlotte must have been lost to her own reverie, because she gave a little start when he addressed her, and had to drag her gaze up from the floor to land on him. When she saw his offered arm, she colored slightly. "Of course, Crispin, dear."

They proceeded towards the doors to the library arm in arm, very decorously. Aunt Roz snorted and renewed her efforts to get me up the stairs.

EIGHTEEN

Christopher left us on the landing, when Tom Gardiner
and Detective Sergeant Finchley came out of the breakfast
room, Tom with a camera in his hand. "Ready to go?" he called
up at Christopher.

Christopher nodded. "I'll see you later, Mother. Pippa." He
started down.

"Be careful," I called after him. "You never know who
might be out there, taking potshots at people."

"If someone takes a potshot at any of us," Tom promised,
"I'll be watching the trajectory of the bullet very carefully."

After a second, he added, more lightly, "You were the one
who was hit, though, Miss Darling. Perhaps you're the one who
should be careful."

I intended to be careful, to be honest. However— "I really
think it could have been either of us. An inch to the right, and I
wouldn't have been hit at all."

"A foot to the left, and you would have had a bullet in the
heart," Christopher reminded me grimly.

"And a foot or two in the other direction, and it would have been you."

He shrugged. "I'll take my chances. I agree with Tom. You're the one who should be careful. Stay with Mother."

He glanced at her. She nodded.

"There's no reason why anyone would want me dead," I told him, although I added, when I saw his mouth open, "but I'll be careful. You be, too. All of you."

They promised they would, and then they headed back out the door to the Hispano-Suiza and the hunt for the bullet, while Aunt Roz propelled me down the hallway past the Duchess's Chamber and towards my room.

"Would you like to take a bath?" she asked as she tugged me along. "Or will a wash-up in the basin and some new clothes do?"

A bath actually sounded lovely, but it involved filling the tub and soaking in it, and getting the bandages wet and having to replace them, so I told her a turn with the basin would be just the thing. "Mostly, I can't wait to get out of these clothes. Christopher was very enthusiastic when he pushed me into the ditch. And the sleeve itches my arm where the blood has dried."

Aunt Roz nodded, guiding me around the corner into the west wing and towards my door. "A bird bath it is, then. I'll help you undress. It'll be difficult for you to move that arm."

It probably would. An exploratory lift from the shoulder sent a stab of pain down to my elbow. "Yes, thank you."

"Don't thank me yet," Aunt Roz said grimly. "This is very upsetting, Pippa. What have you done? Who would want to kill you?"

I had no idea, and said so. "You heard me just now. It might as well have been Christopher."

"It wasn't Christopher," Aunt Roz said and pushed the

door to my room open. She looked around briefly, but when nothing jumped out to harm either of us, she shoved me across the threshold ahead of her. "It was you. You must have done something to someone."

"I can't imagine what. I don't know anything more about these murders than anyone else in the household. Honestly."

"Perhaps you know something you don't know you know," Aunt Roz said, and grabbed the collar of my jacket. "Careful now."

She nudged it down off my shoulders and over my arms. I held my breath when the sleeve dragged over the bandage, hoping it wouldn't dislodge the doctor's handiwork, but the bandage was tight enough, and the rayon of the blouse slippery enough, that the jacket came off with little difficulty and no damage to the wound.

"So far, so good," Aunt Roz said. "Such a shame about your new blouse. It was so becoming to you, too."

"It's fine. Could have been worse." It could have been a bullet embedded in my arm, or my head, or my chest. Or Christopher's. The loss of a blouse, even a brand new one, was minor compared to that.

"It'll have to come over your head," Aunt Roz said, looking at it, "unless you want me to cut it down the middle?"

I glanced at what was left of the sleeve, stiff with blood and with the bottom already cut away by the doctor for easier access to the wound. I had the missing part of the sleeve in the pocket of my jacket, but... "I don't think there's any way to mend rayon, so you might as well finish the job. There's a pair of scissors in the escritoire over there."

Aunt Roz headed that way, and turned around a few seconds later, scissors in hand. And here's where I have to admit that as she approached me with them, with the sharp points aimed at me, my stomach clenched. I didn't think Aunt

Roz was the one who had shot at us—she wouldn't have risked Christopher, and I thought she was rather fond of me, too—but there was just something about having someone come at me with a sharp implement after what had happened, that struck me as profoundly unsettling.

"This will be easier from the back," Aunt Roz said, and walked around me, to where she could grab the bottom of the blouse and apply the scissors to it. "Stand still, dear. I don't want to scratch you by accident."

I froze and held my breath as the scissors made short process of the back of the blouse.

"There we go." Aunt Roz tossed the scissors in the direction of the bed, where they landed on the counterpane with a soft *flump*, and walked around me. "Breathe, Pippa."

I breathed, and continued to do so as she eased the rayon off my shoulders and down my front. "Pity. It was a nice garment."

She tossed it after the scissors, but instead of landing on the bed, the soft fabric fluttered to the floor, short of the goal, with a soft sigh that mirrored my own.

"Oh, well."

Aunt Roz shrugged and unzipped the back of my skirt. "Can you make it out of this on your own?"

I could, and did. I was able to toe the brogues off, and roll down my own stockings, too, one-handed, although I needed help getting the new pair on. Aunt Roz slipped the blue and white afternoon dress back over my head after I had washed the blood off my hands and arms and face—my hair was all right— in the basin, and then she helped me buckle my shoes. "We won't dress for dinner tonight," she told me. "That way you can stay as you are for the rest of the evening. If you need help getting ready for bed later, just let me know."

I said I would. "Listen, Aunt Roz. Do you know anything about St George's... I mean, about Crispin's birth day?"

She blinked. "Crispin's birthday? June 5th, isn't it?"

I nodded.

"No," Aunt Roz said, "I can't say I do. Is something happening that we should know about? A party? It isn't an important year. He's turning twenty-three, isn't he?"

"He is. But I meant his birth day. The day he was born."

"Oh." Aunt Roz dropped down on the edge of the bed, hands in her lap. "No, I can't say I know much about that, either, Pippa. I had a newborn of my own, you know. Christopher was just a few months old. And I had two other small boys, as well, so I had my hands full."

I nodded. Of course she had.

"I remember he came early. By several weeks, as I recall. And Charlotte was very worried. It had taken her several years to get pregnant, and she spent the entire term, from the moment she learned that she was with child until she went into labor, terrified that something would go wrong. I'm not sure she stirred from the grounds the entire eight months. Carrying that baby to term, making sure Harold got his heir, was her sole concern. If anything had happened, I'm not sure she would have survived it."

"But it all went well."

Aunt Roz nodded. "As well as any childbirth ever does. They're a painful, messy business. But I think it was pretty quick, once it started. And he would have been a small baby. That makes it easier."

No doubt. I refrained from contemplating the process too hard.

"We didn't travel here until the next week," Aunt Roz added, "and by then, of course, everything was wonderful.

Charlotte was up and walking, the baby was healthy—*so* tiny, but perfect—and Harold was back from the Continent."

"He wasn't here when his son was born?"

"I'm sure he would have been," Aunt Roz said, "but again, the baby came early."

Right. Of course. "But there wasn't anything unusual about it, that you can remember?"

"Unusual?" She gave me a look. "What sort of unusual?"

When I didn't answer, because I had no idea what sort of thing might have struck Grimsby, she continued. "No. Nothing unusual. Unless you mean that the baby came early and his father wasn't here and his mother was frantic that something would go wrong. None of which turned out to be a problem. He was born healthy, he turned out perfectly fine—"

"That's debatable," I said.

Aunt Roz leveled an amused look at me, but forbore to comment, "—and although Charlotte never did manage to provide a Spare, Crispin made it to his majority in one piece. Harold got his heir, and everything turned out as well as one could hope for."

"So nothing strange about it?"

"No," Aunt Roz said firmly. "What sort of strange?"

I threw subtlety to the wind. "Something that would have struck Grimsby as being out of the ordinary. I saw some of his notes, that he'd taken about people in the family—"

Aunt Roz sucked in a breath and turned pale.

"—and he circled Crispin's birth date and wrote the initials L.M. with a question mark next to it. But I asked the doctor—Lionel Meadows—and he didn't remember anything out of the ordinary."

"Perhaps L.M. is someone else," Aunt Roz said, and her complexion was slowly returning to normal.

"Perhaps. But I asked about it—you were there at the

luncheon table; you heard—and he seemed to be the most likely choice. He was alive at the time, and delivered the baby. He was definitely involved. But he said no, that nothing extraordinary happened."

I brooded for a moment. "Crispin brought up Lady Laetitia Marsden. You know, of the Dorset Marsdens? She was mentioned by name in Grimsby's notes. Maybe it's her."

"St George comes into some of his inheritance on his twenty-fifth birthday," Aunt Roz said. "I know that's two years from now, but perhaps Lady Laetitia is holding out for something like that. And Grimsby saw fit to make note of it."

Perhaps. It made as much sense as anything else. "I don't suppose you know this Eton chap that Christopher mentioned, do you? Langston Mariner?"

Aunt Roz shook her head. "I'm afraid not, Pippa. I hadn't heard his name until Christopher brought it up at lunch."

I nodded. "Me, either. Thank you. For the help and the information."

"It was my pleasure, Pippa, dear." She smiled up at me from the bed. "Did the doctor give you something for the pain? Would you like me to try to find you an aspirin?"

"I'm all right," I said, since the idea of accepting medication from anyone, in a house where someone had, or so it seemed, been killed by an overdose of medication a few days ago, wasn't particularly pleasant.

Again, I didn't really suspect Aunt Roz of wanting to do away with me. But it was better to be safe than sorry, I felt.

"I wouldn't mind a cup of tea," I added. "It must be close to tea-time, surely?"

Aunt Roz sprang to her feet. "Capital idea. Perhaps with something stronger in it. Brandy is good for blood loss."

Is it? "I'm sure that'll be perfectly lovely," I said. "Shall we?"

"Let's." Aunt Roz tucked her hand through my (good) arm and guided me towards the door. "I'm so glad you're in one piece, Pippa. You know I love you like you are my own."

"I know, Aunt Roz," I told her. "I love you like you are my own, too. Christopher is more my brother than anything else, you know."

"Oh, my dear, I'm well aware." She squeezed my arm as she pulled the door open. "If I didn't know, we would have had something to say about your living arrangements, believe me. But we're well aware of how the two of you feel about one another."

"Thank you, Aunt Roz." I sniffed back a wave of emotion that was, most likely, exacerbated by the brush with violent death I had just experienced, as I followed her into the hallway. "Being accepted into your family is the best thing that ever happened to me."

"Dear me," a languid drawl said from across the corridor. It didn't belong to Aunt Roz. "It appears I've arrived at an inopportune time. Again."

"Crispin." Aunt Roz looked taken aback, while I, I'm sure, looked suspicious.

"What are you up to, St George? Eavesdropping again?"

How long had he been leaning against the wall outside my door, exactly? Had he been there when I'd asked Aunt Roz my questions about his birth? Had he heard our thoughts on his relationship, what there might be of it, with Laetitia Marsden, and her possible designs on his inheritance?

We hadn't said anything particularly accusatory, I thought. It had been Christopher who had been on the receiving end of all my speculations on Crispin's guilt earlier. I hadn't mentioned any of that to Aunt Roz, so at least he wouldn't have overheard me practically accusing him of murder.

"Have you been discussing anything worth listening to?" he

asked, uncoiling himself with a rather serpentine movement from the wall. When neither of us said anything to deny or confirm, he added, "I came to see whether you needed help getting downstairs, Darling, since Kit went off to play Cops & Robbers with the detectives, but I see you're in good hands."

"Actually," Aunt Roz said, as Crispin fell into step behind us, "if you don't mind helping Pippa downstairs, Crispin, I'd like to stop off in my own room first."

Neither of them paid any attention to my comment about not needing anyone's help, of course.

"Delighted," Crispin drawled, with an elegant, if abbreviated bow, and appropriated my arm from Aunt Roz when we reached the corner where the west wing met the central portion of the Hall. "Come along, Darling."

He tugged me towards the main staircase while Aunt Roz disappeared into her room.

"You're being ridiculous, St George," I grumbled, even as I allowed myself to be drawn along. "I needn't help getting down the stairs."

"Now, now, Darling." He smirked at me. "If I can behave like a gentleman for long enough to help you, you can act like a lady for long enough to let me."

"A gentleman?" Was that what he thought he was? "Surely that's beyond your ability, St George."

"Do you really think so, Darling?" He looked left and right, up and down, before pulling me determinedly towards the top of the staircase. "This is not the time to antagonize me, you know. It's a long way down, and if you're not careful, my degree of concern might just..." He paused, "—drop."

Drop?

I stopped dead—pardon the pun—at the top of the stairs and twitched my arm out of his hold. "Are you threatening me, St George?"

That left-and-right, up-and-down... had that been to make sure no one was around to see him push me down the stairs? Was that the reason he had come up to my room? He knew I suspected him, and he wanted to eliminate me before I could tell Scotland Yard what I suspected?

His lips curved up. "Would I do such a thing, Darling?"

"I don't know," I said, sticking my chin out, pugnaciously. "Would you?"

The smirk turned into a grin, one that curved his cheeks and made his eyes sparkle. It didn't even look malicious, although I'm sure, somehow, it was. "I swear, Darling, sometimes I worry about you. Truly, I do."

As I blinked up at him—what on earth did *that* mean?—he snagged my arm again and pulled. "Come along, there's a good girl. You can trust me, you know."

I hadn't much choice, of course—he was much stronger than I was—so perforce, I came along. And while my heart tripped a little, none of the rest of me did. We made it safely to the bottom of the staircase and onto the foyer floor. Crispin even kept his hand under my arm until it was time to enter the tea parlor. "After you, Miss Darling." He let go and bowed me in.

"Thank you." I crossed the threshold into the parlor, where Aunt Charlotte was presiding over the teapot in lone majesty.

I eyed the empty room. "I guess Christopher isn't back yet?"

"Not yet," Crispin confirmed, coming in behind me. "And Father and Uncle Herbert rode off to inspect the fences or some such thing."

"Crispin, dear," Aunt Charlotte murmured, in what I supposed was a very gentle admonition to not speak so cavalierly about the estate that would one day be his.

He rolled his eyes. "Yes, Mother."

Aunt Charlotte smiled politely at me. "Tea, Miss Darling?"

"Please," I said. "I don't suppose they went armed, did they?"

Crispin's eyes met mine for a second, startled, before he said, blandly, "Is there any reason they would, Darling? Surely there's no danger of dangerous beasts in the wilds of Wiltshire?"

Of course not. "Just a thought," I said, and reached for the cup of tea Aunt Charlotte had poured just as Crispin did the same. He knocked my hand out of the way, or perhaps I was the one who did it to him. The cup flipped over and splashed hot tea on my fingertips.

"Ow!" I yanked my hand back. Luckily it was the non-injured one, or the movement would have hurt. "What on earth, St George?"

"For God's sake, Darling!" He stuck two fingers in his mouth and sucked the tea off them while Aunt Charlotte stared at the mess on the table. Luckily, the cup hadn't cracked in two. It was hundred-year-old Spode, hand-painted in a puce and gilt floral pattern, circa 1820, and I would have hated to be responsible for its demise. Even if it *was* just as much St George's fault as mine.

"What's wrong with you?" he added, taking the fingers back out of his mouth and wiping them on a napkin while he fixed me with an outraged look. "I was trying to be polite, Miss Darling."

"Well, perhaps that was your problem," I said, snatching the napkin out of his hand and using it to wipe the tea off my own fingers. "You're never polite. How was I supposed to guess you had turned over a new leaf?"

He rolled his eyes. "Humor. Har."

I rolled mine right back. "You're being ridiculous, St

George. It's my left arm that's hurt, not my right. I don't need your help lifting a cup of tea."

"In that case—" He reached down, grabbed the pot out of his mother's hand, filled another cup, dropped a sugar cube and a splash of milk into it, lay a spoon on the saucer next to the cup, and dragged the whole thing across the table until it was in front of me. "There you are, Darling. Pick it up yourself."

"Don't mind if I do," I said, while Aunt Charlotte, abruptly brought back to herself by her son's overbearing ways, got busy straightening up the overturned cup and saucer. "Will it be just the four of us for tea? Where is Francis?"

"Haven't seen him today," Crispin said, dropping into a chair on the other side of the table. "He's either still in his room, sleeping off yesterday's excesses..."

"It's five o'clock in the afternoon!"

"As I was saying. Or he left while we were in Salisbury this morning, and hasn't come back yet."

"Would Scotland Yard let him do that?"

"They let *us* leave, didn't they?" He shrugged. "I'm sure he's somewhere. Here's Aunt Roslyn now. You can ask her."

I turned towards the foyer, just in time to catch Aunt Roz sweeping into the parlor. "Ask me what?" She headed for the chair next to me.

"Where Cousin Francis is," Crispin said, before I could. At the head of the table, Aunt Charlotte began to prepare another cup. "We haven't seen him all day."

"Francis is resting." Aunt Roz folded herself into the chair next to me and accepted the cup and saucer. "Thank you, Charlotte."

"What's wrong with Francis?" I asked, sipping from my own cup. I had no idea how Crispin knew how I liked my tea— dumb luck, probably—but it was perfect.

"He woke up feeling unwell." Aunt Roz didn't look at me,

or at anyone else, as she leaned forward to put her cup and saucer down. "I told him to stay in bed."

Crispin's eyes found mine across the table, and the corner of his mouth pulled up in a smirk. I scowled at him. Yes, we both knew that Francis had been under the influence of something beyond alcohol when he went to bed last night, but I certainly wasn't going to share enjoyment in that knowledge, and certainly not with St George.

Francis was here, though, and that was something to keep in mind. If Uncle Harold and Uncle Herbert had been away from the Hall all day, and it could be proven that the shot had come from the Hall... well, if it hadn't, then I guess Uncle Herbert and Uncle Harold might be guilty. But if not, then it was down to the handful of people left in the manor when Christopher and I left for our walk. The servants, of course. The detectives. Francis, up in his room. Crispin, off somewhere sulking about the way his mother had chastised him earlier. Aunt Charlotte and Aunt Roz.

And of the four, I'm sure I don't have to spell out who my money was on. He was sitting across the table from me, watching me intently, with an amused, slightly malicious expression, quite like a cat at a mousehole, just waiting for me to make the wrong move.

NINETEEN

Christopher, Tom, and Finchley arrived in time to partake in a spot of tea—Aunt Roz insisted, probably so she could have an excuse to interrogate them about any progress they had made—and then they went off (without Christopher) to search the Hall and grounds for any evidence of a rifle or a shooter.

"Hunting rifle?" Crispin inquired. It was now the five of us in the parlor: Francis hadn't come downstairs, and Uncles Harold and Herbert were still off on the grounds somewhere.

"Military," Christopher said, "I think. But I don't know much about it."

"Nor do I." Crispin agreed. "Born too late, the both of us."

"And a good thing, too," Aunt Roz said firmly. "I lost one son to the war. That was enough. I'm glad I didn't have to risk another. Or my only nephew."

"But you gained a daughter," Crispin pointed out, with a glance at me.

Aunt Roz shot one at him. More like a glare, really. "They're not interchangeable, Crispin. I didn't have to lose Robert just because I gained Pippa. It doesn't work that way."

"Of course not, Aunt Roslyn." Crispin glanced at his mother, who had been very quiet this whole time. The almost-demise of a Spode teacup seemed to have unsettled her. "Have you heard, Mother? We're not dressing for dinner tonight. Darling feels unequal to another costume change."

"Crispin..." Aunt Charlotte sighed, and sounded exhausted with it.

"My apologies, Mother. *Miss* Darling."

"You're awful, St George," I told him, with a sigh of my own. "I don't know how your crowds of women put up with you. Truly I don't."

"Upon my word, Darling, neither do I. And yet, somehow they manage."

He smirked. And that might have been what did it. That awful, self-congratulatory smirk. The words fell out of my mouth without conscious thought; I think I just wanted to say something, anything, that would wipe the self-satisfied look off his face.

"I was curious... Not that it's any of my affair—I'm sorry, my business—but the young woman with the baby, the one who showed up at Sutherland House. That worked out all right, it seems?"

I got my wish. The smirk dropped off his face so completely it was like it had never been there at all, and was replaced with a look of malice so concentrated I wouldn't have been surprised if I had dropped dead from the sheer impact, right then and there.

At the head of the table, Aunt Charlotte straightened in her chair. "Baby? Did you say baby? Crispin...!"

"Thanks ever so, Darling," Crispin told me through gritted teeth. "How do you even know about that?"

I glared at him. "I notice you're not denying it."

"Would it do me any good if I did?" He shook his head. "You could have just left it alone, couldn't you?"

"That's rather rich, coming from you," I fired back. "You could have left *her* alone, first of all. And when you leave *me* alone, perhaps I won't bring up your shortcomings as often as you feel you have to bring up mine."

"It wasn't a shortcoming, Darling."

"It most certainly was not. In order for her to claim paternity, you had to have—"

"Not that! For God's sake, Darling—!"

My mouth was still open, but before I could respond, Aunt Charlotte's voice cut through the bickering. "Crispin! What woman with a baby?"

He closed his mouth, turned to her, and waved a languid hand. "Just some poor waif with a newborn, Mother, who thought I'd be stupid enough to take her at her word."

I rolled my eyes. "Clearly she doesn't know you at all."

He sneered. "No, Darling. She doesn't."

"So you didn't...?" Christopher began.

Crispin cut his eyes to him. "No, Kit. I did not."

Christopher nodded.

Crispin looked from him to me and back, accusingly. "How do the two of you know about this, anyway? I thought my affairs were my own."

"Your affairs are very much your own," I said, and watched him sniff in annoyance.

"You know what I mean. How did you find out about it? Not even my mother knew, as should be very evident to you both. How did *you* know?"

"Grimsby knew," I said, and had the pleasure of seeing St George speechless for once.

"And he told you? He told *you*? Why?"

"He didn't. He had information about several of us."

"Me," Christopher said, "Pippa, Francis, Mother..."

I could see the gears inside Crispin's head engage as he put things together. "Is that why he was killed? He was a blackmailer?"

He sounded shocked, like this was entirely new information. And, of course, if he had killed Grimsby and it was because Grimsby had seen him do away with his grandfather, then Crispin might not have known about the blackmail at all.

"We have no idea why he was killed," I said, "although we assume so. Of course, there could be other reasons. But that seems like a good enough motive to go on with."

He looked uneasy. "And is that what the police think, as well?"

"I assume so," I said. "They haven't exactly been forthcoming with me, as you can imagine."

Crispin glanced at Christopher. "Have they been forthcoming with you?"

"No," Christopher said. "Tom and I are friendly enough, but we're not on those terms. I only went with them this afternoon to point out exactly where we were when the shooting happened, so they'd have an easier time finding the bullet. No other reason."

Crispin nodded. Nobody else said anything. I waited for the silence to become oppressive, and then I cleared my throat. "How about we go upstairs, Christopher? You're still in the suit you wore earlier. There's rather a lot of dirt and grass stains on you. And some blood. Mine, I hope."

"Oh." He looked like this hadn't even entered his mind. "Yes, of course, Pippa."

He pulled my chair out and helped me up, hand under my (good) arm.

"Please excuse us," I said formally. "We'll see you all for dinner."

Aunt Roz nodded. Aunt Charlotte ignored me. I waited for Crispin to make some kind of pointed remark about Christopher and me going off together to get Christopher out of his suit, but when he didn't, I realized he probably hadn't even noticed me speak.

"What was that all about?" Christopher asked as soon as we'd cleared the parlor door and were on our way towards the staircase.

"Your cousin, you mean?" I glanced over my shoulder to make sure no one was around to hear. "He's been a nuisance all afternoon. For a second or two earlier, I thought he was going to push me down the staircase."

The same staircase we had just started up.

"He wouldn't do that," Christopher said. "Although for a second or two in there, I thought he was going to strangle you."

That thought had crossed my mind, too. However— "Not in front of his mother. Or yours."

"That was quite a big bombshell you threw at him. And at Aunt Charlotte." He climbed for a second in silence. "Why did you do it?"

"Wanted to wipe the smirk off his face," I said.

Christopher nodded. "I'd say you succeeded. I guess we can conclude, at least, that if Crispin is the guilty party, he didn't kill Grimsby because Grimsby was blackmailing him."

"Clearly not," I agreed, catching up to him at the top of the staircase. "Did you and Tom and Finchley discover anything useful, or was it just as you told us?"

"A bullet from a hunting rifle," Christopher said, and fell into step with me as we headed for his room in the east wing. "It was just lying there in the grass, spent. With a bit of blood on it. Yours, we assume. But apparently that's enough to give them a start. They were going to the gun room to see if anything else is missing, and if not, I guess they're doing another door-to-door search for the weapon."

"It could be outside," I said, and Christopher nodded.

"Of course it could. And if it is, I'm not looking for it. I've had enough of the great outdoors for today."

"Your father and uncle seem to be still out there. They've been gone a long time."

Christopher paled. "Good Lord. You don't think anyone shot *them*, do you?"

"I think we would have heard it if someone did," I said. "I'll admit I was pretty distracted, but I think I only heard the one shot. Didn't you?"

He started breathing again. "I guess so, now that you mention it."

"They probably just have a lot to discuss. Their father just died."

"Of course," Christopher said, looking relieved. "I'm sure you're right."

"Although if they don't come home within the next hour, we could say something to someone. We don't want them traipsing around on horseback through the fields in the dark."

"No," Christopher agreed, "we definitely don't."

After a second, he added, "You don't think Crispin...?"

"I have no idea. He was here at the Hall, so he's part of the suspect pool. And if Uncle Harold turns up dead, then I'd say we should definitely consider him. But until then, I'm not sure that he's any more of a suspect than anyone else."

Christopher nodded and sank his teeth into his bottom lip.

By now we had turned the corner into the east wing, and were making our way towards Christopher's room. Francis's closed door was on the left, and I slowed my steps. "You haven't spoken to Francis today, have you?"

"No," Christopher said. "You don't think...?"

"Aunt Roz said he was feeling under the weather this morning, and she told him to stay in bed. Although I don't think it could hurt to knock, just to make sure he's all right."

Although now that I thought about it, that might have been just what Aunt Roz had done after she sent me downstairs with Crispin earlier. Gone to see how Francis was doing.

Christopher applied his knuckles to the wood. "Francis?"

There was no answer from within, not even a disagreeable mutter, and Christopher shot me a look.

"Try the knob," I suggested.

He did, and when it turned in his hand, he pushed the door open. It was dark inside, with the curtains drawn across the only window, and it had that pungent odor you usually associate with sickness.

"Francis?" We tiptoed towards the bed. The drapes around it were closed, and Christopher fumbled with one until he found a place to stick his head through. "Francis?"

Now, that disagreeable mutter came, and I felt my heart kick in again.

No, I guess I hadn't really believed that Francis had been murdered in his bed—that would be rather a lot of murders for one country house in one weekend—but given his physical state last night, I wouldn't have been terribly surprised to learn he had succumbed to whatever drug he had been using, and had died overnight.

"Just checking that you're all right," Christopher said brightly, and Francis's grumbling resolved itself into recognizable words.

"...sick, you impudent monkey. Go 'way and let me sleep."

"Sure thing, old bean." Christopher withdrew from the drapes and twitched them shut again. "Let's go. He's obviously alive."

Obviously. "One less murder to worry about, then."

"That's not helpful," Christopher said as we scurried back across the carpet and into the corridor. He closed Francis's door carefully behind us and continued down towards his own door, with a glance at me over his shoulder. "You didn't really think...?"

"Not really, no. But with bullets flying and people dropping dead left and right, it's hard not to worry."

Christopher nodded and reached for his own doorknob. "At least there's nobody we have to worry about in here."

"Famous last words," I said dryly, but of course he was right. There was no one else in his room, dead or alive. What there was, leaned up against the wall under the window, was a rifle.

Both of us stopped in the middle of the floor and eyed it.

It made a certain sort of sense that it would be here, of course. Christopher's room had been empty this afternoon, because Christopher and I had been walking down the road towards the village. Francis's room next door had not been empty, and Aunt Charlotte was around, so might have gone into her own room at any moment. Or into Uncle Harold's, for that matter. She was the mistress of the house, and could go wherever she wanted. Much safer for the shooter to utilize a room he—or she, to be fair—would know was empty.

But this was the part of the house that faced the copse of trees and the road, so it made sense that the shot would have come from up here. I walked to the window, careful not to upset the rifle, and peered out. "Nice view from up here. Clear shot at the road as it comes out from behind the trees."

Christopher nodded. "I should get Tom."

"Probably a good idea. I'll wait here."

"Don't touch anything," Christopher said, and turned towards the door.

"Of course not."

I watched from in front of the window as he ducked out into the hallway, leaving the door half open behind him. A few seconds later, I could hear the door at the end of the hall, into the servants' staircase, open and shut, as well.

The rifle leered at me from beside the window. I scowled back.

It wasn't difficult to figure out what had happened. Someone had walked into the gun room when Scotland Yard's back was turned—they really ought to have locked and warded the room, although perhaps they had, and the shooter had gone in anyway—and picked a rifle and ammunition from the cabinets. The breakfast room, where the detectives were doing their work, was in the east wing, pretty much directly below this one, the better to get morning sun, while the gun room, box room, and other utilitarian spaces were all in the west wing. They would have had to set a guard to prevent it from happening, really, and of course they hadn't brought enough personnel with them for that.

Nor did I think anyone had expected another assault on the gun room, honestly.

The shooter had most likely come up the servants' staircase on that side of the house, the one that came out next to my room, since the likelihood was less that he'd encounter anyone that way. I was out walking, and the detectives were all downstairs. The entire west wing was reliably empty, in other words, most likely on both floors. Uncle Herbert was out riding with Uncle Harold. The only two variables were Aunt Roz and Aunt Charlotte, and I had no idea where they'd been when this was going on.

But clearly the shooter had made it to Christopher's room unmolested, along with the rifle. He had opened the window and waited for Christopher and me to come out from behind the trees down on the road, and had aimed for us. It was a half mile by road, less as the crow—or bullet—flies. And then he had quietly put the rifle down below the window—there was no sense in risking discovery by taking it back to the gun room— and walked across the room to the door, and vanished.

Where?

Into Francis's room next door? Sickness made a handy excuse for not facing anyone, and I imagined it would be hard to face the rest of the family after you've aimed a gun at your only surviving brother.

Or perhaps across the hall into Crispin's rooms?

I'd certainly made a very convincing case for his guilt earlier, to Christopher and to myself. He'd had means and motive for everything that had happened so far, and at least he'd had means for this. Motive was a different story. I knew we bickered a lot, but killing me because of it seemed a step too far.

Although motive, as I understand it, is really of the least consideration to a detective. If someone has access to the weapon and the murder site at the time the murder takes place, their motive doesn't much matter. And I could place Crispin in this room, with this gun, at the time when the shot fell, at least in my mind.

There was the sound of footsteps outside the door, and I turned that way as a figure appeared in the doorway. I had expected it to be Christopher and Tom, of course. When I found myself face to face with Crispin, especially after the thoughts I'd just had about him, I must admit that my stomach gave an uncomfortable sort of lurch, like all my intestines were being squeezed in a vice.

The look on his face did nothing to make me feel better. "Darling."

"St George," I said, and did my best to keep my voice steady.

He looked from me around the empty room. If he noticed

the rifle, he gave no sign of it. Perhaps I had inadvertently put myself in front of it.

When his attention returned to me, he asked, "Waiting for Kit?"

"He went downstairs to fetch Tom Gardiner." I might as well make it clear that there were reinforcements coming, and soon, in case he decided to strangle me on the spot.

That irritating eyebrow quirked. "A threesome?"

"Don't be disgusting, St George," I told him. "Your life may be full of perversions, but don't assume that mine is."

"Of course not." This time it was his mouth that quirked, and with what looked like genuine amusement. "I haven't forgiven you for that conversation downstairs, you know. What on earth would compel you to bring *that* up in front of my mother?"

"You annoyed me," I said.

"I see."

"And I'll admit I found the information shocking."

"I'm sure you did." And it was beyond clear that he meant the remark as an insult. As if I were some backwards provincial who didn't understand how things worked up in Town.

I did my best to dredge up some patience, when what I really wanted to do was wallop him upside the head. "I'm sorry you can't have the girl you want, St George, but punishing your family by ruining your reputation and possibly the rest of your life—"

His jaw clenched. "Thank you, Darling, for your care and concern."

"It's not care and concern," I told him, "you absolute tosser. Your family worries about you. And just because the girl in that particular scenario was lying—I assume you were telling the truth about that?"

He raised a shoulder, looking sulky.

"Just because she was lying, doesn't mean you won't get caught in the same trap another day, with a girl you've actually dallied with. You have to be careful, St George. You have a family name and a title to worry about—"

"Sod my family name and title," Crispin growled. "Nobody cares about that anymore."

"Everyone cares about that! Or do you really think these women all flock to you because of your good looks and charm?"

"Why, Darling..."

"They don't! They want the money and the title, not you!"

"I know," Crispin said coldly. "You've already made it clear this weekend that that's all I have to offer."

"Oh, sod off!" It was really terribly rude of me, but I was at my wits' end. "Go away, St George. I have things to do. And if you want to wrap your new car around another light pole or get yourself caught by another gold-digger with a baby, then don't come crying to your family about it afterwards."

"I didn't come to you this time!" Crispin snarled. "It was nobody's business but mine, at least until Grimsby dug it up. And I don't want your sympathy, you muppet. Or your care or concern or worry or whatever it was you threatened me with. You're awful, Darling, and I don't care if I ever see you again for as long as I live."

"Well, that's just lovely," I told him darkly. "I hope it'll be more than two months this time, then, before you show up at the flat."

"Don't worry, it will be!"

He vanished from the doorway. Three seconds later, I heard the door across the hall slam.

No more than three seconds after that, the door to the servants' staircase opened, and then Christopher came into the room, followed by Tom Gardiner. "Was that Crispin?" the former asked, with a look at the door that still vibrated in its frame.

I nodded. "He wanted a chat about what happened downstairs."

"What happened?" Tom asked, and I turned to him.

"I brought up a few of the things from Grimsby's dossier in front of his mother. He didn't like it."

Tom nodded. "I wouldn't have liked that, either."

"It was his own fault," I said. "He was being a git."

Tom shrugged. "So about this rifle..."

"Over there." I pointed.

"Ah." He brushed past me towards it. "There it is."

"We didn't touch it," I said, as I pivoted to watch him approach the window, "although I doubt there are any fingerprints on it."

He shook his head. "There's been so much talk about fingerprints lately, that everyone knows to wear gloves. But it's always good to have the weapon."

"Can I suggest that you lock the gun room and take away the keys this time?"

"We already had," Tom said. "Someone must have known where to find a spare."

Interesting. Yet another finger pointed at someone actually living in the house.

I glanced over my shoulder—not at anything in particular, more at the two walls and the hallway separating us from St George's rooms—and then back at Tom. "Do you know who the murderer is? Are you getting any closer to figuring it out?"

"We have an idea," Tom said cautiously, "but I'm not going to tell you."

I put my hands on my hips. Or rather, I put one. The other arm twinged at the movement, so I dropped it. "Why not?"

"Because we don't want anyone to tip this person off that

we're suspicious of them. They've committed two murders and tried to commit a third, and we don't want to give them any more of a reason to try again."

"If you wanted to use me as bait, to try to catch them in the act...?"

"Absolutely not," Christopher said firmly.

Tom glanced at him before shaking his head, too. "We're Scotland Yard, Miss Darling. We don't do things like that."

"Pippa," I said firmly. "And really? Whyever not? Because it seems like a good idea...?"

"No," Christopher said. "It's not a good idea. Absolutely not. I won't hear of it."

I turned to him. "I wouldn't be in any danger, Christopher. You'd all be there to make sure nothing happened to me."

"No, Miss Darling."

I looked at Tom and he rolled his eyes. "No, Pippa. We're not going to use you as bait. And furthermore—"

"He absolutely forbids you to do it yourself," Christopher cut in. "Tell her, Tom. Tell her you forbid it."

"I forbid it," Tom said. "You are to behave exactly as normal, Miss Darling. Go down to supper, say the things you'd normally say, do the things you'd normally do. Don't say anything suspicious and don't look sideways at anyone. Try not to antagonize St George any more than you have to. And also, don't do anything stupid, like have any long walks in the garden by yourself before bed."

No, it was probably a good idea to avoid that. Especially if it hadn't been planned beforehand and no one would be skulking in the shadows to intercept any further attempts on my life.

"I suppose supper will be safe?"

"As long as you eat from the community plates," Tom said. "Anything handed to you specifically is suspect."

I nodded. "I'll be careful. But are you really not going to tell us who you suspect?"

"I'm really not. It's a suspicion, nothing more. We don't have the proof yet. And with someone as volatile as this, we don't want to risk tipping them off that we suspect them. All of you are people with money and resources and connections. It would be very easy for any one of you to disappear."

That was true, of course. At least for all of us of the younger generation. And it wasn't like the older generation was even that old. If Uncle Harold or Uncle Herbert wanted to disappear, I'm sure they'd manage.

And speaking of that...

"You don't think that's what Uncle Herbert and Uncle Harold are doing, do you? Disappearing?"

"No," Tom said. "I'm sure His Grace and Lord Herbert will be along in time for supper. And on that note..." He reached for the rifle and wrapped a (gloved) hand around it. "I'd better get this downstairs. Once Finch is finished with it, I'll send him up here to have a go at the window. Don't touch it."

We shook our heads.

"A shame you touched the doorknob, but I guess there's nothing to be done about that."

"We didn't realize that anything was wrong until we were already inside the room," I said apologetically. "Otherwise we would have been more careful."

For all the good it would have done, when all the suspects were people who lived in the house, and could touch anything they wanted. Finding Crispin's fingerprints on Christopher's door wouldn't prove a thing. Nor would finding Francis's fingerprints, or Uncle Herbert's, or Aunt Roz's, or for that matter Uncle Harold's or Aunt Charlotte's. Any one of them could have come up with a reasonable excuse for having tried the handle on Christopher's door, and I was as certain as I could be that the rifle itself would have no helpful prints at all on it.

Tom vanished out the door and down the servants' stairs with the rifle.

"I guess it's you and me until supper," I told Christopher.

He nodded. "At least I can make sure nothing happens to you that way."

TWENTY

Tom was right: Uncle Harold and Uncle Herbert did make it back to the Hall in time for supper, and after a long afternoon of riding around the estate, were quite happy not to have to dress for the meal. Uncle Herbert was shocked, of course, to hear that there had been an attempt on my life, or perhaps Christopher's life, while he'd been gone.

"Insanity!" he exclaimed, thumping his fist on the table. "People running around taking potshots at my son and my niece in broad daylight! And what is Scotland Yard doing about it?"

"I'm sure they're working hard," Aunt Roz said. "And Christopher and Pippa are both just fine, Herbert. Calm yourself. Have some more veal."

She put more veal on Uncle Herbert's plate, and went so far as to almost force it into his mouth. It was one way to shut him up, I suppose.

Other than Uncle Herbert carrying on, it was a very quiet meal. The detectives took dinner on their own again. Francis stayed in his room, as he had done for breakfast and luncheon. I asked Aunt Roz whether we should arrange for a tray to be sent up to him, and she informed me that when he was hungry enough, he'd come out.

The same ought to be true for Crispin, who didn't show up, either. But Aunt Charlotte was cut from a different cloth than Aunt Roz, so she prepared a tray with her own hands, from the dishes on the table, and sent it upstairs with the second footman. When he came back, he told her that he had left it in front of the door when the Viscount St George didn't respond to his knock.

"Are you certain he's inside?" I wanted to know.

Everyone turned to look at me, and Aunt Charlotte gave me a stare down the length of her nose that was quite well done considering that she's no taller than I am, especially not sitting down. "Whatever do you mean, Miss Darling? Why wouldn't he be inside?"

"No reason," I said. Other than that I had Tom's comment about people vanishing on my mind. But it was undoubtedly best if I didn't articulate my suspicions of St George in present company. "And I didn't mean to imply that he wasn't. I more wanted to make sure nothing had happened to him."

Aunt Charlotte gave me a nasty look. "I'm certain he's just fine, Miss Darling." She turned her head regally. "Alfred?"

The footman jumped when Aunt Charlotte addressed him. "Your Grace?"

"My son," Aunt Charlotte said. "Was he inside his room when you knocked?"

Alfred nodded. "I imagine so, Your Grace. I heard sounds from inside."

"Sounds?"

"Drawers banging, m'lady. Things moving around. Muttering."

"Packing?" Christopher suggested, with a glance at me.

Alfred looked like he didn't appreciate being put on the spot. "Might be, Master Christopher. Though I wouldn't want to say for sure."

"I'll go talk to him," Uncle Harold said and pushed his chair back. "No, Charlotte—"

For Aunt Charlotte had started to get to her feet, too. "I'll handle this. You coddle him too much. He isn't a boy anymore."

He tossed his napkin on the table and strode out. Aunt Charlotte wound her hands together in her lap, biting her lip.

"He'll be fine, Charlotte," Aunt Roz said comfortingly. "Harold's right. Crispin's a man now. He can deal with a conversation with his father."

Aunt Charlotte nodded, but for the next ten minutes, she merely moved the food on her plate around, instead of actually eating any of it.

Uncle Harold came back down carrying the tray, still full of food, and dropped it, almost literally, on the table. "Says he's not hungry. If he changes his mind, he can get his own food."

He took his own seat again, flapped his napkin open over his lap, and went back to enjoying his supper.

"But he's all right?" Aunt Roz asked.

"Right as rain," Uncle Harold nodded. "Up there having a sulk, is all. Obstinate little popinjay."

You'd have thought he'd have a little fondness in his voice when he applied this appellation to his only son, but you'd be wrong.

"Leave the boy alone," Uncle Herbert grunted. "He'll come out when he's ready. Pass the butter, Kit."

Christopher passed the butter. Conversation lagged. Eventually Aunt Charlotte excused herself and headed upstairs. We all knew she'd gone to check on Crispin, but none of us said anything about it. Uncle Harold rolled his eyes, but didn't do anything to stop her.

All in all, it was a very strange meal. At the end of it. Uncle Harold and Uncle Herbert went into the billiards room with Aunt Roz, where they talked Christopher into making a fourth for bridge. Aunt Charlotte never came back downstairs, or if she did, it wasn't into the game room. We didn't see Crispin or Francis for the rest of the evening, either. I thought about retiring to my room, or to the library or somewhere else in the manor, but whenever I looked like I thought about getting up, Christopher sent me a warning look. Instead, I spent a couple hours watching other people play cards, and then Christopher and I headed upstairs. Via the servants' staircase in the east wing, because I wanted to see, or at least hear, for myself, that Crispin was still in his room and hadn't, as the books say, done a bunk with his guilty conscience while we were all sitting around the dining table.

The light was on in his sitting room, and when Christopher knocked on the door, it took a moment, but eventually a voice from inside said, "What do you want?"

"It's Kit," Christopher said. "And Pippa."

There was a beat, and then— "Go away. I don't want to talk to you."

"We just want to make sure you're all right," I tried.

There was a snort. It was clearly audible through the door. "Of course, Darling. I know how much you care."

"I don't want you dead," I told him, which was the truth as far as it went.

"I'm flattered, Darling. But missing supper once isn't going to kill me."

No, of course it wouldn't. "Just don't do anything stupid," I said.

There was a beat. Perhaps he was thinking about asking me what I might have meant by that. Or perhaps he knew exactly what I was talking about.

"I'll do my best," came the answer eventually. I glanced at Christopher, who shrugged.

"Good night, Crispin."

"Night, Kit," Crispin said. "Sleep well." The admonition could have been sinister or smug, or perhaps simply honest. Hard to say through the door.

"I'll walk you to your room," Christopher told me as we continued down the hall. "I'll check on Francis on my way back, and make sure he's all right. But first I want you safely tucked away in your own room. Unless you'd like to stay in mine tonight?"

"I'm afraid your aunt would have a heart attack if I did. There's a reason she put me in a room clear on the other side of the Hall."

"She wouldn't have to know," Christopher said.

"I'm sure she'd figure it out somehow. And while I honestly don't care what your Aunt Charlotte thinks of me—" Not much, anyway; or at least not when she wasn't snubbing me to my face, "—we are guests in her home. Besides, no offense to you, Christopher, I feel safer in the other wing, surrounded by Scotland Yard detectives."

"It's hard to blame you there," Christopher admitted, as we turned the corner into the central wing. "Maybe *I* should stay in *your* room."

"You're welcome to, if you'd like. The bed is big enough for two."

"I'd better not," Christopher admitted, if a bit wistfully. "As you said, we *are* guests."

I nodded. "Hopefully not for much longer, though. And then we can go back to London and our own lives. I'll be glad to get away from here."

"You're not the only one," Christopher agreed. "It's been a horrid weekend. Two deaths, one attempted murder..."

"Much too much St George."

He sniggered, and I added, "On the other hand, there's been Tom Gardiner."

"That's true."

I slanted him a look. "He seems to like you."

"What's not to like?" Christopher wanted to know, facetiously. "I've known him since I was thirteen. Of course he likes me, Pippa. Don't turn it into something it isn't, please."

"If you say so." If he didn't want to talk about it, I certainly wasn't going to force the conversation on him. We turned the corner into the west wing in silence. "He made it sound like they have strong suspicions of someone, as far as the murders go."

Christopher nodded. "Maybe by tomorrow we'll be able to go home. Or Wednesday, at the latest."

"That would be lovely." The idea of our own flat, with just the two of us inside it, no St George, no Scotland Yard, no murderers taking pot shots at me... it all sounded too good to be true, frankly.

He came to a stop outside my door. "I'll come in with you and make sure everything inside is all right. That no one is lying in wait behind the draperies with a dagger."

"It would have to be your aunt or your brother," I said, "since everyone else is downstairs, and we know Crispin was in his room when we went past."

"Humor me." He pushed the door open and stepped over the threshold. And yes, did proceed to check behind the curtains and under the bed and inside the wardrobe for unauthorized visitors. That done—no one was there, of course—he took my water jug down the hall to the washroom, where he emptied out the water, dried the inside of the jug, and filled it up again from the tap. "Better safe than sorry. Anything else you need help with?"

I hadn't needed help with any of what he'd already done, but I didn't have the heart to tell him. "I'm fine," I said. "I can get my own dress and shoes and makeup off. Go to sleep, Christopher. If anything happens tonight, I'm sure you'll hear about it."

He nodded. "Wedge a chair under your doorknob, just in case."

I promised I would, before I saw him on his way. "You do the same. I still think that shot might have been meant for you."

Then I checked the draperies and wardrobe and under the bed again myself—not because I didn't trust him, but because we'd been outside the room for a few minutes—before I did, indeed, wedge a chair under the knob of the door. Feeling a little safer, I wrestled my shoes off and my dress onto a hanger and crawled into bed in my unmentionables, instead of trying to fumble myself into my pyjamas.

You might think I'd have a problem falling asleep after the day we'd had. That I'd lie awake reliving the moment I was shot, the moment Christopher pushed me into the ditch, the moments we lay there, waiting to see whether there'd be more shots coming our way.

You'd be wrong. I fell asleep a few minutes after crawling into bed, before I got halfway through the long list of reasons why Crispin was the most likely murder suspect at Sutherland Hall, and why Francis wasn't. If I were honest, I knew in my heart of hearts that it might equally well be Francis, that his (hypothetical) motive for wanting his grandfather dead was as strong as Crispin's (hypothetical) motive, and they'd both had access to the gun room and the rifle and the pistol and the maze... but I'd much rather see Crispin in the dock, so I kept telling myself all the reasons I thought it might be him.

I drifted off to sleep in the middle of it, and of course the neuroses of the day came out in nightmares. I felt like I spent hours running for my life, through fog and dark forests and the streets of Little Sutherland, while bullets pinged off the walls around me. I heard the sound of footsteps getting ever closer, and felt hot breath on the back of my neck.

And then, in the blink of an eye, we were in the salon at Sutherland Hall, and—

"Drink your tea, Darling," Crispin told me, holding out the same cup and saucer he had knocked out of his mother's hand earlier today. The liquid inside looked like a lovely milky tea, just the way I liked it... until a death's head formed on top, shimmering a pale greenish white. The cup moved closer, insistently. Crispin smiled, but his eyes were a bright silver, flat and hard...

I sat bolt upright in bed, gasping for air, my own eyes wide and staring.

It took a while after that before I was able to sleep again. And from then on, I hovered just on the edge of consciousness, jerking awake every so often to scan the room and make sure I was alone.

I always was. At no point did anyone actually try to invade my room. The doorknob never moved, the chair stayed in place, and I heard no noises from outside in the hallway. I should have spent a peaceful night. I laid it at Crispin's door that I hadn't. Not that I ever planned to tell him so.

I got up in the morning fully expecting to learn that he had vanished during in the night. He hadn't heard, the way Christopher and I had, that Scotland Yard was coming close to naming a suspect. But surely he had to expect that the investigation would conclude sooner or later, and that he'd eventually be held to account for his crimes.

Or perhaps he was so sure he had covered his tracks that he thought he didn't have anything to worry about. When I walked into the dining room for breakfast, he was standing at the sideboard looking quite as blasé as he always did. His tie was perfect, and so was his collar. His flannel bags had a knife-edged pleat, and he had topped the ensemble with a gray, blue, and red pullover in a diamond pattern, quite vivid enough all on its own to assault the retinas.

I probably would have winced even if I hadn't been surviving on a night of very bad sleep. "Good Lord, St George."

He sniggered. "Morning, Darling. You look rather haggard. Rough night?"

"You have no idea," I said, and then rolled my eyes when I saw his expression. "Come off it, St George. You know as well as I do that there's nothing like that going on. I didn't sleep well, that's all."

"Bad dreams?"

He poured a cup of coffee and handed it to me. It was quite nice of him, actually, although after the nightmare I'd had—bad dreams, indeed—I must admit that I gave it a dubious look. I couldn't see any way that he could have managed to put anything into it, but I still had that image of the floating death's head in my mind, and it was hard to unsee.

"Don't worry," he told me, obviously noticing my hesitancy, "it isn't poisoned."

"I didn't think it was," I lied, and took a seat at the table. "Thank you."

"Of course." He sat himself and his plate down across from me and eyed me across the heaped serving of eggs, sausages, and toast. His eyes were a clear gray, and for once they held no malice or artifice whatsoever. "I wouldn't poison you, you know."

"I believe you," I said, even if I didn't, wholly. But since he was being semi-polite, or at least cordial, to me this morning, I figured I could return the favor. "I guess you never did end up eating anything last night, did you?"

He shook his head, sending a lock of fair hair flopping over his forehead. Between the casual bags and the pullover, I guessed he hadn't taken the trouble to thoroughly brilliantine his hair this morning, either. "Mother sent some dinner up to my room, and then Father came and took it away again, as punishment for bad behavior. As if I'm still nine years old. So I stayed in my room and drank my dinner, since I'm an adult and I can do that."

I tilted my head to look at him. "Have you considered that you might have a problem?"

"With alcohol?" He shook his head. "Francis has a problem. I can stop any time I want to."

"Isn't that what they all say?"

"I don't know," Crispin said, "is it?"

I didn't know either, so I didn't respond. "I'm sorry I put you on the spot yesterday," I told him instead. My revelation about the girl with the baby was, at least partly, what had put him in such a bad mood and had gotten him in trouble with his father—and no dinner—so I felt I bore some of the responsibility. "I shouldn't have done it."

"It's all right. I don't enjoy having you—having anyone— know everything about my affairs. But I guess that's what I get for making Sutherland House my base in Town. I should have done what you and Kit did, and gotten my own flat."

"Something to consider for the future," I said lightly, while I tried not to think about the fact that if I was right about him, he had no future to speak of. At most it would be a cell at Wormwood Scrubs, and at worst, a trip to the gallows.

Besides, when he acted like this—like a normal human being, and one who didn't go out of his way to antagonize me— it was hard to reconcile him with the murderer I had convinced myself he was.

"Excuse me," I told him. "I think I'm ready for some food now."

He nodded, and devoted himself to his breakfast while I wandered over to the sideboard and filled a plate of my own. Slowly, while I considered the situation yet again, just in case I'd been wrong.

Someone had murdered Duke Henry and Grimsby, and had shot at me and Christopher.

If not Crispin, then who?

It hadn't been Aunt Roz in the garden maze, because her hair was dark. And it hadn't been Uncle Harold or Uncle Herbert with the rifle yesterday, because they'd both been out of the Hall when the shot fell.

Besides Francis, who else was there?

And what was my subconscious trying to tell me with that trip back to the tea table and the poisoned cup of tea I had dreamed last night? I had taken it as proof of Crispin's guilt, that my subconscious agreed with conscious me, but what if I had been trying to tell myself something different?

In the dream, Crispin had clearly been offering me poisoned tea. But in reality, the tea had not been poisoned. Or at least the tea he had slopped into the fresh cup, and doctored with milk and sugar, and put in front of me, hadn't been. The tea Aunt Charlotte had poured was what had ended up soaking into the tablecloth after Crispin had knocked it out of my hand.

And out of his mother's hand.

His mother, who had fair hair and access to the gun room, and who had been home yesterday while Christopher and I had been walking to the village.

That's as far as I got before Christopher joined us, just ahead of Aunt Roz and Uncle Herbert. My mind was still trying to grapple with the problem, but it got harder as people started talking all around me.

"Francis is still among the living," Christopher said as he sat down beside Crispin. "I checked before I came down. Morning, St George."

Crispin grunted something, but didn't respond beyond that. His mouth might have been full, to give him the benefit of the doubt.

"Well, really, Christopher," Aunt Roz sniffed, "was there any doubt?"

Christopher looked at me, and I at him. Neither of us said anything. Aunt Roz turned to Uncle Herbert.

"Now, listen here, Kit—" Uncle Herbert began, clearly about to do his duty as head of the household and take his recalcitrant son to task for his flippancy. But that was as far as he got before there was a clatter of footsteps on the stairs and then across the foyer.

"St George," Uncle Harold's voice called out, and Crispin raised his eyes towards the doorway. "St George, where are you?"

He burst into the doorway and skidded to a stop, breathing hard. "St George!"

"Good morning, Harold," Aunt Roz said pleasantly. "Coffee? Tea?"

Uncle Harold shook his head without so much as looking in her direction. "There you are," he said, which was quite a lot like pointing out the obvious. And Crispin must have thought so, too, because he inclined his head with all of his customary attitude.

"Here I am. May I ask what's wrong, Father?"

"It's your mother," Uncle Harold said, without any effort to soften the blow. "I think she's dead."

TWENTY-ONE

CRISPIN STAGGERED. It's hard to do while sitting down, but he managed. And I wasn't the only one who noticed, either, because Christopher scooted his chair a bit closer and actually put his shoulder against Crispin's upper arm to keep him steady.

"Dead?" Aunt Roz managed. She had gone pale, too, but not to the degree that Crispin had. If I hadn't known he was very much alive, I would have thought he was a ghost. The usually faint circles under his eyes stood out against his pale skin like bruises.

Uncle Harold nodded, looking around distractedly. "We need the police."

"I'll get them," I said, since everyone else was busy: Christopher with his cousin and Uncle Roz with Uncle Harold.

Uncle Herbert gave me a distracted nod, and I jumped up from the chair and ran out of the room and down the hall to the breakfast room, heels clicking rapid-fire against the marble. "Tom! Inspector Pendennis! Detective Finchley!"

By the time I had the Scotland Yard detectives following behind me like a row of ducklings, the rest of the family was on its way up the stairs. Or rather, Crispin was almost at the top, taking the stairs two at a time, while Christopher scrambled after, a few steps behind. The older generation, meanwhile, was at the bottom, starting up. I abandoned the detectives and took off, pushing past my aunt and uncles with a breathless, "Pardon me."

I was overtaken before I reached the top by Tom and Detective Sergeant Finchley, both of whom had much longer legs than mine, and no heels on their shoes.

By the time I made it off the staircase and could see the end of the central wing, the door to Aunt Charlotte's room stood wide open. Crispin had disappeared into his mother's bedroom, and Christopher was just about to do the same. Tom and Finchley were halfway down the hall past the Duke's Chamber, feet thudding on the carpet.

In the few seconds it took me to reach the door to Aunt Charlotte's room, Crispin had crossed the floor to the side of his mother's bed, and Christopher had joined him there. They had their backs to me, but I could see quite clearly the rigidity of Crispin's shoulders.

Tom and Finchley quickly made their way to the other side of the bed. "Don't touch anything," Finchley warned.

I stepped across the carpeted floor as quietly as I could in the presence of death. Because yes, it was very clear that Aunt Charlotte had left us. I had no idea how Uncle Harold could have made it sound like there was any doubt.

She was lying in bed as peacefully as a doll, with her nightgown buttoned to the neck, the counterpane tucked under her arms, and her hands folded across her chest. Her silvery curls framed her face like a fluffy nest. Her eyes were closed and her face smooth and peaceful. There were no signs I could see of foul play. It looked as if she had simply fallen asleep and then not woken up again.

Very much the same way the late duke had looked two days ago when we'd stood in front of his bed, in fact. So that wasn't necessarily an indication that she hadn't been murdered.

There was absolutely no way I could fit this murder, if it was one, into my theory that Crispin was the murderer, though. While I could think of reasons for him to have killed almost anyone else, I couldn't make sense of him killing his mother. Certainly not with the way he was looking down at her now, with his eyes wet and his lips trembling.

Looking at him was painful, so I focused on the rest of the room instead, while my thoughts, once again, click-clacked down the track they had derailed themselves onto in the dining room.

Aunt Charlotte had slept alone. I had already known that, but the information was borne in on me again as I glanced around her bedchamber. Everything in here was feminine, from the pale-blue-and-cream damask wallpaper and matching carpet, to the spindly rococo-style escritoire with its gilded legs over by the wall.

The writing surface was down, and what looked like a sheet of paper lay in the middle of it. I wandered that way, while over by the bed, Christopher reached out and put a supportive hand on Crispin's shoulder. From the back, the two of them looked like twins: identical in everything but dress, save for Crispin's slightly lighter hair.

For a second I thought he might shrug off Christopher's attempt to comfort, because he stiffened visibly when Christopher's hand landed on his shoulder, but then he made an equally visible effort to relax.

I turned back to the escritoire.

There was indeed a note in the middle of the writing surface, and I scanned the first couple of lines rapidly.

My darling boy, it began. *If I am still alive when you find this, do not try to revive me.*

"There's what looks like a letter over here," I announced, to nobody in particular.

Under normal circumstances I might have picked it up and handed it to someone, but these were not normal circumstances. As evidenced by Finchley's immediate cry of, "Don't touch it!"

"I wasn't planning to," I told him. "I think we've all learned better than to touch things by now."

He flushed—his skin was as fair as Christopher's—but he didn't say anything, just came to stand beside me.

Meanwhile, I read another line or two.

It was I who killed your grandfather and Simon Grimsby. They had discovered my secret—

"For her son," Finchley said.

I nodded.

"Is that her handwriting?"

I glanced at him. "As far as I can tell. I don't have much occasion to see it." She certainly didn't send me little love notes. "Although from the Christmas cards I can remember... it looks like it."

"I'm sure her husband and her son can confirm it."

No doubt. "Go get your fingerprint paraphernalia, would you? I'm sure St George would like to read his letter sooner rather than later."

Actually, I wasn't sure about that at all. Crispin didn't look like he was aware of much of anything right now. But there was no sense in dilly-dallying. If Finchley was going to dust the paper for fingerprints, he might as well get on with it.

"Make sure no one touches it," he told me. I nodded,

although by then he already had his back to me and was moving across the floor towards the door with long strides.

Aunt Roz, meanwhile, drifted my way. "Poor Crispin," she said softly. "It looks like she did it herself, doesn't it?"

From the half-full waterglass and the small, empty vial on the night table, to this letter addressed to her best-loved, yes. It looked exactly like that.

Aunt Roz sank her teeth into her bottom lip. "Why on earth would Charlotte do away with herself?"

The obvious reason was that she had killed Duke Henry and his valet, but I didn't feel like I ought to put it quite that bluntly. Not out loud and in front of everyone, at any rate. And not now.

"That's for the police to determine," I said instead, "I imagine."

Aunt Roz nodded, still worrying her lip.

Over by the bed, Pendennis had taken charge, and was bending over to peer at the vial on the night table, hands behind his back. "Veronal," he read.

Aunt Roz made a startled sort of movement. I glanced at her, and she made a face. "Francis," she whispered.

"That's what Francis takes? Veronal?"

It was a sleeping medicine, wasn't it? Almost a hypnotic? Quite easy to overdose on, and Agatha Christie's story, *Who Killed Ackroyd?* had made liberal use of it when it was serialized in the London Evening News last summer, as I recalled. One of the characters in the story, Mrs. Ferrars, used Veronal to kill both herself and her husband.

I wondered whether Aunt Charlotte had taken the London Evening News.

I also wondered, for just a moment, about Francis, until I told myself that Aunt Charlotte had left a note in her own hand, and she wouldn't have lied for Francis.

No, it was far more likely that she had gotten hold of some of his Veronal without his knowledge. He'd been sick enough yesterday that practically anything could have happened in his room and he wouldn't have been aware. And if he had noticed her coming in, all she'd have had to say was that she was worried about his health and making sure he was all right. He'd have no reason to doubt that, as Christopher and I had done the same thing, and so had Aunt Roz.

I turned back to the note, surreptitiously, to see whether I could manage to read another line or two, but a clatter outside the door heralded the return of Detective Sergeant Finchley and his fingerprint powder. Aunt Roz stepped aside, back to her husband and brother-in-law, while I moved back a step, only far enough to get out of Finchley's way as he, dressed in rubber gloves now, dusted fingerprint powder over the front and then the back of the sheet of paper.

"Single set," he announced. "Small. Looks like Her Grace's."

Pendennis nodded and snatched the piece of paper off the table. "Vial next," he told Finchley, "and waterglass. Meanwhile—"

He stalked over to the bed, and Crispin. "Lord St George."

Crispin blinked, but reached out. And stared at the heading of the letter in his mother's handwriting for several seconds before he began reading. His face had a blank sort of look, an emptiness that I remembered from losing my own parents. Christopher gave him a worried look, and then dropped his own eyes to the letter, as well.

They both read for a moment, and then Crispin's hand clenched around the paper. I was standing close enough to hear his indrawn breath. He let it out again, deliberately, and handed the letter across the bed, to Tom. "You'd better have this."

Tom nodded. "We'll get it back to you."

The sound Crispin made sounded like it was half laughter, half tears, all of it wrenched out of him by force. I didn't even like him—actively abhorred him a lot of the time—and I felt my heart break at the level of emotion he was trying to contain.

"Don't bother," he told Tom. "I don't think it's anything I want to read again."

"Come on." I tucked my hand through his arm. "Let's go downstairs and find something to drink. Brandy sounds good."

"It's ten in the morning," Aunt Roz said, mildly shocked.

"We'll mix it with tea, then."

I tugged, and Crispin came away from his mother's bedside with something of the feeling of a cork from a bottle. Reluctantly at first, and then more easily the farther away from the bed we got. "Come on, Christopher. Give me a hand."

Christopher nodded. Uncle Harold watched us until we had passed him, but he didn't move forward or address his son. Perhaps he was simply too overcome with shock and grief himself, which would be understandable, although it seemed to me that he could have spared some comfort for his only child.

THE THREE OF us ended up downstairs in the library. Christopher opened a bottle of brandy and poured a stiff drink into a glass, which he pressed into Crispin's hand. As far as I was concerned, there was no point in diluting the medicinal effects of the alcohol with tea, and Christopher seemed to agree with me. Crispin appeared to still be in shock, because while he accepted the glass, he made no move to lift it and drink.

"Go on," I told him, wrapping my hand around both the glass and his fingers and attempting to raise it to his mouth. "Have a sip."

His eyes snapped to me, and they were empty, too. Until

something sparked, some indication of life, and he finally looked at me like he knew who I was, but had no idea how I'd gotten there. "Darling?"

I nodded. "Drink, St George. It'll help."

He looked from me to the glass in his hand, like this was the first time he'd noticed that it was there, and then—finally—he raised it to his lips and took a sip. And let his breath out with a shudder.

"I'm sorry for your loss," I said, formally, now that I knew he was capable of hearing me.

"Thank you, Darling." He finally started to behave like a normal human being, if not quite like himself, and leaned back, putting his head against the back of the sofa. "My mother is dead."

I nodded. "I'm sorry."

"My mother killed herself."

I exchanged a look with Christopher, who was perched on the edge of the sofa on the other side of Crispin. "So it seems."

"Did the letter say why?" Christopher asked tentatively, and Crispin rolled his head to look at him.

"She confessed to killing Grandfather and Grimsby."

"Why?"

"He'd been digging up secrets," Crispin said, staring up at the ceiling. The glass was resting on his stomach, but his hand was wrapped securely around it. "She had one. Apparently Grimsby found out, and told Grandfather. She wanted to make sure my father didn't find out."

"What was the secret?" Christopher wanted to know, but personally, I thought I could make a good guess. There are only so many secrets married women keep from their husbands. An accidental-on-purpose pregnancy to force a proposal is at the top of the list, but of course that wasn't the case here. Aunt Charlotte and Uncle Harold had already been married quite a long time before Crispin was born, as both Doctor Meadows and Aunt Roz had assured me.

No, she had probably had an affair at some point, and she had been afraid her husband would cast her out if he found out about it. With the title and all the money on the line, it made sense—in a twisted sort of way—that she'd murder her father-in-law and his valet rather than face the consequences of a misstep like that. Especially since removing the late duke would only improve her position anyway. She had died being Duchess of Sutherland.

"I guess it must have been Aunt Charlotte I saw in the maze the night Grimsby was shot," I said, and Crispin turned his head to look at me.

"I suppose so? She would have had to have been there in order to shoot him."

"I can't imagine why I didn't think of her. I knew it was someone with fair hair, but I didn't even think about your mother..."

Not until this morning, at any rate.

"And why would you?" Crispin asked disagreeably. "It would be quite impolite to suspect your hostess of murder, wouldn't it?"

Of course it would. And just as bad to suspect her son, when he hadn't been guilty. "I'm so sorry."

"You already said that. Why do you continue to apologize?"

"Well," I admitted, "I guess it's because up until this morning, I mostly suspected you."

At that, he sat up, eyes widening. "Me?" The brandy sloshed around in the glass, and he moved it over to the table before turning back to me. "Why on earth would you suspect me, Darling? It was clearly all about the secrets, and I don't have any. My life is an open book."

That was nowhere near true, of course, and I had my

mouth open to tell him how very wrong he was, but Christopher got in first.

"We thought Grandfather wouldn't agree to let you marry... um..."

He hesitated, seeming to search for the right terminology, unless he was hoping Crispin would slip up and provide a name. Crispin must have thought so, because he arched a brow. I rolled my eyes at them both. "We thought the duke wouldn't let you marry this girl you seem to have convinced yourself you want, and so you decided to eliminate him. But Grimsby saw you do it, and so you had to get rid of him, too."

"Ingenious." Crispin put his head back against the sofa again. "Your idea, Darling, I'm sure?"

"Of course," I said grumpily. "Christopher actually likes you, you know. And you can't really blame me, St George. The indications were all there. Who else but you would want me dead?"

He opened his mouth, but Christopher spoke over him. "Did your mother confess to shooting at Pippa and me yesterday, too?"

This time, Crispin hesitated. "I don't know. Maybe in the latter part of the letter? I didn't read the whole thing. Once I got to the confession, I thought it was better off with Tom."

"So was it someone else, then?" Christopher asked.

Crispin shook his head. "I'm sure it was my mother. I wouldn't shoot at either of you, and Francis was in no position yesterday to aim a gun. That leaves my mother and yours."

He eyed Christopher. "I don't think your mother did it. So it must have been mine."

Christopher nodded, since neither of us believed it was Aunt Roz on the other end of the rifle, either. "I wonder why she found it necessary?"

"Probably imagined Darling knew more than she did,"

Crispin said with a look at me. "You made some fairly cryptic comments from time to time, you know."

I made a face. "If I did, I directed them at you, not at her. But I suppose that's possible."

"Or perhaps she knew you suspected Crispin," Christopher suggested, "and she tried to get you out of the way to protect him."

"Surely there were better ways to do that than shoot at me? Especially when he'd be on the suspect list, too?"

Neither of them answered. Until Crispin reached over to the table, grabbed the glass of brandy, and tossed back what was left inside. Then he breathed out with a whoosh, his eyes glassy, but at least there was color in his cheeks again. "I'm sorry, Darling."

"It was her doing," I told him, "not yours, so no apology necessary."

He grimaced, but didn't say anything else. I thought about that upended teacup yesterday, and the tea Aunt Charlotte had prepared for me pouring all over the tabletop instead of ending up in my mouth. And I wondered whether he had suspected at that point that his mother was guilty of murder and attempted murder. There were some indications that he might have, the teacup being just one of them. But in the end I decided against asking. He was dealing with quite enough as it was, really.

We were still sitting there in silence several minutes later, when Chief Inspector Pendennis walked through the door and gave us all a look, including the glass, before fastening his eyes on Crispin. "If I could ask you to come with me, Lord St George?"

It was posed as a question, but was clearly not meant to be one.

Crispin nodded and got to his feet without looking at either of us. I thought about throwing a "Good luck," at his back, but I didn't think he'd need it—there was no danger for him in this conversation, even if it would surely prove to be uncomfortable —and besides, it might give the wrong impression.

I did send the well wishes after him silently, though. I still wouldn't say I liked Crispin much better than I had before this weekend, but I did feel sorrier for him right now than I would have thought possible. He'd lost his mother on top of losing his grandfather, and he knew that she was responsible for two murders. And then there were the other issues I had read about in Grimsby's notes: the drinking, the carousing, the women. All in all, he had quite a lot of burdens heaped on his shoulders. Add in my own guilt over having assumed him capable of murder when he wasn't, and I was feeling quite bad, indeed.

They passed through the door and into the hallway, and Christopher and I looked at each other.

"Go upstairs and pack?" Christopher suggested. "If we hurry, we can catch the 14:21 from Salisbury and be home before tea."

I thought about it. That sounded like a lovely plan, and now that Pendennis and company had a viable suspect in their sights—even if she was dead, or maybe especially because she was dead—there was no reason for Christopher and me to hang around Sutherland Hall any longer.

"Do you think they'll let us leave?"

Crispin and Uncle Harold would have their hands full with funeral arrangements shortly, not to mention the task of downplaying Aunt Charlotte's crime to society, I assumed. I had no desire to get mixed up in it.

"I don't see any reason why not," Christopher said. "We had nothing to do with any of it, and all our statements are on file."

"Tom knows where to find you anyway, if he needs you."

"I'm not sure I want to contemplate what you mean by that," Christopher said, "but certainly, Pippa."

He offered me his arm. I stuck my hand through, and together we headed up the stairs to the first floor, to pack our bags and get as far as we could from Sutherland Hall before anyone tried to stop us.

EPILOGUE

"It's good to be home," Christopher said several hours later, as we exited the cab outside our mansion block of flats and paid the cabbie. "Good evening, Evans."

"Evening, Mr. Astley." Evans tipped his hat and held the door as we brushed past and into the lobby. "Evening, Miss Darling."

"Good to see you, Evans. Has anything happened while we were gone?"

"Not that I know of, Miss Darling." Evans pocketed the coin Christopher had given him. "A quick trip to the country, wasn't it?"

Well, when we left Saturday morning, we had certainly intended it to be a quick trip to the country. And I supposed to Evans, who didn't know what we'd been dealing with, it might still seem like it had been a quick trip to the country. A few days longer than expected, certainly, but what are two days when you're not dealing with murder and mayhem?

I'm sure, to Christopher as well as to myself, it had felt more like a month's holiday in purgatory.

"Yes," I told Evans, with a grin at Christopher, "a quick trip to the country. Any mail?"

He fished a couple of envelopes—bills, of course—out of the cubby and handed them to me. "Anything else I can do for you, Miss Darling?"

He started edging towards the front door, where I assumed he could see someone else approaching for entry.

"Nothing at all," I told him, and gave Christopher a nudge with my shoulder. "Let's go, Christopher."

Christopher headed for the lift with me right behind. We were just pulling back the grille when a voice rang out. "Hold the elevator!"

I looked over my shoulder and, in a moment of inverted déjà vu, saw Florence Schlomsky steaming towards me, scarves fluttering and heels clicking. "Hullo, Pippa."

"Florence," I said primly, while Flossie bared every one of her teeth in Christopher's direction.

"Hullo, Mr. Astley."

"Miss Schlomsky." Christopher managed a truncated bow, even as he gave the impression of trying to squeeze himself into the corner of the lift to avoid her. He kept his weekender bag in front of him as a barrier.

"Oh, don't be such a stickler, Mr. Astley. You know I've told you over and over again to call me Flossie."

She sidled closer while I occupied myself with getting the lift going. Christopher appeared to have abandoned the ship to save himself. "Say, it seems I ran into your cousin last Friday, Mr. Astley, and made the mistake of thinking he was you."

She giggled at the silliness of it.

"St George," I said darkly, while Christopher nodded.

"My cousin Crispin. Yes. He mentioned it."

The lift started moving with a jolt. We all staggered before we found our balance again.

"You don't know where I could find him again," Flossie asked, "do you?"

I rolled my eyes. St George, or more likely his money and title, had made their usual impression, it seemed.

"At the moment he's in Wiltshire," I said, "and not likely to make it up to London again for a fortnight, at least. His mother and grandfather both died this weekend."

"Jumping Jehoshaphat!" Flossie looked from me to Christopher. "Is it like the Wild West out there in Wiltshire?"

I managed an almost passable smile. "You'd think so, wouldn't you?"

"Well, I should write him a note, then," Flossie said, eyes and teeth shining, "and express my condolences."

"Capital idea," Christopher agreed. "If you give it to me, I'll be happy to ensure he gets it."

Flossie hesitated. She looked at him, and then at me, and for once, there were absolutely no teeth in evidence.

"Or if you'd prefer," Christopher added, since it seemed very much like Flossie would like a different, perhaps more direct, solution, "you can drop a note at Sutherland House. It's in Mayfair. The staff will make sure it gets to him."

There would be plenty of sympathy notes dropped off at Sutherland House over the next few days, I imagined, once the news about the late duke and about Lady Charlotte got out.

By that point, the lift had reached the second floor and jolted to a stop, and I pulled back the grille and reached for my bag. "You go on ahead, Florence. We have the bags to manage. It was lovely to see you."

Flossie nodded. "You too, Pippa."

She sounded about as sincere as I did, I imagine.

"Come on, Christopher," I said, as I watched her flounce down the hallway with her panels fluttering. Christopher, of course, didn't move from his corner until she was gone, with the door shut behind her, when I told him, "It's safe. You can come out now. She's inside her flat."

Christopher extricated himself from the lift with a shudder. "Horrid."

"She's not so bad," I said, although I'll admit I felt a little less friendly towards Flossie today than I had on Friday, too.

"You're not the one in her sights." Christopher shivered exaggeratedly as we made our way towards the door to our own flat.

"It doesn't appear as if you're at the top of her list anymore, either," I pointed out. "It seems she has dropped you for your cousin."

"Better him than me," Christopher said, and pushed open the flat door and bowed me in. "Here we are. Home, sweet home. Finally."

"Indeed." I headed for my bedroom door, swinging the weekender bag as I went. "See you in the sitting room in thirty?"

"Make it forty-five," Christopher said. "I have a note to write."

I nodded. "I might put down a few words, myself."

"Taking a leaf out of my mother's book and submitting a piece of gossip to the tabloids?" He grinned.

I grinned back. "I'll leave that little sideline to Aunt Roz. But it seems only fair to warn St George that Flossie Schlomsky has her eye on him, doesn't it?"

"Oh, it does, indeed. You're trying to ensure that he never comes back to the Essex House Mansions again, I assume?"

"You know me so well," I said, and shut the door to my room.

———

Letter from Miss Philippa Darling, the Essex House Mansions, London, to the Right Honorable Viscount St George, Sutherland Hall, Little Sutherland, Wiltshire:

April 27th

~~Dear Lord~~ St George,

First, let me tell you again how very sorry I am for the loss of your mother. As you know, I lost my own a few years ago, ~~under much different circumstances, of course, but~~ and I can empathize with what you're going through.

Please accept our very heartfelt condolences, from both Christopher and myself.

Secondly, you probably noticed our rather precipitate departure from the Hall this afternoon. Under the circumstances, we thought it best to let you and your father get on with the ~~murder investigation and~~ arrangements without unwanted houseguests underfoot.

And also, with no offense towards your ancestral home, it was an awful weekend and I couldn't wait to get away.

Finally, I feel I ought to warn you that Flossie Schlomsky seems to be on the hunt, and you seem to be the intended quarry. She cornered us upon coming home, and winkled your direction out of Christopher~~, who has never been very successful in withstanding pressure from determined females~~. It might be best if you avoid London, Sutherland House, and especially the Essex House Mansions for the foreseeable future.

Yours,
Philippa Darling

———

Letter to Miss Philippa Darling, Essex House Mansions, London, from the Right Honorable Viscount St George, Sutherland Hall, Little Sutherland, Wiltshire:

April 29th

Darling,

Yours? Really?

You and Kit will be coming back for the funerals, won't you?

StG

———

AUTHOR'S NOTE

Dear Reader,

Just a few notes about this book. First, the language:

I was born, lo! these many years ago, in Northern Europe, where I started learning English as a second language around the age of 10. Due to proximity, it was mostly British English, although we got exposed to plenty of other forms of the English language, too, both in school and outside. There were American and Australian TV shows, movies, books, and music, in addition to Canadian, Scottish, and Irish, and a lot of other languages. And then I moved to New York City at 20, and pretty much switched to American English from there. At this point I have written more than 40 books in that particular version of the English language.

All of which is to say that this book is a bit language-confused. Pippa, of course, is British. (And half German, but that's not important to this particular issue, although I can personally relate to the dual-country thing.) She and Christopher live in London, where they share a flat with a lift, partly because I couldn't bring myself to have my thoroughly British characters call those things anything else, but also because it allows my American character to tell Pippa to "hold the elevator!" so she can get up to her apartment.

The floors are British: ground, first, and second. Or at least I think I managed to keep that straight. Cookies are biscuits, diapers are nappies—not that there are any of those in this book—and I've tried to leave out any anachronisms that struck me as particularly American. But I'm only human, so there are going to be mistakes, both in the American-to-English thing, and the 2023-to-1926 one. And also, the spelling is mostly American even while the words are British. All the -our words, for instance, are spelled -or. Color, rumor, etcetera, instead of colour and rumour. I figure the books will be read mostly by an American audience, and they'll have it easier that way.

In other words, feel free to tell me that I've made mistakes, but you won't be telling me anything I don't already know. I didn't have this manuscript, as they say, Britpicked, and I don't expect the book to be perfect. You shouldn't, either. It's meant to be entertainment, and if the mistakes take away from that, then I apologize, but I did the best I could.

Secondly, there really was a Bodley Head Press, and they really did publish Agatha Christie's first book, *The Mysterious Affair at Styles*, in 1921. (T. Fisher Unwin also existed, and published Dorothy L. Sayers's *Whose Body?* a few years later.) But if anyone named Mr. Bancroft worked at The Bodley Head, it's news to me. I picked his name out of the ether, and the story of the divan is not intended to cast aspersions on any company or person. This is fiction. Mr. Bancroft is fictional, and so is Pippa, and so was their interview, whatever may have happened during it.

Thirdly, there really was a Lady Austin who hosted drag balls in London during the late 1920s. I don't think he/she was in action as early as 1926, but it's close enough that I figured I'd fudge the numbers a bit and bring in a real personage for that job. Of course, her—or more likely his—name wasn't really Austin, so in that sense he was as fictional as anyone else in this book. But the balls were real, and the Bright Young Things were quite sanguine about the issue of homosexuality—and sexuality in general—even though the London police were not. The raids were real, too, and so were the laws and the legal ramifications of being caught.

And speaking of real people, the Jungman sisters, Zita and Teresa, were real members of the Bright Young Set. In 1926, Zita was a few months younger than Christopher and Crispin, born in September 1903, and Teresa—called Baby—was still just 18, born in July 1907. Both married multiple times, and died, four years apart, aged 102, which just goes to show that living a long life doesn't necessarily mean living a blameless one. Neither of the Jungman sisters dallied with Crispin, and the list of his conquests that Grimsby compiled is made up entirely of fictional girls.

Finally, I am not trying to make any political statements with this book. For purposes of this story, Christopher is a real person with as much right to happiness as any of my other characters, and if the way he finds his bliss is by putting on a pretty dress and going to a ball where he can dance the night away with other men, that's no more my business than the fact that his cousin is a womanizing cad who has cut a wide swathe through London's Bright Young Set chasing his own happiness. Neither of them is a perfect being, and I try to take them at face value, the same as Pippa—who admittedly has a harder time dealing with Crispin's antics, but that's because she likes Christopher better.

Or perhaps not.

But at any rate, there you have it. Thank you for reading

this book, and if you feel moved to leave a review somewhere, I'd appreciate it. If you decide to read the next book, I'd appreciate that even more. :)

Till next time!

ABOUT THE AUTHOR

Jenna Bennett is the *New York Times* and *USA Today* best-selling author of more than forty books, most of them in the genres of mystery and suspense.

For more information, please visit Jenna's website, www.jennabennett.com

9 781942 939481